SHADOW OF THE ETERNAL WATCHER

JOSH MENDOZA

Published by Inkshares, Inc., Oakland, California
www.inkshares.com

Edited by Noah Broyles
Interior design by Kevin G. Summers

ISBN: 9781950301775
e-ISBN: 9781950301782
Library of Congress Control Number: 2024952941

First edition

Printed in the United States of America

For my parents, Mike and Jude.
Thank you for encouraging me to chase my dreams.

For my wife, Mary.
Thank you for always believing in me.

And for my kids, Abigail and Anderson.
You are loved.

PROLOGUE

THEY'RE COMING FOR YOU.

The First Consul woke in a panic, gasping for breath like a drowning man pulled back from the brink. What had he been dreaming about? His frantic pulse made him certain it had been a nightmare, but the memories of it vanished faster than wisps of smoke flitting into a night sky. All that remained was an anxious need to flee, chiseling away at his chest with the rhythm of his racing heart. *Thump. Thump. Thump.* Over and over and over, driving him mad with a desperation to make it stop.

Disoriented, he stared into an inky darkness at what he assumed was the ceiling. Something was wrong. Or had he done something wrong? He couldn't be sure. None of it made sense in the delirium of sleep. Most people would've dismissed their worries as nonsense and gone back to bed. But he wasn't most people. His instincts told him to make sure. And listening to that little voice in his head was the only reason he was still breathing.

Pushing through exhaustion, he forced his aching body to sit up. Detecting motion, the lights in the room came to a dim but acceptable level, a fire crackled to life in the hearth, and the internal temperature began to rise to his preferred settings. As his eyes adjusted, the Consul found himself staring directly into the unrelenting eyes of the first emperor, stitched into a cut silk tapestry hanging above his fireplace. The grim face gave him a start that nearly sent him toppling from bed. He'd had the wall hanging brought up from the lower levels earlier that month, and he still wasn't used to its ghastly occupant. The museum curators had objected to his taking the artwork—or, as they had put it, an irreplaceable piece of early imperial antiquity—but they had eventually settled on praising his good taste and giving him what he wanted.

A wise decision when it came to their own self-preservation.

The tapestry's depiction was well known to any descendant of the imperium. East meets West. The unification of two great empires. At the center of the tapestry stood the unifier—with his dead stare—always portrayed in both the classical Roman toga and the traditional Chinese robe. Beneath the man, two dragons consumed one another in the fiery pits of hell. One was white and muscular in the ancient Western motif and the other depicted as sinewy strands of black smoke in the Eastern tradition. A symbiotic circle of death and rebirth. Day and night. Yin and Yang. The Eternal Watcher.

The Consul slipped out of bed and immediately wished he'd waited for the heaters to finish their job. The clammy marble clung to his skin. He despised the primitive stones and wood paneling that decorated this extravagant penthouse. But tradition was important to the masses, and presenting stoic austerity with imperial decadence gave him legitimacy.

The balcony door slid back easily as he approached, letting in the semblance of crisp autumn air that the climate control system estimated to be appropriate. The air was stale from the recirculation, poorly hidden beneath artificial air fresheners mimicking a pine forest. Another illusion for the masses. There hadn't been a forest on this planet in nearly two hundred years. *Was this even what a pine forest would smell like?* Who the hell knew? But his scientists assured him their calculations were precise.

All this pretending was an inconvenience. He preferred to live with the reality of their predicament. To celebrate the technology that allowed them to survive on their ruined planet and keep their enemies at bay. Dreaming of something that hadn't existed in their lifetimes was a distraction for the weak. But again, he wasn't most people. He took another deep breath of this fantasy, wishing for the stench of the city or the bustling noise of metropolitan mayhem, something that might remind a man they were alive. But none of it reached the Consul through the invisible energy shield enclosing his balcony.

Safety at a cost. A trade-off. Debatable if it was a good one.

At least he could see his city. The evening sky thrummed with activity, lit up by the red running lights of the maglev trams whirring between the sheer ebony towers of the capital. He strained his eyes, focusing past the towers and blinking lights, beyond the incessant glow from the floating neon advertisements and shop windows below. All that sweat, desperation, and sin pulsed under his feet. But up here at the pinnacle of society, the First Consul stood alone.

In the distance, he caught a glimpse of what he'd been looking for in the faint but distinct vibration of the shield that enclosed the entire city grid. Its nearly invisible net pulsed with a shimmering azure energy. He let out the breath he hadn't realized he'd been holding. All was still. All was quiet. All was as it should be.

He shivered. If that was true, then why did he have this lingering dread in the pit of his stomach?

Returning to his room, he found himself very much alone save for that unnerving yet watchful gaze of the tapestry. All that chaos with one great power at its center. A vortex of certainty. Reaching the top of any organization was difficult. No one knew that better than him. He'd scraped and hustled, toiled and suffered, cheated and lied his way to the head of the largest mining conglomerate Earth had ever known. But that wasn't enough. Wealth was only an instrument to greater power. Even as a child dreaming of a better life, he'd known that to be true. So, with his newfound tool, he'd bought himself an army and united his two strongest political foes by force, establishing a peace that had lasted over a decade. Balance in the triumvirate. A precursor in early times to the glory that became the dyad of the imperial dynasty.

Perhaps history would echo itself. A First Consul could easily become an Emperor. A new dynasty to rival anything seen in Rome or Xi'an.

A goal for you to strive for in these trying times.

He'd no sooner decided to go back to bed then the lights in his quarters pulsed off and then on again. A power surge? Unlikely but possible.

You can only hope.

That knot in his stomach returned as he hustled back to the balcony. His palms sweated with anticipation at the danger he might find lurking. On the horizon, the faint blue hum of the energy shield was still there. And then, in the blink of an eye, it wasn't. The alarm klaxons blared an instant later, warning of the imminent threat that he'd instinctively known was coming since the moment he woke.

The First Consul swore to himself but didn't hesitate. He'd always been a fighter and he'd prepared for this very eventuality. Next to his bed, he ripped open the drawer of his end table and pulled out a standard-issue military sidearm. He spun the knobs on the pistol, bringing its emitters to full power. Next to where the pistol had been was his communicator. He activated it but was met by only static.

The power surge could be an accident. Energy reserves had been dwindling dangerously low the last few years with mining operations at a near standstill. But the jammed internal communications could mean only one thing. He'd been betrayed.

He heard the danger before he saw the flash of emerald light, a deep guttural issuance that seemed to precede the monster that would surely come for him now that the shield had failed. Spinning to face his attacker, he saw only the swirling mist of green eyes as the creature's stone-like talons slashed across his chest. Pain seared through his torso and he wheezed a cry of surprise. The damn things were fast.

He staggered back, wounded but alive, and fired his pistol.

But the shot missed the creature because it had vanished the moment before he pulled the trigger. The crackling blue projectile flew across his quarters and ripped through a terra-cotta statue. Its burnt-orange bearded face and traditional chain-link armor disintegrated before the two-thousand-year-old relic had a chance to explode. The energy pulse slammed into the wall behind where the statue of the ancient Chinese warrior had been, sending marble and wood flying in all directions and dissipating in the reinforced titanium wall hidden behind the classical facade.

The Consul was on his feet, his soldiering taking over. He checked his surroundings. Every shadow could be the death-blow. Again, he heard the slow guttural roar that preceded the return of a Stone Tail. He spun and fired the weapon, not waiting to see his attacker. The blue sphere slammed into a flash of green light as a reptilian monstrosity began to coalesce into existence. The gravity pulse did its job, disrupting the monster's inter-dimensional phase, stopping it between realities and neutralizing the creature. Even though the light simply blipped to nothing, the First Consul liked to imagine he'd heard the horrified screech of an animal as the primitive lizard was sent back to its Maker.

The main door to his quarters flew open as three troopers dashed into his room, pulse rifles at the ready. Their sleek black armor glistened in the glow of the blinking red alarm lights. None of the soldiers had taken the time to don their helmets, and he recognized two of them as his personal bodyguards, though he couldn't remember their names. The third woman he didn't know. While she scanned the area for another attacker, his two protectors came directly to him without a sideways glance.

As if they aren't worried they'll be attacked . . .

Or know they won't be. You know what has to be done.

Without a second thought, the First Consul unleashed two quick blasts from his still fully charged pistol. The bodyguards actually did scream as the pulse energy connected with their armor and began to melt them from the inside out. A blast at this range was deadly no matter what. The First Consul watched as the bodyguards disintegrated, trying to determine if they'd known the plan all along. The soldier he didn't know froze in horror, her deep-brown eyes dancing between the vaporizing men and her leader, wondering if she was next. But she did not raise her weapon to attack him. That, as far as he was concerned, was the definition of loyalty.

"What's your name, soldier?" the First Consul asked.

"Kai, my liege."

"Well, Kai, I've been betrayed. And those two were either complicit in my assassination or inept for allowing it to happen. I won't abide either."

"Of course not," she said, regaining her composure. "What are your orders?"

"Go to the hangar bay and prepare my shuttle. We're leaving this planet. The sailors on my flagship are all loyal."

"I can't leave you, sir. You've been injured."

"Just a scratch. Besides, I can take care of myself. But I want that shuttle gears-up when I'm on board. Understood?"

The trooper slammed her fist to her armored chest in the traditional imperial salute and ran for the door.

"And Kai," the First Consul called after her. She turned back at the door, eager to serve. "Tell no one. I'll be to you shortly."

Alone again, the First Consul hurried back into the living room where the fire in the hearth still burned. Above it, the tapestry hung in tatters. Stray energy and bits of exploded wall from his previous shots had ruined the once-priceless heirloom. He stooped down and picked up a remnant of the artwork, the black dragon consuming the tail of the white one. He crushed his fist around the silk and felt it turn to ash in his hand.

The First Consul slid back a false compartment, hidden behind where the tapestry used to hang, revealing a safe. He inputted his command code into the keypad and let the machine scan his eye. With a satisfying click, it opened to reveal a simple metal lockbox, a stark contrast to the embellished artifacts displayed around his room. He pulled the box out, almost dropping it from the sheer weight of the thing. The metal top lifted off easily. The heaviness of the container came from what was held within it. Inside, a stone the size of his fist glowed with swirling green clouds, just as the eyes of the monster who'd come for it had.

He reached down and stroked the stone.

And instantly, everything around him phased out of existence, seeming to morph into gray smoke. His insides lurched, and he felt as if he'd been hurled across the room. But he hadn't moved an inch. There was a ringing in the air, though he was certain he hadn't hit his head. He glanced around, the place was exactly as it had been, smoking cinders, broken stone, and charred human remains. But lying nearby at the base of the fireplace was something that hadn't been there before: himself.

Or at least some other version of himself he barely even recognized.

He stared at the unconscious man lying at his feet, knelt down and shook him. The other him did not stir. Then he heard it again, that incessant ringing. He rifled the man's pockets until he found the source of the noise, a cumbersome plastic brick with a retractable antenna. He put the archaic communication device near the sleeping man's ear and waited.

The man's eyes fluttered open, glassy, maybe drunk. But they were the First Consul's eyes. The two of them locked gazes. The other man blinked away sleep, seeing his double, but obviously not believing him to be real. That was all right. The First Consul hadn't believed the stories when his workers started reporting strange hallucinations in the mines. The impossible was meant to be doubted until it became the only probable solution.

The First Consul smiled at the man who was nearly the spitting image of himself. "You'd better answer that. It might be important."

The other him blinked again stupidly and fumbled with the ringing contraption.

"And be careful, Duster Raines," the First Consul said. "If they came for me, they'll be coming for you, too. Hopefully I'll get to you first."

The other him flipped open his communication device. The ringing ceased and the duplicate vanished as if he'd never been there to begin with. But he knew exactly where to find that man when he needed him.

The First Consul readied his pistol, hefted the green stone, and hurried through the ravaged artwork of a once-great empire to his waiting command ship and the civil war he'd been trying to avoid.

CHAPTER 1

My beater of a Ford Galaxie swerved across Wilshire as I fought to keep it between the white lines. I probably shouldn't have driven. It was late—after midnight—and I'd already had a few too many. Though that'd never stopped me before. The car groaned as I jerked the wheel back to center. Missed the sidewalk but might've taken someone's mirror with me. Impossible to know for sure. Didn't feel too bad about it either way. People knew the risks parking in LA.

At least I'd made incredible time. Threw the jalopy into park just past Fairfax and stared at the neon sign for my favorite watering hole. The thing sputtered, missing a few letters, but clearly read *The Lazy Giant*. The street was deserted except for a few homeless catching a wink in the cold. This bar defined dive. And not in a hip way that made it a draw. That's why I liked it.

Out of the glove box, I grabbed my wallet and cell phone, leaving behind my 9mm. Guess I felt lucky on a couple of counts that night. Checked myself quick in the reflection of the window. Looked like I'd been living out of the car, which wasn't far from the truth. Straightened my hair, ran my fingers over my mustache, pulled at my sport coat—it needed a press—and made my way across the street. Hopefully my date had low standards.

The Lazy Giant attracted a loyal crowd because of the cheap drinks and friendly pours. But that evening was sparse, even for a Tuesday. Jeff tended bar most nights, though my knowledge of his personal life ended with the name. A big guy, overweight but strong, with a jaw that could crack walnuts—if one ever had the disposition or desire to do such a thing—he didn't move much behind that bar, no space for it, but he always sweat like he'd just run a marathon. He cleaned a glass in the sink and, when he saw me, tossed a dirty look my way.

"We're closing up, Raines."

"But you aren't closed yet."

Jeff sighed, grabbed the bourbon bottle, and began mixing my drink.

"Perfect Manhattan on the rocks," I said out of habit. "Little dry. Little sweet."

"Tell me something I don't know."

A couple of the low-life regulars slouched over their cocktails, dead to the world. Some twentysomething grad students in loose-fitting USC sweatshirts played darts in the corner. Never seen them before. Probably thought it a joke to have date night in a shithole like this. I didn't see a woman by herself. Let alone one that belonged to the voice I'd heard on the phone.

"Anyone ask for me tonight, Jeff?"

"Nope." He set the Manhattan on the bar and smirked. "If someone had, I'd have locked the door."

"Funny."

My would-be employer went by Madison Andrews, and she'd roused me from the warm embrace of an alcoholic stupor with an unwanted phone call. I didn't know her. Trust me, I would've remembered that voice. It had a rasp that caught in the back of the throat and sounded like broken glass grinding together in a bag of marbles. Just my type. I felt bad about Carla but she'd abandoned me, not the other way around. That's always a tough pill to swallow. The rejection, I mean. We should've been keeping each other warm in bed. Instead, I'd had a few drinks alone and tried to lose consciousness on the cold linoleum of my run-down apartment in Koreatown. Probably that very whiskey giving me delusions of grandeur about this nightcap with Madison being a date.

Making myself at home in a booth, I got to work nursing my drink. It went down smooth and cool with the ice and settled in my stomach, fortifying with the other bourbons I'd already enjoyed. That easy feel of the buzz slid over me in waves, blurring life's problems with the incessant throbbing in my head and the spinning sensation of the booze. I leaned back, closed my eyes, and enjoyed the fall.

"You didn't order me one?" that unmistakable rasp of a voice asked.

My eyes snapped open to meet one dangerous woman. She had dark hair, brown skin, and olive eyes to match her very expensive-looking cocktail dress. My date belonged at the lounge of the Beverly Hills Hotel, not this storied establishment. But she couldn't care less. This lady had confidence to spare, and she'd lowered herself to my level because she needed something from me. And it obviously wasn't my good company.

What a letdown for you.

Depression took hold as I imagined returning home to my instant ramen and pet cockroaches. I banished that despair with a gulp of whiskey. Madison flashed a fake smile and the entire night felt disingenuous. In an instant, self-pity gave way to a bitter fury I barely recognized as my own. All I wanted was for her to shut her damn mouth and leave me be. But she persisted, you had to give her that.

"Aren't you going to ask me to join you?"

Vaguely, I motioned across the booth and Madison sat. In her eyes, I thought I caught a glimpse of disdain. Maybe fear. But it disappeared faster than it arrived. I chalked it up to the booze and let it go.

Jeff sauntered over, and she ordered a gin and tonic. I got a refill. We stared at each other for those moments it took the bartender to make the drinks and bring them back. Awkward. We drank in silence until she broke it: "I'm afraid you have me at a disadvantage."

"How's that?"

"Well, you got my name over the phone. You haven't even introduced yourself."

"My name's Duster Raines. Raines'll do. I'm a private investigator. But based on the fact you called me and mentioned work, I assume you already knew both those things."

"Cute."

"So, you going to tell me what you want, or we just going to sit here and pretend this is a social call until the bar closes?"

"You're handsome, Mr. Raines. Bet you'd clean up nice."

"I'm tall, too. Still doesn't explain why I'm sitting in this dump."

"You picked it." Madison took a long sip of her cocktail. "Most men would be excited to have a drink with me."

"Oh, don't get me wrong. That voice of yours is killer. And anyone can see you're beautiful. And that dress . . ." She shifted uncomfortably under my lingering gaze. I chased the crude moment away with more whiskey. "But I see the depression on that wedding finger, and I don't make a habit of messing with other men's wives. Usually ends with someone in the hospital. And it's never me."

She rubbed the place where her wedding ring had been. I loved being right.

"You're a mean drunk."

"It's past my bedtime."

She laughed. "I like you."

"Well, now we have something in common," I lied. "So how about you tell me what this is all about?"

"My husband."

"Where's the ring?"

"Somewhere safe. I took it off because . . ."

"You don't have to explain to me."

"That's kind of you." She downed her drink. Liquid courage. "He disappeared three days ago."

"Police?"

"What can they do? They have no idea what's coming. None of you do."

She stared at me with an intensity I'd only seen matched a few times in my life. And one of those was a dirty little incident from the Gulf War I preferred to forget. Her gaze burned straight through me, as if she'd forgotten we were talking, seeing something beyond this place. A skill I could relate to. Should've gotten up right then and left. But I didn't.

"What do you think happened?" I asked as kind as I could manage.

"That he's been abducted," she muttered, snapping back from wherever she'd been.

"Did they leave a note?"

She laughed wildly, which in my experience only happened in bad movies or right before someone shoved a knife in your neck. "No, don't be silly." Madison leaned across the table so her lips nearly brushed my ear and whispered, "Aliens don't leave notes."

* * *

Back out on the road, I let the car do its job. Flew down Fairfax to God knows where. But anywhere sounded better than where I'd just been. The engine complained as I turned hard onto Sunset and headed into the heart of Hollywood, making my way through light traffic towards the sign—you know, the famous one—which burned bright in the night sky against the black backdrop of the mountains. Strangely, I didn't recall the sign ever being lit at night. But there it shone, like a beacon leading me to safety.

Rain started to fall. Bizarre because it never rained in Los Angeles. Or was that the Valley? I couldn't remember the last time it had rained so I left it at that.

Even at this hour and with surprise rain, the streets bustled with tourists, homeless, drunks, hookers, and all other sorts of undesirables. The rest were aspiring actors and screenwriters. That was my town. Los Angeles. La-La Land. A fantasy of broken dreams and lost hope. Believe me, there's plenty of both to go around in this city.

Started to feel bad about how I'd run out on Mrs. Andrews. I'd dropped some cash and gave her my business card to be polite. Call me in a day or two, I'd said. A line of bull. Hoped she got the message. She'd grabbed my arm, asked me to stay with a desperation I pitied. But I didn't need another crazy person in my life—I was crazy enough for one lifetime already.

Why had I agreed to meet with her in the first place? I couldn't remember.

Was it money? No, that'd been the excuse.

The reason had something to do with lust but that self-deception was long gone. Now, I just felt uneasy I'd been too tight with a paranoid delusional. Don't get me wrong, I was used to wacky stories. In my line of work, you hear a lot of them. But something in Madison's eyes told me she'd seen things, real or imaginary, and they'd damaged her beyond repair. No payday could've gotten me to stick around.

Stop worrying. No need to ruin your buzz.

So, I wasn't worried about the money I'd just passed up. Or the back rent I owed. Or Madison needing my help. I had a bad habit of falling for the hard-luck cases, and that needed to stop. Bound to be easier money just around the corner.

Be patient. Don't look back.

But for some reason, I did look back. Probably the wailing sirens got my attention. Flashing in my rearview mirror were the red and blue lights of a police cruiser. They were hot on my tail. How long had they been there? No time to think. I threw on the blinker and pulled off the main road into a back alley.

My car lit up as the high beam spotlight from the cop's car focused on me. I squinted through the light, barely able to see the silhouette of a man making his way towards my driver's-side window. He walked slow, methodical, almost gliding. Not a man at all but the reaper coming to take me to the great beyond. Fear took me. I couldn't move. This demon of darkness in control. The ringing in my ears intensified, a death knell of my impending doom.

You knew he'd be back. Blood demands blood. Fate always gets paid.

"Leave me alone," I grunted. Shook my head, gave it a solid slap, broke up my crazy apocalyptic thoughts into a million tiny pieces. Hallucinations be damned.

Truth be told, I'd had too much to drink. And this probably wasn't good. But I knew I could get this car home safe. Just needed to explain that to the cop. It'd be all right. I sat up straight, put on a smile, and rolled down the window. Cold air hit me in the face like a wet blanket. "What seems to be the problem, officer?"

"I've been following you for the last four miles," the rain-drenched policeman snapped. "You been drinking?" Young kid, probably twenty. Smug. Knew he'd scored a bust. Gloating. Rookie cop. Plain as day. I'd been like him once. If I played my cards right, this would end with me asleep in my bed. No worse for wear.

"I had a drink or two. But I'm good to drive." I flashed my PI badge, a polished silver crest with the Justice Department emblem. The metal glistened in the high-beam light. Sharp. Impressive. And a complete fake. I'd had the thing made about five years back to get past doormen and bouncers. It was illegal to impersonate an officer in Los Angeles but hopefully this kid didn't know that law yet. Besides, I still felt lucky.

The rookie eyed the badge incredulously. Unable to tell if it made an impression, I pulled out my retired police officer ID card and passed it over. This one was real. "I used to be a cop."

"License and registration." The kid tossed my retired cop card at me like trash.

Who the hell did this guy think he was? For a moment, I considered getting out of the car and teaching him a lesson. But I thought better of it and handed him my license instead. Time for cooler heads to prevail. The glove box popped and out came the registration. As I went for the insurance, I accidentally knocked my concealed 9mm onto the passenger seat.

In a blur, I hit the wet pavement. Out of the corner of my eye, I could see the cop aiming his pistol at the back of my head. He had a look on his face somewhere between rage and terror. I can tell you from experience there's not much difference between the two when you're on the receiving end of a loaded firearm.

"Whoa. What's the big idea?" Tough to talk. Might have been slurring. Or I'd hit the concrete too hard.

"Stay on the fucking ground. Keep your hands where I can see them."

"I was just getting you my registration."

"Shut up." He grabbed my right arm and cocked it behind my back. "You're under arrest for driving while intoxicated, impersonating a police officer, and carrying a concealed weapon."

"I'm permitted. Christ. Just told you, I *used* to be a cop."

His knee went into the small of my back. Despite my better instincts, I cried out in pain.

As he shifted off me, he put most of his weight into his other leg. He'd lowered his gun, pointing the weapon straight into the ground. Rookie mistakes. Off-balance and the gun no longer a threat, it would only take a little thrust forward and I'd have the kid on the ground. Snap his wrist, another grab, and the gun would be out of his hand and in mine.

Time slowed as the fight played in my mind.

Out of my body, I watched from above as every move I'd imagined occurred in perfect synchronization. The kid flipped over me and hit the asphalt. As I rolled up onto my feet, I broke his wrist and yanked the gun free. Took aim. Stared down on him. In control. Goddamn, I was good. Part of me wished I'd actually done it.

Then, my watching spirit slammed back into my body. Reality gripped my mind and shook it back to the now. And a terror sank in at the realization that everything I'd just witnessed had happened.

Oh, shit.

The young cop's hands—both the good one and the broken one, which flopped about because it no longer attached at his forearm—were out in front of his face to block bullets he had no chance of stopping. Tears already streamed down his cheeks. "Please don't kill me, man. I got a wife. Kids."

Dazed, I said, "I'm sorry. I didn't mean it."

"I won't tell a fucking soul. I swear."

Cop was a liar. Bad one, too. Had to shut him up.

Stop. No more blood. There's always a price.

Fine. Have it your way.

The gun clip hit the ground and I unchambered the loaded bullet. Then I pistol-whipped the kid hard across the face a few times until I knew he wouldn't get up for at least an hour. Poor rookie. He'd landed in deep shit. Lost his gun and everything. Probably going to lose his job next. But at least he hadn't lost his life.

You're welcome.

Wiped my prints off his gun and dropped it by his side. Grabbed my paraphernalia and got back in the car. Dripping wet, I shivered. My breaths came out panicked. What the hell just happened? Couldn't think about it now. I gave the car gas and left the unconscious cop in my rearview.

CHAPTER 2

BARELY ABLE TO SEE THROUGH THE DOWNPOUR, I DROVE ON instinct. This was bad. Really bad. But they'd never put me away. No time for that. My greater destiny called. I needed a fixer and I needed one fast. And the list of people who could get me out of this jam was short. One name short. Too bad she probably wouldn't help me. Damn, had to try.

That's the truth. You've got no choice.

The only certainty now, my lawyer wouldn't be happy to see me.

Everything looked the same to me as I cruised the recently gentrified streets of the Miracle Mile arts district. Rows upon rows of newly built, meticulously maintained trilevel townhomes muddled together in the darkness and incessant rain. Pounding on the door of what I hoped was my lawyer's residence, I resisted the urge to scream her name. Repeatedly rang the doorbell, over and over and over, echoing that annoying chime into the home.

Carla opened the door in a loosely cinched robe with her golden hair pulled up in a sloppy bun. She wore no makeup and the wrinkles at the corners of her eyes showed. We'd both aged. Me more than her. But it didn't matter. I could see her

mind working overtime, trying to figure out what I was playing at by showing up unannounced. She was the only person I
knew who could run circles around me in an argument. I loved
that about her most. But it also scared the shit out of me.

"What the hell, Raines?"

She white-knuckled a baseball bat in her right hand. I
probably deserved that. She waited. I didn't really want to talk
first. But I'd come to her and she was the lawyer. So, I gave
in and started with the uncomfortable pleasantries this formal
meeting stipulated.

"Hey, Carla. Sorry to bother you this late."

"Save the bull."

"There's no bull."

"You're drenched."

"It's raining."

She hid her pity quick, but I knew her too well and caught
a glimmer of sympathy before she buried it beneath anger.
Couldn't blame her for that, either. Not with our history. We
tended to run hot and cold. Long story. And it was late. She'd
been asleep. What time was it? No clue. But no doubt I'd
woken her.

Carla said, "I can't believe I'm even giving you the time of
day."

"I know it's been a minute. I'm sorry for all that." I hesitated,
unsure of what to say. I hadn't really thought this through. So I
went with the truth. "Something's happened."

"What do you mean?"

I told her about the cop. Skipped over the out-of-body
kung fu battle.

"What were you even doing out?"

"I couldn't sleep."

"So you went and assaulted a police officer?"

"That's a vast oversimplification of my predicament."

"You're drunk."

"Not really. If I was, this headache would be manageable."

She smiled in spite of herself. "Good. You deserve a little pain. Way I see it, you've got one play here. You need to turn yourself in."

"No way."

"If you do, I might be able to help. Otherwise, you're a fugitive."

"Isn't there someone you can call? Pull in a favor."

"You're delusional."

She had me there. This was insanity. All the options in the world and I came to visit my ex-girlfriend. Stupid.

"Raines, look." Carla struggled for the words. "I don't know what you want from me."

"I made a mistake."

"Yeah."

"I'm sorry I woke you."

I hustled out into the rain. Carla didn't try to stop me. The door slammed and I was alone again. On the road, I didn't see my car. Where had I parked? I made my way up and down the different streets, but the car wasn't where it should've been. I doubled back.

Hold it together, Raines.

Freezing rain fell with purpose, soaking me to the bone. My muscles rebelled, brutally shaking and out of control. It was all I could do to keep moving through the chills. Completely dark. The streets deserted. The storm clouds roiled above in a violent torrent of milky grays and blacks. Rain pummeled me as I struggled up the flooded street, which was a slick of oil and other pollutants. Gutters and sewers overflowed, the smell of urine unbearable. The city morphed into a swamp, and it swam at my feet in waves of purple, gold, and black—a rainbow of toxic death.

Keep moving. Don't drown us in this poison.

Guess I didn't take my advice because I jolted awake as a black SUV roared past at a dangerous speed. Probably one of those ride-sharing cars. Hate those things. The SUV hydroplaned, skidding in the rain, and threw a black sludge from the street all over me. The vehicle came to a halt a few yards in front of where I slumped against a building. The black slime dripped from my clothes as I pulled myself to my feet.

Plumes of exhaust rose from the SUV's tailpipe in the frigid air. The car rattled there, the only thing for miles. Its vibrations were ominous, the machine seemingly ready to pounce. Part of me thought to run. I didn't need to meet anyone else that night. But my body wouldn't have been up to the task even if I'd tried. So, I waited. The back door finally opened and a woman in a suit with an umbrella stepped out. Between the rain and the low light, I couldn't make out much about her.

"Duster Raines?" the woman shouted to be heard over the rain.

"Who wants to know?"

"Old friends."

No. That didn't feel right.

"You look like hell, Duster."

My mind hazy, I tried to jump up and down to get the blood flowing. But instead, I swayed a bit and almost fell over. I focused on the woman and her ride-sharing service. Stared through the rain at the shadow. The more I stared, the more I couldn't shake the feeling I should know her. But this lady wasn't my friend. Only my mother called me Duster.

"How about we get you home safe?" the shadow asked.

The question didn't feel safe. Nothing about this night felt safe. But sleeping in the downpour had made things worse on my body. My teeth chattered, and I knew getting my feet moving again wouldn't be easy.

And where the hell did you park our car?

If I didn't get out of this storm, losing consciousness seemed likely. Some kids playing hooky would find my waterlogged corpse in the morning. Not a great way to go. And the thought of those kids throwing rocks at my dead body made my stomach turn. So, I let my imagination convince me that the car was the best bet and got in the back.

The SUV had seat warmers, a welcome reprieve as my soaking clothes stuck to the black leather seatback and began to cook. I put my pruned hands near the air vents and let the heat blow over them. The feeling started to come back, and they ached.

The driver turned and forced a friendly grin my way. He had a baby face and wore a neatly trimmed beard meant to hide his age. His blue suit appeared tailored and freshly pressed. The kid looked as familiar as the shadow of the umbrella woman had. But I couldn't place him. That bugged me almost as much as his bullshit smile. These two were trying hard to be my friends and probably wanted something I didn't want to give.

Umbrella woman got in the back with me. Young, just like her counterpart, but with cold eyes that longed to be forgiven. She'd done things she wished to forget but knew she never would. I recognized that look because I saw it every morning staring back at me while I brushed my teeth. A nasty scar ran from the edge of her left eye to the corner of her mouth, a wound meant to end her life. She didn't try to hide the disfigurement, instead wearing it like a trophy with her black hair pulled into a tight ponytail to accentuate the blemish.

The SUV's wheels squealed as the driver gunned the throttle. I could barely see where we were going between the blinding headlights and the sheets of rain hammering down. The windshield wipers worked in constant flux, their percussive scraping of glass blending with the roar of the storm. But amid that cacophony, something felt off. The suited duo sat silent. Brooding. This was no normal ride-sharing service.

"So, what's the deal?" I finally asked.

"What do you mean, Duster?" umbrella woman said flatly. Those cold eyes stared dead through me, giving little in return. Couldn't read her. A great poker face.

My mind leapt at the thought of playing games, and that nagging sensation at the back of my mind scuttled to the forefront. These two were the college kids who'd been throwing darts at The Lazy Giant. They'd stood out in their USC sweatshirts, sipping canned hard seltzers. Not the usual sordid inebriates The Lazy Giant tended to attract. I'd thought they'd been goofing around coming to that dive, being ironic, but now I wasn't so sure. Part of me was relieved to have solved the mystery but the other part was deeply disturbed at how little sense my discovery made. How had these two found their way to me on this stormy night? Why had they changed into suits? Why were they operating a ride-sharing service on their date night? Probably only one answer and I didn't like it.

"I remember you two," I said.

Umbrella woman frowned. Front seat guy turned back to face me with that big dumb grin. Stupid because he drove way too fast in the rain and now he wasn't even watching the road. But he didn't seem to care. In turning, his jacket fell open, and I saw his underarm-holstered Glock 23, standard issue among the FBI, and that confirmed my suspicion. These two were government agents. They were young to be in the field but that probably meant they were good.

What did you blunder into, Raines?

"Told you he'd make us," the driver said to umbrella woman.

"Yeah, you did. You're a better detective than I gave you credit for, Duster."

"Thanks?"

"Don't mention it."

"So, am I getting your names?"

"Nah. Names only complicate things. You just need to know that we're friends."

"Doesn't feel too friendly."

"Not with that attitude, Duster," the driver said. "I mean, a guy with your record, you'd think you'd be working with us. In fact, that's why we're here. You love your country. Right, Duster?"

Guy worked hard pretending to be my friend. Constant use of my name. A tactic so blatant it insulted. But I let it slide. Had to since I was trapped in a speeding vehicle with two armed spies.

"What do you know about my record?" I didn't have to ask twice.

"Captain Duster Raines, United States Air Force," umbrella woman said. "Honorably discharged from service nearly twenty years ago. Served during the first Gulf War as a fighter pilot. Dropped some big bombs. Got a lot of medals."

"But you had some bad luck, too," the driver added. "Your plane crashed somewhere in the deserts of Iraq after an apparent mechanical failure. Was two weeks before a SEAL team extracted you. You evaded capture. Killed a few enemies."

"Pretty impressive stuff," umbrella woman said. "After the war, you joined the LAPD. Rose through the ranks to detective quicker than most. Like all those people you killed dropping bombs, you put a lot of bad guys behind bars."

"Maybe a little too impressive for your own good," the driver said. "There were widespread rumors you'd been fixing cases. Couldn't be proved in an internal investigation but the department buried you at a desk. Apparently, you lived off the action. Couldn't handle the office. When you took a nosedive into the bottle, it was suggested you find other employ. You retired six years ago. Opened the PI firm. And that brings us to today."

"So you guys can use Google," I said. "Big deal."

"You know we didn't use Google," umbrella woman said.

She was right. Google didn't bring up half the stuff they'd said, although it did find a great image of me wearing my flight suit in front of an F-15 Eagle. Not that I ever googled myself. No, these two weren't the internet trolls I wished they were. They were spooks. And I'd fallen into something deeper than I'd imagined.

"If you want my help," I said, "just ask for it."

"See," the driver chided umbrella woman. "I told you Captain Raines was a patriot."

"Don't gloat," she said. "It doesn't suit you."

"Listen, Duster," the driver said. "We know you met with Mrs. Andrews earlier this evening, and that she talked to you about her husband. Probably gave you some line about aliens. That about right?"

I nodded. Better to let them tell me what I knew. Maybe learn something I didn't.

"We'd like you to find those aliens," umbrella woman said.

The car hit a pothole and we all jolted around the car. My mind raced at her request; this night kept getting weirder. "So let me get this straight, the FBI thinks that missing husband case will lead them to a clandestine group of alien kidnappers?"

"He even made us on the FBI thing." Guess the driver was a fan.

"Shut up," umbrella woman snapped. "You just made it for him." The driver sulked while umbrella woman kept talking. "No, Duster. She's not going to lead you to aliens. She's going to lead you to her husband, Dr. Steven Andrews. We'd like him back. We think she knows where he is. And for whatever reason, she called you. She must trust you. We figure it'll make our job a lot easier if you just help her."

"What's this Dr. Andrews do?"

Umbrella woman smiled. "Just find him, will ya?"

"I usually get paid up front."

"How about we make that *unfortunate* run-in with the police disappear?"

There it was. These two owned me.

"Consider it a test," the driver said. "You pass, we might have more work for you. And if you don't . . ." He shrugged. I caught his meaning.

As if on cue, the SUV skidded to a halt and umbrella woman rolled down her window. My vanished car sat there, parked in front of my apartment building. Eerie.

"Get some sleep," umbrella woman said. "You look like hell. And see what you can find out about Mrs. Andrews and her missing husband in the morning. Okay?"

Back out in the rain, I could tell the sun had risen because the light bounced down through the clouds in sporadic golden beams. The streets were still abandoned, like some sort of zombie apocalypse. I leaned through umbrella woman's rolled-down window. "Just find Dr. Andrews, huh? Got any suggestions where I start?"

Umbrella woman handed me a small piece of paper with an address scrawled on it. "Maybe start with where he used to live. You're the sleuth, right? Sure you'll figure it out from there."

"And how do I get in touch with you when I find him?"

"Don't worry about that," she said. "We'll be watching."

The SUV tore off down the road and disappeared around the corner.

CHAPTER 3

Nauseous with a bad hangover, I woke in bed. Usually, I could manage the pain. Control it. Today, not so much.

The room turned erratically, quickening when I sat up. So I stayed put, kept my eyes closed, and tried to convince myself the room was still there. Vertigo took me hard into free fall through a black nothing. More than my stomach could handle, I took the only other option available and opened my eyes again.

Unbalanced, the ceiling fan thrummed. But I was thankful for the counterpoint of motion—spinning room versus fan—calming my nerves. Kept me grounded. The bitter taste of bile burned the back of my throat. I ignored it, instead concentrating on how I'd ended up this way in the first place. The night blurred together. I knew I'd done something terrible but couldn't remember what.

Carla. Remember her?

Yeah . . .

Needed to call her. Apologize. Set things right. Definitely a priority.

Dread grabbed hold about the conversation we'd have. It wouldn't go well. It rarely did. I buried that thought and tried to ignore the crushing-rock anxiety just placed on my chest. Had to keep going. Ignore the trap of self-pity. Otherwise, I'd be locked down tight. Unable to function.

Deep breaths. Slow it down. Focus on the now.

Unfortunately, as the minutes ticked by, I remembered every detail from the previous night's misadventure. And the more I thought on it, the crazier it seemed. Slowing time. Uncanny ninja skills. Out-of-body observations of said amazing skills. Probably hadn't happened. No. Definitely didn't happen. There were explanations. Alcohol poisoning. Psychosis. Video games. Mania. Rotten milk. Something.

Carla's right, you're delusional.

Who asked you?

Other than the valid concerns over my mental state, the more pressing issue was owing my freedom to a couple of FBI stooges who could send me to jail on the slightest whim. No two ways around it, I had to do what they said. Looked like things were just getting started between me, Madison Andrews, and her alien-abducted doctor husband. I'd have to see if she'd still pay me to find him.

I rolled out of bed and fell hard to the ground. Second attempt went better. Up on my feet, I embraced the pulsing beat in my head. It reminded me I still lived despite best efforts.

The blinding white light in the bathroom flicked on. Sink water hit my face. Head throbbed. More regret. Dry swallowed a couple aspirin. Breakfast of champions. Focus regained, I started a hot shower.

The building's pipes were as old as the city itself, and it took a good ten minutes of waiting for the water to get to the right temperature. So, I waited. Rocked back and forth—probably still drunk—stared at myself in the mirror. Didn't even recognize this guy. His yellowed skin sagged at the jowls. Apparently, he was still in shape despite his lifestyle. But haggard. Too skinny. His haunted eyes, hollowed into a sallow face, judged me.

This wasn't a man. It was a ghost. A shadow of its former self. A fraud.

Mustache looked classy, though.

My reflection disappeared behind a fog of steam. Shower must be ready.

That first hit of hot water gave nothing but relief. Who knows how long I stood there? Let the soap wash away my pain. Hoped it would make me feel whole. Watched my demons swirl in that dank water, swallowed by the drain. They'd be back. But for the moment, I was free.

Dripping wet and draped in a towel, I picked up a box of ramen off my kitchen floor. The three minutes it took to heat in the microwave felt like an eternity. *Ding.* I devoured my soup, burning my mouth as I went. The warm noodles tasted like nothing but delicious salt.

After breakfast, I changed into a clean brown suit with a checkered pattern to the jacket. Then I dug through my sock drawer and pulled out an old snub-nosed revolver I kept in the apartment for protection. It didn't have the same reliable feel as my 9mm, but it would put a hole in anyone on the receiving end. Always good to have a backup. I grabbed my cell phone off the nightstand and put it in my jacket pocket without turning it on.

My collection of bottles beckoned. Thinking more about Carla and making that call to apologize only made matters worse. A siren's song. The drink a dark temptress. I knew better. I'd been to the meetings plenty. Gone through the steps. But they never stuck. The longer I went without a drink, the more I saw the faces of the people I'd put away—or worse, killed—and started to think maybe everything I'd done to atone for my sins hadn't been for the right reasons.

Shook that thought. Ignored the booze. Alcohol got me into this mess and I didn't need to go back down that hole so soon. But the longer you think about a thing, the more it sounds like a good idea. I had to get out of the apartment. Keep myself busy. This case needed solving, and that seemed as good a place to start as any.

Out the door, I made my escape. But I didn't get far. Halfway to my building's ancient elevator, down that shabby hallway with peeling paint and stained carpets, a worn and shrill voice reverberated off the haphazardly installed drywall.

"Raines!"

Damn. So close.

Hongsik Kim, my portly warden that the law called a landlord, hurried to my side. He wore baggy jeans, white tennis shoes, and a yellow Lakers T-shirt that was two sizes too small and barely fit over his beach ball gut. Guess that was his idea of business casual. He had a mean streak in him a mile wide, and his wrath was usually directed in my general direction.

His lackeys were always after me about my rent. Sure, I owed it. But that didn't mean they needed to be so hard on me about it. I was tired of thinking about my empty bank account, and Mr. Kim did nothing but remind me.

"Raines," Mr. Kim said again, out of breath as he reached the elevator.

"Yes, Mr. Kim?"

"You owe me rent."

"I already told that child collector of yours you'd get your pound of flesh next week."

"It's always the same old story with you, Raines."

"Relax," I said. "I'm on a job right now."

"You've got until the end of the week. Then, I call the sheriff. You get me?"

"Yeah, I get you."

Mr. Kim got on the elevator and waited for me to follow. When I didn't get on, he let the doors slide shut with a glare. Instead, I hoofed it the six flights down. Didn't need one more minute spent with that guy.

Outside the building, the street clamored with pedestrians. The clouds still rolled by overhead, giving everything a dreary and oppressive feel. But it had stopped raining. The Galaxie waited for me, front and center. I almost hated to move it from such a great parking spot. The FBI had done something right.

As I forced the driver's-side door open with some effort, a kid sitting on the stoop of a building across the street caught my eye. I stared, waiting for him to disappear—a figment of my imagination—because sometimes I see people that aren't there. But when he didn't vanish, I had to accept that the boy was who he appeared to be. Juan Escalante.

I dodged through oncoming traffic to reach him. "Hey, kid. I thought I told you I'd pay next week?"

Juan glanced up from the weathered magazine he'd been reading. On the cover of the old rag was the image of a large satellite in orbit above Earth. The word *CODE* was set in large block letters. Before he tossed it aside and frowned at me, I caught the subheading: *Understanding AI Systems in a Global World.* No idea what that meant. I knew Juan had a reputation as a bit of a math whiz—his propensity for numbers was why he was employed by Hongsik Kim as the rent collector. Did I mention Mr. Kim owned three buildings on this block alone? I digress—but computer systems was a whole other level than I'd realized.

"Why'd you stick the fat man on me?" I demanded.

"Didn't. He just doesn't like you much."

"That's obvious. Fucking asshole should . . ." I lost my train of thought. "Shouldn't you be in school?"

"It's three o'clock. School's out for the day."

I looked at the overcast sky. Realized I'd slept the day away. I asked, "Your mom good?"

"You don't know my mom."

"Just being polite. What're you doing out here?"

"I live here."

"You do? Huh, never seen you coming and going."

"I've seen you." Sounded like an accusation. I let it go.

"You into computer stuff?" I asked lamely, gesturing at his discarded magazine.

"No, I just read it for the pictures."

"Think you're clever?"

He shrugged, glanced at his feet, a bit uncomfortable at being called out. Seemed pretty obvious he was usually a polite kid. The tough-guy bit was an act for me.

I said, "They let you do a lot of that stuff in school?"

"I go to a STEM magnet."

"Stem of what?"

"Never mind," Juan said. "Yeah, we do a lot of computer stuff there."

"Cool. You know, I used to fly planes. Still do sometimes when I can scrape together the fees to take one up for a few hours. We had a few computers in them, used to be considered state of the art."

Juan stared at me, neither smiling nor frowning. Progress.

"I could take you up some time."

"I don't really like to fly."

"You're kidding me."

"Makes me nervous."

"The crashing?"

"Obviously."

"I crashed once . . ." I trailed off, thinking back to the moment. The crash wasn't the part that kept me up at night, but I wasn't about to tell the kid that.

"You're not making me feel too confident for that flight."

"What?" I said, coming back from the memory. "Sorry. Right. Yeah, well, the point is I survived. And it doesn't happen that often. I had a mechanical failure. Uncle Sam's fault."

"Don't let my dad hear you say that. He's an Army engineer."

"No shit? I'd love to meet him some time."

"He's deployed." Juan looked at his feet again. Missed his dad. I couldn't really think what to say. The silence lingered between us. I wasn't very good at chitchat. Especially with a teenager.

"Next time I tell you I'll get you the money, cut me some slack. Okay?"

"How about you just pay your rent so I don't have to come knocking?" Kid was a know-it-all. I'd had enough. But before I could bolt, Juan stopped me short. "Mr. Raines, can I ask you something?"

"Raines'll do. Mister reminds me of my dad and he was a real piece of work."

"Right. Sorry. It's my cousin. Drek."

"Your cousin's named Drek?"

"It's a nickname."

"Gang?"

"Can we not get into that?"

"Fine. What do you want, then?"

"Well, he got arrested the other day. Wasn't doing nothing. Just sitting out front like I am now. Minding his business."

"Name like Drek, doubt he was doing nothing."

"That's the same shit the police sling. Last I checked it's not a crime to be Mexican."

"But gangbanging and drug dealing are."

"He's just surviving like everyone else."

"You're not living that life."

Juan nodded, then frowned, looked down at his feet for the third time. Sore subject. Cousin was probably trying to drag him down into the gutters. Kid was too smart for that. But sometimes that didn't matter.

Regaining his confidence, Juan asked, "Do you know someone who could help him? Like a lawyer."

"You got a pen?" He reached into his backpack and pulled out a pencil. I jotted Carla's number down on one of my business cards and handed it to him. "Tell her you know me but that you don't really like me. And say I said you're a good kid."

"Seriously?"

"Long story. She'll help you though. Best there is."

"Thanks. I owe you. My family—"

"Don't mention it." Another urge struck as I started to go. "That's got my cell phone, too. You ever need anything, you can call me. Cool?"

Juan looked the card over, then stuffed it in his jeans. He didn't say anything else but the fact he had my number made me feel like one of the good guys.

CHAPTER 4

My rocks glass glistened, sweating beads of condensation onto the bar at The Lazy Giant. The melting ice glowed in the mustard-colored light, swirling as the brown liquid danced a slow and methodical waltz around it. The sickly sweet stench of that bar mixed with the smoky musk of my whiskey. It was the smell of dirt. Toil. Pain. But there was no sadness here. Only relief.

I tried to think of reasons not to indulge but that list wasn't very long.

The incident with Mr. Kim had put me on edge—that guy was a real piece of work—and I needed to soften the blow. So, I'd made a small detour on my way to see Madison Andrews. And Jeff had put the one thing in front of me that always made everything seem all right.

But not today. After last night, my steadfast friend seemed a betrayer.

What did I ever do to you, whiskey?

The drink didn't respond. Obviously. But we both knew the answer was nothing.

We'd done plenty together, though.

The front door opened with a ding, drawing me away from my cocktail. A welcome distraction from my battle with sobriety. Shock overwhelmed me as umbrella woman and her driver, both clad in their college apparel, walked in.

These two had guts. Ordered a couple of drinks from Jeff without so much as a glance in my direction. Cold shoulder. Didn't even have the decency to take a couple of sips at the bar. Instead, they threw darts in the corner. So, that was how they were playing it. I couldn't believe it. They were mocking me, their backs turned in those stupid disguises. It told me I meant nothing. I couldn't let it stand.

My beverage clenched tight in my grip, the glass surprisingly heavy—I'd never held a full glass this long—I took up a stool at a nearby high-top and stared. They threw dart after dart at the board, refusing to acknowledge my existence.

My blood boiled. But I stayed cool.

The few looks I did catch gave little in the way of recognition. They played the part to perfection. Impossibly so. Even the best can't hide from someone they know. There's almost always a moment of recognition before a person buries it down. A trained eye can catch that flash as the soul betrays the mind. And I was trained. But these two didn't have it. If you asked me, I'd say they'd never met me before. Generally, only sociopaths and the most elite of the government could be so detached. Maybe they were both.

Cleared my throat. "We getting on a first-name basis today or what?"

Umbrella woman gave me a dirty look and said, "Shove off."

"You're just gonna keep on pretending?"

"Look, man," the driver said. "We're just trying to play a little game here. Why don't you leave us be?"

"Oh, sure. I'll leave you be."

Back at the bar with my cocktail, I watched them play for another twenty minutes. They snuck a few looks at me. Nervous. Just a couple of uncomfortable twentysomethings having a few drinks after a long day of classes in their graduate program. Didn't make any sense. They knew I had to help them find Dr. Andrews. Otherwise, I'd be rotting in a jail cell for the rest of my good years. So why this college kid charade? It didn't fit.

"Something wrong with the drink?" Jeff asked from behind the bar.

"You know those two playing darts?"

"Those two?" Sounded like he'd never given them much thought. "They started coming in about a month ago, I'd say. Order themselves a couple cans of them hard seltzers the USC kids drink nowadays. Always play darts."

"Funny. I only ever noticed them last night."

"Don't know why you'd notice them in the first place."

"It's what I do."

"Right. So, the drink's okay, then?"

"Wouldn't know."

I left my Manhattan swimming in a pool of water on the bar. Jeff said something about paying for it but I ignored him because I needed to save money.

The brisk night air met me head-on, and I welcomed it with a deep breath. It stung with the bitter cold of the previous night's storm. I made my way towards my car, sober for the first time in a long time. It wouldn't last. But for that moment, I let myself be proud.

* * *

Again and again, I checked my rearview mirror for a sign that I was being followed. Dodged in and out of traffic. Ripped across side streets. Cut through neighborhoods. Flew down back alleys. Made a real show of it. No way I had a tail.

Seeing those two FBI agents on another date night unnerved me. My mind raced, trying to decipher what they were up to. But I couldn't figure their game. And whenever you can't figure something, it's best to assume the worst and go in guns blazing. I already had two guns, but I needed an insurance policy in case this went bad.

I kept an office downtown on the edge of the warehouse district on the third story of a centuries-old brick building. The previous tenant had been my shrink a few years back when I had a steady income and could afford such things. Place wasn't anything fancy. Simple waiting room with a single office. I'd kept my doc's old furnishing and set it up like I had a secretary. Office even had a fish tank. Though after my first fish died from negligence, the tank had remained empty.

Working where I used to spill my guts about life's little problems was disconcerting. But I'd gotten the lease for a steal since my former psychiatrist had hung himself in the office after killing one of his patients. I'd only seen the lady he murdered once in the waiting room. She'd had soft, green eyes that shone out from under a cloud of sadness. That day, she'd been reading a *Vanity Fair* and kept crinkling the corner of the pages after she finished them. That really struck me because it wasn't her magazine. All these years later, she still burned in my memory. Probably because they found her the next morning shot dead with my therapist swinging from a rope. Tale as old as time.

The landlord had been pretty lax on the rent after that grisly affair. In the intervening years, I may have mentioned it wasn't beneath me to remind potential tenants of the gory details. As such, I still had the place for a song. I'd considered ditching the apartment and just living out of the office, but sometimes it's nice to have somewhere to go. You know, work-life balance. Otherwise, you never get anything done.

Coming into the waiting room, I immediately noticed something was off. Things were straightened. A small package, about the size of a tissue box, sat on the table atop my six-year-old magazines. It was addressed to me with no return. The delivery date read three days prior.

Ripped that thing open like a kid at a birthday party.

Inside was an intricately designed bronze key with double-sided locking grooves etched with the number 406. A tag was attached at the end with a perfectly handwritten address for the Bank of the West in Santa Monica. Underneath it all lay a note written on crisp stationery with a gold crest. The paper felt thick, expensive, and had an embroidered pattern of flowers at the border. Written in the same meticulous scrawl as the address was a simple note:

Dear Mr. Raines,

> *I'm afraid I don't have much time and am forced to send this prior to our meeting. Ironically you may be the only person in this universe I can trust. I just hope I'm right.*

Madison

The jilted style didn't surprise me. Madison seemed the stuffy sort. I checked the date on the packaging again to make sure I'd read it right. Three days ago. Like she'd said, before we met. But why? What could be in this safe deposit box that she couldn't have given me in person? And what was this about the irony of trusting me? I had no idea and couldn't begin to guess. I'd have to ask her. And I needed to do that fast because I got the sense I didn't have a lot of time.

Inside a filing drawer in my desk was a small safe, and in that safe were the two things I'd come for in the first place: a box of bullets for the snub-nosed revolver and a wad of cash. Counted the money quick, about three hundred dollars. I wasn't sure what I'd find at Madison's house, but I knew I wouldn't have access to this office for a while after tonight. I stuffed the money into my jacket and took the box of bullets.

Back outside, the biting air burned my face. Punishing me. Trying to stop me from my course. Ignored that, too.

As I drove off, I watched my building disappear. A sense of loss pressed on me. The sadness of nostalgia. Not sure why I felt so much for an office I never used. Place wasn't even that nice. But it turned out I'd been right about needing the bullets and money because it was the last time I'd ever be back there.

CHAPTER 5

Streetlights flickered on, illuminating a narrow road in a swanky part of the Hollywood Hills. Clock on the dash read just after five but the sun had already set. My car lumbered up an incline, passing mansion after mansion. I'd only been in these neighborhoods a handful of times in the twenty years I'd lived in Los Angeles. Not my usual clientele. Andrews must have been a good doctor to afford a place up here.

Almost by accident, I came upon the address I'd been given by the FBI. Because it was situated back off the road and defended by a twelve-foot privacy hedge, one could easily pass by without knowing. At the street stood a blood-red wooden gate with an intricately designed wrought-iron top shaped like a dragon—it reminded me of one of the Japanese gardens on the outskirts of town. The home beyond the fence looked like a modern art museum featuring an exhibit in the abstract, poured concrete combined with slats of red-stained wood. Massive ceiling-high windows broke up the rest of the monotonous cement structure. But they were completely blacked out. A hollow box without a soul.

Obsessively, I checked my rearview as I circled onto a different street and parked the car a few blocks downhill. Since I figured no one would be stealing my car in this neighborhood,

I left the keys in the ignition. That way I could get the engine started fast without fumbling in my pockets. You never knew what a few seconds might buy you. No sign of the FBI agents yet. But they knew I'd be coming here. Maybe I was being paranoid. But whatever their plan was for me, best to keep them guessing at mine.

Popped the glove box and went for my 9mm. It wasn't there. Checked again. No gun.

Shit. You should've looked when they moved your car in the first place. Sloppy, Raines.

My hand flew to my jacket pocket where the snub-nosed revolver rested, its weight a reassurance. Again, I checked the chamber. Fully loaded. Six shots. Opened the box of bullets I'd taken from my office—there were six here, too—one full reload. My hand trembled as I pocketed them and put the gun back in my jacket.

Deep breath, Raines. Steady your nerves.

My newfound sobriety had made me skittish with withdrawals. Plus, I had a bad taste in my mouth about this gig. The FBI didn't need me and I knew it. They thought I was a drunk they could use and toss aside. An expendable pawn in a chess match. They were toying with me, that much was obvious, but the why still didn't make any sense. I needed to be careful. One wrong step could send everything spiraling out of control.

There wasn't a single person on the street as I made my way back the few blocks to the darkened house. The neighbors had fled into their own fortresses, defending themselves against one another. Fine by me. I welcomed the privacy.

Hoisting my body over the wrought-iron fence, I landed with a thud. Not smooth. The yard was covered with nothing but gravel and, as I made my way towards the front door, every step ground those rocks together in a racket. But there was no one around to hear it except me so I kept going.

Bang. I knocked on the front door. No answer. *Bang-bang-bang.* Silence. I tried the door handle. Locked. I peered through the decorative windows but couldn't make out much.

Crunching through the rocks along the perimeter of the home, I looked for anything out of place. Side gate had been left ajar, so I made my way into the backyard. Wet grass stuck to my shoes as I moved past a large swimming pool, which was the only thing lit up in the yard. It shone bright like a portal to an underground world, reflecting waves of shimmering white light into the surrounding darkness. The entire cityscape twinkled below, mixing together with the night sky. An infinite galaxy of stars. An endless expanse of other lives.

I found the back of the home much like the front, dark and impossible to see into. Tried the sliding glass door, and to my surprise, it slid back with little effort. Examined the lock, no sign of forced entry. All the same, I pulled out my revolver and felt its grip. Reliable. Ready. Deep breath. I stepped into the home.

All was still. Cautiously, I made my way through a kitchen filled with brand-new, stainless-steel appliances that looked like they'd never been used. The wood floors sparkled in the moonlight, immaculately clean. And noisy as hell, squeaking as my wet rubber soles stuck with every step. I took off my shoes and left them in the kitchen.

Ducking through a doorway, I found a formal dining room that had never seen a meal. Another hallway led to another. Each room filled with never-used, handcrafted furniture. The walls were sparse. No family photos. A few Cubist paintings. Other than that, everything was stark white. No personal touches to make it feel like home. Nothing about this place felt right. The woman I'd met at the bar had struck me as old timey. I'd been expecting rich colors, plush furniture, thick rugs, classic art. But I'd found the opposite. This modern Japanese minimalism couldn't possibly be the taste of the woman I'd met at The Lazy Giant.

My labored breaths were the only sounds in this empty shell of a home. My hands sweat fear. I wiped my palms on my jacket, switching the gun back and forth as I did so. My jaw shook. My teeth clenched tight to control it. I was out of practice and it showed.

Turning another corner in this labyrinth, I came to the top of a staircase leading down. I descended to a landing with a large metal doorway that looked like it belonged in a missile silo rather than a residence. Next to the fortified door blinked a high-tech keypad. It required a thumbprint and combination. No way I'd get through this thing. But lucky for me, the door had been left open.

Readying my gun, I took a quick step into the room and covered the corners. There was no one here. The walls were made entirely of CCTV screens, one of which was splintered like a spiderweb. Looked like an errant bullet strike had destroyed it. Below the screens were a couple top-end computers. Panic room. Lot of good a panic room did with the door wide open. The screens blinked between different camera angles throughout the home. If someone were here, they'd have watched my every move.

Hustling around the desk to one of the workstations, I tripped over something and fell. Rolling on the ground, I came up fast with my gun at the ready. But all I met was the blank stare of Madison Andrews, her eyes frozen in the past. She wore a gray T-shirt with a logo for a local Pilates studio. It had been stained red with blood from a single gunshot wound to the chest. I touched the blood gingerly with the tip of my finger, cold but viscous, not yet hardened. Murder happened some time that afternoon. She'd been wearing jeans but they were pulled down to her ankles. Looked like the assailants had searched her body thoroughly. The key to her safe deposit box felt heavier in my pocket. I didn't need anyone to tell me that its contents had been reason enough to take Madison's life. I hoped she'd been dead when they'd done their searching. She deserved better.

Her dead stare told a story of betrayal. She'd known her assailant. That would explain the open panic room door. I looked into those eyes, tried to see into her past to know what had happened. But they glared back. Deep in my bones, I knew she blamed me. That hurt most of all.

With a tenderness that surprised even me, I closed her eyes. She stopped judging.

My stomach lurched. I swallowed vomit back down—*don't panic, Raines*—and tried not to lose it completely.

I wanted to get up and leave. Let her rest. But I couldn't. Gently, I tucked some stray hairs back behind her ear. I regretted the way I'd treated her at The Lazy Giant. I hadn't even bought her a drink.

Yeah, you're a real class act.

Mind your own business.

As I focused on Madison's lifeless body, the guilt overwhelmed me again. I knew I couldn't leave her like this. I owed her that much. When I moved her body out from under the desk to let her rest with dignity, a matte black gun fell onto the ground. Instinctively, I picked it up and immediately wished I hadn't. I now held the murder weapon and my prints were all over it.

Get your shit together, Raines. You're going to get us killed.

The damage already done, I gave the gun a once-over. Felt better about the fingerprints because they didn't matter. This was my gun. The 9mm missing from my glove box. Presumably taken when the FBI agents moved my car to that incredible parking spot in front of my building.

Shit. Shit. Shit.

Now I really lost it. Luckily, I found a nearby wastebasket to hold the contents of my stomach. Finished, I wiped my mouth and swallowed the sour bile still caught in the back of my throat. I'd been set up. But why? They had me dead to rights on the assault charge. Easy jail time. Depending on the judge, could've landed me fifteen years. Maybe more if they'd trumped up some gun charge. But they'd wanted a patsy for the death of Madison Andrews, and she'd delivered me to them on a silver platter.

And it had worked. I'd technically broken into this house, there was video of me searching rooms armed with a gun, and there was a dead body shot by a firearm registered to me. I'd go away for life if they caught me.

Maybe I'd just been an opportunity for those agents to hang this murder on. Wrong place. Wrong time. But that didn't feel right. One thing had bothered me since the moment I'd answered Madison's call. No one knew that number except Carla, creditors, and my very short client list. So how did this woman I'd never met magically have it? I didn't exactly advertise. Had the FBI agents given it to her? That would explain why she was dead in her panic room with no signs of forced entry. She knew them and let them in to kill her with my gun. But that line of thought led to one conclusion: the FBI had targeted me from the beginning.

A piercing alarm broke my train of thought. The incessant sound emanated from a blinking red button on one of the workstations. I pressed it. The alarm immediately stopped, and some of the surveillance screens snapped to the perimeter of the home. Six people had just broken down the wrought-iron fence—fanning out across the front lawn like they were taking a hill in a war—clad in black assault gear, riot helmets, and armed with fully automatic weapons. There were no markings on their gear, but they looked like SWAT. Their timing was impeccable. And my fear of a setup now felt confirmed beyond a shadow of a doubt.

I didn't have much time before they'd be in the house and on top of me.

I hurried to the panic room door, shut it, and hit the biggest and brightest button on the keypad next to it. Multiple locks engaged, securing me in the room. Safe for now but trapped. Didn't matter. No way I could fight my way past that crack team. And since the FBI agents were framing me, I knew they'd picked their guys right. Made sure to have a few loose triggers on the squad. Shoot first and ask questions later over my dead body. There would be no surrendering.

Back on the computer screens, the death squad methodically cleared the house room by room. They'd be to the panic room door in three minutes tops. And I bet it would only take them about five minutes to get the appropriate amount of explosives to blow the door. I'd be in their custody in less than eight minutes. If the blast from the explosives didn't kill me first.

I checked the room. Found a small hatch in the corner, tucked behind one of the desks, which looked like it might access a ventilation duct. In a rush, I yanked the desk aside. The hatch opened with no argument into an adjacent, spherical room. There were two metal rings secured perfectly within the sphere and designed to swing and pivot around the room. Between those two rings stood a platform with wires and cables running into it. There was enough space for one person to stand atop the platform between the two rings. The entire place had a secret-lab vibe going for it. But with Madison dead and her husband missing, I had no way of knowing its function. And I doubted the rifle-clad warriors on their way to kill me would allow the time I needed to figure it out. But frankly, unless it was a teleportation device, I was out of luck. This was a dead end.

I crawled back into the panic room.

Poorly crafted industrial-grade carpet lined the floor, which seemed odd since the rest of the house had cost a fortune. Then I saw it. At one corner, the carpet didn't meet the wall flush. Improperly laid, it had been rolled out quick as if to cover something up. I grabbed the corner and pulled hard. It ripped up fast, as if designed to do so. Underneath, another metal hatch led directly into the ground. I popped it open and found a tunnel with a ladder descending into the darkness.

A deafening bang sounded from the other side of the panic room door. Then another. I checked the screens. Two of the SWAT struck the door with a battering ram. That certainly wouldn't work. Another SWAT member shouted into a walkie-talkie, probably requesting the explosive ordnance that would bury me under a pile of rubble. Five more minutes tops.

Even though I had no time, I tried to leave Madison with as much dignity as I could. Pulled her pants back up. Straightened her hair. Folded her arms across her chest. "I'm really sorry about this, Madison." I could feel a welling in my eyes as I spoke. "I should've helped from the beginning. Don't worry, though. I'll find your husband and make those two FBI hacks pay. I owe you that at least."

My stomach tied up in knots, I dripped sweat. Spiraling. Losing control.

The other side of the door banged from a battering ram strike, snapping me back to the reality of my imminent demise. I had to keep going or this would be my tomb. Madison's corpse lay at my feet but I couldn't look at her anymore. I'd failed her.

Ashamed, I hurried to the hatch and descended into the abyss.

CHAPTER 6

AT THE BOTTOM OF THE LADDER, I DROPPED DOWN INTO A pool of muck. Ice-cold water soaked through my socks. Wished I hadn't taken my shoes off in the kitchen. But I had. My feet would keep.

Darkness enveloped me but my eyes had adjusted on the climb down. I could make out a latticework of pipes and wires on the ceiling. They ran past where I could see into what appeared to be a tunnel. The sound of slow-flowing water echoed around me. With the reverberations and tight spacing, the noise of the water raged like a river roaring out to sea.

Probably about three minutes before SWAT was on my trail. I'd pulled the carpet back over the hatch as I closed it, but that would only slow them down for so long. And they'd have a distinct advantage down in these catacombs with night-vision goggles. I needed a head start, and it should've started five minutes ago. I plunged into the darkness.

The space was cramped and I had to stoop to keep moving. I gasped in breaths that should've been easy. The dank air felt packed together, like it didn't flow outside in any natural way. I ignored that thought. There was an exit to this maze somewhere. Had to be. No use worrying about it now because there was no going back.

Doubled my pace.

To keep from falling, I steadied my hands along the walls. They were rough, some type of stacked brick with patchy cement keeping them together. The masonry was subpar and certainly hadn't been built by whoever constructed that concrete monstrosity I'd just escaped. No, this place felt old and slapped together.

Alone in the dark, my mind raced. How long had these tunnels been here? Were they an old LA sewer system? Was I going towards the outskirts of the Hollywood Hills or deeper into them? Maybe this wasn't an escape route at all. Maybe it was leading to an old fallout shelter: a defense for the rich against imaginary nuclear wars. Idea after idea flowed through me, none of them good, the possibilities making me jumpy. Claustrophobia struck next, the walls closing in all around. Suffocating.

My heart hammered in my ears. I stooped down a little farther, took my hands off the walls, tried to keep from being crushed.

Keep going. Back only leads to death. Or worse.

It felt like miles before the tunnel came to a sudden stop at a T-intersection. The ground dipped down, and the gathered water flowed at the lowest point. I'd found my river. I decided to follow the water and made a hard left into a giant pipe. From there, the straightness of the tunnels came to an end, twisting and turning into an abysmal black hole. I continued to follow the flow of freezing water at my feet. Hopefully it flowed somewhere worth going.

In the distance, I heard the reverberations of an explosion. The SWAT team had blown the steel door. They'd be in the tunnels and coming after me soon. Hopefully my route would throw them off but following the water seemed obvious.

Run, Raines. You can't let them capture you.

My feet pounded the water, numb from the cold, prickling with an odd sensation that wasn't pain but still hurt. In spite of that, I kept moving. Tried to find a rhythm for my pace. But my breaths were coming out hoarse and ragged. Despite the fact that I drank too much, I kept myself in decent shape—old Air Force habits die hard—and I still ran every day. Sometimes nights because mornings are tough when you're on a binger. But none of that mattered down here with the tight air and the constrained spaces.

My eyes danced with bizarre halos of light that didn't exist. I thought I could just make out another T-intersection ahead. No time to think, I went left.

And ran straight into a wall.

The impact put me on the ground. Wind knocked out of me. Dazed. My entire body ached. But I had to keep moving. Shaking away the cobwebs in my head, I dragged myself up and turned back the way I'd come. But *something* stopped me short. Two red eyes glowed in the dark maybe thirty feet in front of me. I couldn't hear the breathing of the animal over the deafening sound of my own gasps, but I figured some type of coyote had wandered into these tunnels from the Hollywood Hills.

Fear dissipated to a desperate relief at seeing this creature. There must be a way out near here. But that elation disappeared faster than it came.

The noise told me the beast had moved before I could see the shadow of the animal emerging from the dark. The red eyes grew larger, covering the distance at an incredible speed—faster than any animal I'd ever seen. As it closed in, I saw its claws digging into the stone floor with an awesome power that didn't seem possible. This was no coyote.

With no time to react, I fumbled for the gun in my pocket. Wasted precious seconds finding the grip. Took aim without pulling the revolver out of the jacket. Sighted down what I thought was the barrel. Right between those terrifying red eyes.

Pulled the trigger.

The gun kicked with incredible force that almost tore my jacket at the seams. I missed—at least I think I did—and those eyes continued closing in. The beast let out a terrible roar. My heart stopped. I was a dead man.

Round after round erupted from the gun until it went *click*.

Bullets ricocheted off stone, pipes, and metal. No way I hit the creature. But then, just as suddenly as they'd appeared, the eyes vanished. The shadow of the creature's body hit the ground and skidded to a stop about fifteen feet from where I stood.

Nice shooting, Raines.

Thanks.

Taking the gun out of my now ruined jacket—occupational hazard—I quickly reloaded it with the last six bullets. Readying the revolver, I inched towards the downed animal. It didn't appear to be moving. No labored breaths or whimpering to indicate I'd only wounded it. The beast was dead. I smiled. Still had my shot.

As I got closer, I noticed sparks coming out of the animal's carcass. Certain in my safety, I hustled over and saw the impossible. The animal looked like a small cheetah crossed with a dog. Maybe four feet across, with long legs, sharp teeth, the whole nine yards. Except it was made of some type of reflective metal. My bullet had struck it in the skull and blown it open, revealing a mess of wires, circuit boards, and other electronics I couldn't begin to comprehend.

No, this wasn't an animal. It was a robot.

CHAPTER 7

MY FEET CARRIED ME FASTER THAN I'D EVER RUN BEFORE. I wasn't worried about cramped spaces, blind turns, or the screaming numbness in my shoeless feet—all of which said I needed to stop. No time for any of that. My mind was resolute and focused only on escape. Escaping SWAT, the FBI, and the insanity of robots, aliens, or whatever else this case intended to throw my way. I was done. But first, I needed to get out alive.

There's a fucking robot after us. Don't you think we should talk about that?

I just said there wasn't time. Shut up while I save our asses.

It's always later with you.

Even though it hadn't been a coyote wandering in off the hills, I'd been right that the creature had entered the tunnels another way. Soon I found myself standing at the end of a drainage pipe, taking in the panoramic city lights of Los Angeles. I'd never been so happy to see that view. Water gushed out of the pipe over my feet and rolled down the hillside into another drainage system.

My initial thought: *Get back to the car.* But that would be the wrong call. My old Galaxie couldn't handle a chase or a firefight. I'd miss her but tough choices needed to be made.

Daggers pierced my legs as I ran. My feet weren't so numb anymore and they hurt like hell. But there might be a pack of ravenous robot cheetah dogs on the prowl. Keep moving. My heart raced, oddly excited. I was on the lam. My instincts kicked in. I'd always been a survivor. They'd never catch me. Not alive anyway.

At the bottom of the hill, I came out of the bushes near the Sunset Strip. Countless cars flowed into the upscale neighborhoods above, their drivers oblivious to the mechanical menaces lurking in the night. Fortunately, I knew exactly where I was and ducked back into the shrubs for a short jog to a popular restaurant just off the main drag, Chez Maison something or other. French. I'd always wanted to try it. But I could never afford the food they served.

Out front of the fancy bistro, two valets took cars from a packed parking lot and drove them off-site. Hidden in the darkness, I bided my time for when both valets were gone and there were no cars in line. Took longer than I'd anticipated, probably ten minutes, but what I had in mind required privacy.

When the coast finally cleared, I went straight to the valet stand and opened the cabinet with the keys. There were a plethora of elite cars: Ferraris, Bentleys, Porsches, Range Rovers. I settled on a worn Mercedes key because it felt the least pretentious of the options. Clicking the lock button, the lights of a nearby car flashed. I'd gotten lucky: one of the early guests that had managed a spot in the lot. I sprinted to the car and got in.

The car was older, early nineties, and didn't have a navigation system or many bells and whistles. Probably better that way. Odds of it having an antitheft tracking system greatly decreased the older the car. I gave the ignition a turn and the engine roared to life. I turned on my blinker and pulled into traffic and cruised west, careful to keep to the speed limit. It was Tuesday evening, just after eight. The bank that Madison's safety deposit key belonged to would open at nine the next morning. No one would expect me there, or in Santa Monica, but I didn't want to risk it—needed fewer prying eyes—so I worked my way towards the 405 and took the freeway north, away from the glowing lights. A few freeway changes and an hour of drive time later, I found myself in the middle of the desert in the city of Palmdale.

This town and I went way back to my early Air Force days. There was a lot of action right off the freeway: bars, restaurants, stores, the usual suburban sprawl. If you weren't a local, you were coming for the gun shops, drugs, or easy tail. None of the above for me—I couldn't afford it.

Throwing on the turn signal, I eased my luxury sedan off the freeway and darted into the city's mall parking lot. As the car coasted through the massive sea of asphalt, I checked the glove box. Inside was a roll of cash—about a hundred dollars—what luck. Who leaves cash in a car with a valet? Trusting sort, I suppose. Guess I'd picked the right car. All told, I had about four hundred dollars to my name. Not bad. Definitely serviceable.

Parking the stolen car at a busy restaurant, I went in and asked them to call me a cab. Then I walked back out towards the freeway. Would've loved to join the raucous festivities of the bar, grabbed a bite, maybe had a drink—after what I'd seen, a few shots to calm my nerves seemed in order—but I couldn't. Not yet anyway. The entire point of coming out here was to lie low. So that was what I was going to do. Besides, I didn't have any shoes.

The taxi didn't take long to find me. Standard yellow. Nothing fancy. The driver was a woman, mid-forties, average build, dark complexion, and didn't make eye contact for very long. She'd seen a few sordid types get in that backseat over the years and knew to keep to herself. Her vehicle was clean, too. No smells. Couldn't believe all this luck. Where had that been last night? Didn't really matter. If there's one truth about luck I'd learned from working on the police force, it's that it always runs out. I needed to get out of sight and fast.

Making myself discreet in the back, I asked her to take me to a cheap place to stay. Away from the action. Fifteen minutes of silence later, the cabbie dropped me at a drive-up motel from a bygone era. Paid her with cash. Tipped the right amount, about 15 percent, didn't want to seem lavish and didn't want her to remember me for stiffing her.

Nonplussed, she drove off. A true pro. Real lifesaver.

Wished I could've given her more. But lingering on such thoughts only made me long for a life I never had. So I buried that sadness and tried to forget the cabbie.

The motel sat on the edge of desert waste, nothing beyond its back fences for tens of miles. Place was small, just an assortment of one-story buildings encircling a yellowed, cracked plaster pool. Everything needed a new coat of paint. The main office light shone bright, and a flashing *Vacancy* sign burned orange through the window. A large marquee read *Desert Palms Inn*. Next to the sign stood a single fifteen-foot palm tree that justified the name.

The lone palm swayed in the desert wind, rocking back and forth, marking time like a metronome for some forgotten deity at a piano, playing a concerto about the fate of us all.

But you don't hear the music so there's no reason to dwell on what you can't understand.

We hear it though.

The office was empty so I rang the bell for service. A skinny teenager appeared from the back. The boy bore a striking resemblance to an Iraqi kid I'd met during the Gulf War. Not something I wanted to think about now. I buried it down. This kid wore baggy jeans and a T-shirt for some band I'd never heard of called the Arctic Monkeys. The motel was probably his parents' business, and he was working the night shift for them. Bet they were proud.

My smile went unreturned.

Rapping on the bulletproof glass that separated us, I said, "Wild West, huh?"

"You want a room?" the child clerk asked. Just stick to business. Smart kid. You probably get a lot of wackos out here.

"Yeah. One night."

"Gotta be cash for one night. We only take credit cards for three or more."

"That'll work."

"It's thirty-five bucks. No smoking. You can use the pool until checkout. Noon tomorrow. There's a vending machine out behind the shed. You might have noticed there's desert on the property line. If you go wandering, watch for snakes and stuff. We're not responsible if you get yourself killed."

"There a liquor store around?"

"About a mile back up the road."

I gave the teen two twenties and took my five bucks change. Said my thanks.

The kid shot me a look like I was just another one of the deadbeat meth addicts he got in here all the time. Probably figured it was three-to-one odds he'd find me dead in my room from an overdose. I'd let him think it. Best to blend in.

* * *

About forty-five minutes later, I sat on the bed of my room getting situated after a walk to the liquor store. I could've made the trip faster, but my feet were killing me and I still wasn't wearing any shoes. Fortunately, the owner of the shop hadn't seemed to care about my shoeless state so long as I had money.

I'd bought an inexpensive handle of Jim Beam whiskey, a bottle of water, a bag of chips, and some beef jerky. After all that, I still had about three hundred and thirty dollars to my name. Enough to last me through the week, even after I bought shoes in the morning. But I'd have to figure something else out soon.

The room was drab. A worn quilt covered threadbare sheets on what barely passed for a mattress. The aged off-white paint was broken up by thrift-store art depicting idyllic landscapes. On a folding plastic card table sat a TV that looked so old I was surprised to find it had color. All of it was held together by worn brown carpet that looked to be original. No frills. Place didn't even have a nightstand for the Gideons to leave a Bible in. I checked under the bed and in the closet to make sure nothing weird had happened before my arrival. There was nothing to find except the smell of off-brand cleaning solutions hiding the unmentionable acts of the room's fifty-odd years of service. Thank God I didn't have a black light.

Sitting on the creaky bed, I ate my dinner, watched TV, and drank whiskey. The burn in my stomach was warm and welcoming. I tried not to think about the insanity of nearly being killed by a robot. I'd hit my head pretty hard on that wall and maybe I'd dreamed the entire episode. I kept telling myself that must be the explanation. But I wasn't buying it so I drank more to cover the worry.

About four swigs and three pieces of beef jerky later, it came to me. A few years ago, I'd seen a machine like that cheetah in a YouTube video. A robotics team was working on it at some university. Their machine could run on a treadmill at incredible speeds. It couldn't really do anything else. But man, could that thing run. Granted, the robot that tried to eat me was more impressive. But with enough money, I didn't see why that YouTube cheetah couldn't have been made into a weapon. Search and destroy. Top secret. Just like the drone program was for years before we started killing terrorists on cable news with them.

Guess the FBI agents had brought out all the stops to catch me. I couldn't help but be flattered. I drank more whiskey. Tried not to be nervous about secret government robots.

A replay of the Dodgers game from earlier that night was the only thing worth watching. It was mid-October so that probably meant it was the playoffs, though I didn't follow sports that much. Some guy I'd never heard of threw pitch after pitch to other guys with bats. It all seemed a little silly but a welcome distraction from the events of earlier.

Madison Andrews. I took another slug from the bottle and attempted to bury the memory.

Eventually, the game ended. The Dodgers won. I tried to take some pride in the city victory. It was hollow.

Flipped more channels. There weren't many of them. Some QVC saleswoman was slinging paste jewelry and telling me I had to get a piece for the lady I loved. Carla would like one. Maybe Madison would've, too.

Another shot of the liquor. *Don't think about it.* Gripped the remote for dear life.

The TV landed on some low-budget space documentary. Images of the Earth from satellites, spinning slowly, a giant blue orb in the vast darkness. Surreal. Then it switched to a panel of scientists on a poorly lit stage in a lecture hall that looked sparsely populated even from this angle. If it had been black and white, you'd have thought you were watching footage from the 1950s of a smoke-filled talk show.

The panelists were discussing a recent mission to Mars. NASA had sent a satellite named *Copernicus* out there, and everyone seemed excited about data they'd gotten back. Unlike anything they'd ever seen, one of the panelists kept saying. The topic seemed dense for TV but apparently public access didn't give a damn.

I took another drink. Ate a few chips.

They cut away from the panel to a few different images of Mars. The moderator rambled off facts about the red planet and asked the panel more questions. I stared at the alien images; the world seemed sad, lost. Then the show came back to the panel discussing an anomaly the satellite had picked up in orbit. I didn't really care, but there was nothing better on so I kept watching.

"It's most certainly a tiny black hole," a small man in a tweed jacket said. The TV flashed his credentials as a professor of astrophysics from Stanford. "This anomaly, something we can actually study, measure, well, it could open a Pandora's box of discovery. It's really a very exciting time for our field.

"The thesis of my recent book contends that the loss of water on Mars had to do with gravitational forces altering the planet's orbit. I believe the discovery of this anomaly points to proof for my theory. There's a possibility that this black hole is tens of thousands of years old and that its formation altered the orbit of Mars, thus making life as we know it impossible. I'm hoping further study and analysis of these readings will prove me right."

"I agree with Dr. Tabel about one thing," a woman on the panel interjected. She was another professor, this time from MIT. The little words beneath her face told me her name was Dr. Eliza Nielsen and that she specialized in applied mathematics. "This is an exciting time in our field. However, I have to disagree with my colleague's theory. The math doesn't support a gravitational pull of that magnitude for that period of time. The planet would've been wiped out, even by such a miniscule black hole."

All this was way over my head, but I liked to see Dr. Nielsen making a fight of it. Tabel was a bit too preachy for my tastes and I got the sense he could talk about himself all night.

"I'd like to point out that it's much too early to know that for sure," Tabel stammered.

Some other guy on the panel started to agree with Tabel, but Nielsen wouldn't let him have the last word. "With all due respect, we've had the numbers long enough to dispute your theories, Dr. Tabel. You can try and sell more books if you like, but what I find much more likely is that this is some type of wormhole, newly formed, and possibly not naturally occurring. But there's really only one way to know for sure, which is why I've proposed altering the trajectory of *Copernicus*. Send it into the anomaly and see what we find."

The other panelists murmured among themselves. Apparently, risking the satellite was not a popular idea. But the moderator jumped in before the panel descended into anarchy. "What precisely do you think we'd find, Dr. Nielsen?"

"Perhaps nothing. Perhaps we'll end up on the other side of the galaxy and have real-time readings of a system we've only seen from millions of years ago through Hubble. But perhaps more incredible than that, we'll find another reality entirely. It could give credence to the idea of myriad universes just like our own, unfolding in similar but disparate ways."

"You're talking about the multiverse," the moderator said.

"Precisely," Dr. Nielsen said. "It has been theorized that anything that does happen will happen in these other universes. Infinite possibilities."

"You think the math doesn't support my gravitational theories of a black hole. Fine," Tabel snapped. "But then you go and talk about parallel universes. Well, that's where I draw the line. You have no proof of that, and you know it. It's just theoretical nonsense. I thought this was a show about science, not science fiction. I strenuously object to . . ."

I didn't hear much else of the argument because I fell asleep.

CHAPTER 8

I'M IN THE IRAQI DESERT. WHERE EXACTLY, I'M NOT SURE. No clear landmarks. Just desert and asphalt. I drag my parachute off the main road and bury it in the burning sands. With that hidden, my thoughts turn to finding cover to avoid detection.

Check my sidearm pistol, 9mm. Doesn't look damaged.

In the distance, I see the fiery wreckage of my crashed plane. That's the first place they'll look. I walk away from the fire.

Sand blurs with that giant blue sky in an endless expanse. No horizon. Only waves of mirage and heat. Hoofing it about five miles, I find a river just over the crest of a sand dune—not all oases are mirages—lush with palm trees, bushes, and other plants. Not a bad place to hide out.

So, I lay prone in some tall grass among the bushes and wait.

Time is endless. It obeys no rules here. Follows no set path. It's been hours. Maybe days. Don't think about it. Keep a low profile. Wait for rescue. But with the war on, and me behind enemy lines, it's hard to know when they'll come.

Will they come?

The thought has occurred that they think I'm dead. No one searches for the dead guy. All I can do is hope they look. The hoping makes time move even slower than before.

Try to drift, maybe get some sleep.

The river flows before me into the desert waste.

My heart skips at the sound of laughter. A boy, no older than twelve, plays down by the river. Must not be far from a village. Couldn't imagine his family wanted him out here with the fighting. But kids are kids. Think they're invincible.

Slowly, I crawl out and check the outlying areas. I don't see or hear a truck. Little boy is definitely alone. Hunker down. Just because you can see someone doesn't mean they see you. Survival one-oh-one. Remain hidden. Don't panic.

He grows bored of his game and throws rocks in the river. Watches the giant splashes they make. After a while, he grows tired of that, too, and walks uphill towards me.

Hold my breath. He's only a few feet away. He doesn't see me. Don't move.

The kid picks some fruit off the bush I'm in. Takes a bite. Tosses it aside. Looks down. Sees my eyes. Recognition. He's made a mistake. Then panic. Fear of me. He runs. Rightfully so, I'm the enemy.

If he gets back to the village, there'll be a convoy of soldiers on me in minutes. I hate myself for it, but it has to be this way.

Him or me.

I take aim. The kid runs in a straight line. It's an easy shot.

Him or me. Him or me.

Exhale. Don't think about it.

Him or me. Him or me. Him or me. Him . . .

Squeeze the trigger.

* * *

In a cold sweat, I wake. My head aches. Clutched tight in one hand is an empty whiskey bottle. My mouth is dry, and it takes me a few seconds to remember that I'm not in Iraq. Haven't been for a long time.

It's hard to catch my breath. But at least I'm not screaming. Nightmares aren't new. But usually when I woke, it was pure frenzy unleashed on the world.

The TV's still on but muted. An episode of *The Twilight Zone* plays in black and white. A man shouts at a woman while she makes toast in a sterile kitchen. The American dream. The man in my magic box is horrified. Agitated beyond reason. His life unravels before my eyes. But his wife, I'm guessing it's his wife, is oddly devoid of emotion. She's the unhinged one, I think. Must be. His rage feels more justified than her automaton neutrality.

But I can't follow the story. Their argument continues in silence.

The digital clock reads 6:24. I check again: 6:24 a.m. Morning. Thankfully.

Around the corners of the mini blinds, an unnatural glow permeates the room, like the yellow-orange flames of an old gas stove. I'm off-balance from drinking as I stumble for the window but thinking clearly because of the nightmare. Outside, the world is blanketed in a wall of dust. The violent winds pelt my window with invisible pebbles, rattling the glass pane. Something emerges from the swirl of all that dirt. At first, I don't believe it; I rub my eyes and check again. But there, standing impossibly still, is a single shadowed figure.

Were they watching me?

I grab my gun off the nightstand. Then I'm out in the storm, squinting into the blinding sand. The wind howls, mournful, stinging my face with a fierce heat. It's disorienting, oppressive. The figure moves away and disappears into the fog of dust. Plunging ahead, I pursue. There's nothing for a long while except for the sand and moaning wind.

Keep moving. They're out here.

Then I'm on the shadow. It turns back and aims a gun. I fire first. The *crack-bang* of the pistol echoes into eternity and pushes away all sound of wind. Silence strikes down on me like a hammer as the shadow hits the ground.

Reality stops.

The sand lurks all around me, held back by an invisible barrier, like the reverse effect of a shaken snow globe. In this bubble, silence reigns.

The shadow's body lies face down in the dirt. We must have wandered into the desert. Looking back, I can't see the motel. The two of us are alone. I flip the body over, expecting one of the FBI agents. But instead, it's Madison Andrews. I've shot her in the chest, and her Pilates shirt soaks through with blood.

Madison's not dead but will be soon. She says, "You did this to me."

I drop the gun. Apply pressure to the wound.

"Try not to talk," I say.

She cries tears of blood as she struggles to breathe.

"You're a murderer," she gasps one last time.

All is still. My hands stained red. I scream into the apocalyptic orange sky.

* * *

Just like before, I woke in the motel room. But this time I screamed.

This was real. Pathetically predictable unlike the dream of waking calm. Knowing I was awake didn't bring me peace.

Checked my hands. Not covered in blood. Not literally, anyway.

Out the window, the sun hung low on the horizon. Dawn. No storm. No dust. No Madison. Just lonely, empty desert.

The boy-wonder manager rushed out of the office, past the pool, and made a beeline for my room. He held a key attached to a large piece of tempered metal. Probably a master.

How long have you been screaming?

Back in bed, the bottle lay on its side. Discarded. But there were still a few drops left of my brown liquid. At least a shot's worth. It went down fast, quenching my burning throat.

A rerun of *The Price Is Right* played on TV. From the look of the contestants' clothes and Bob Barker's youth, it was an episode from the 80s. I turned the volume up and watched as a man correctly guessed the price of a dishwasher and acted like he'd won a million dollars.

The teenage clerk knocked at the door. He was yelling something about a noise complaint, asking if I was okay. I heard his pleas to open the door or he'd do it himself.

But I ignored him.

Sitting cross-legged on the dirty brown carpet, I covered my face and wept.

CHAPTER 9

To preserve my dwindling cash, I walked back to the mall. It was mid-October but the desert sweltered, the sidewalks literally swayed in front of me as waves of heat drifted off the crisp concrete. My shoeless feet throbbed, blistering raw as the hot cement worked another number on them. A few miles back, I'd taken off my jacket and rolled up my sleeves. It didn't help. Sweat soaked my already-wrinkled shirt. Now I needed new clothes to go with the shoes I intended to buy. Home wasn't an option; the police would be waiting for me there. Guess I'd be spending all the money I just saved walking.

My stolen vehicle was right where I'd left it, parked in front of the now-deserted Yard House chain restaurant. But no one seemed to have paid the car much mind. Probably not unusual for drunks to grab a ride home and return for their car the next day. Certainly the respectable thing to do.

Despite the early hour, the Palmdale Fiesta Mall doors were unlocked, the air conditioning working overtime to cool the massive space. The place had seen better days. *For Lease* signs covered most of the storefronts. Regular janitorial services appeared to have been forsaken, and graffiti plastered the walls. Once a pristine mecca of shopping, it was now a fallen relic of the past. But this derelict mall wasn't completely forsaken. Amid the ruins of capitalism, a shantytown had sprung up near the food court. Apparently neither the owners nor the city cared to enforce the *No Loitering* notices posted next to those leasing signs. Probably simpler for everyone to save money on security and let the poor get out of the heat and away from the watchful eyes of those God-fearing, taxpaying, American dreamers who'd claimed this desert in the name of suburbia.

Fortunately, the anchor stores had weathered this economic travesty. So, I made my way to Dillard's and took a seat on a planter that still had a few fake greens to brighten the place up. Nearby, a hodgepodge of lean-tos, tents, and other structures had been erected out of cardboard boxes, tarps, canopies, and suitcases—it's amazing what people throw away. A few of the residents gave me knowing looks as they went about their daily chores. With no shoes and my sweat-drenched outfit, I was beyond the pale of any self-respecting citizen of the Palmdale Fashion Center shantytown. After all, they had running water, multiple roofs over their heads, and affordable food. That shower I'd enjoyed yesterday morning now seemed a distant memory.

As I waited for the shop to open, a glowing storefront down a side corridor caught my attention—mostly because it was the only small business to have survived the massacre. Down by the store's light stood an A-frame sandwich board. There were no words stating what the business sold but bargain rate psychic sprang to mind. On the poster, a large, open-palmed hand with bolts of lightning jutting out from behind it demanded you stop. Embedded in the middle of the palm was an eye, its pupil burning red like the robot cheetah dog that had tried to eat me last night. The iris around the red pupil swirled with hues of emeralds and jades. I stared at that menacing haze of green, unable to shake the feeling I'd seen that tainted cloud before. But I couldn't place the where or the when. A chill went through me. A sinking feeling in the pit of my gut told me to flee.

But I didn't listen. Something called to me from within that drab den of the occult hidden within this oasis of the desert. A lost memory burrowed into the back of my brain like a parasite gnawing away at my soul. That blank space in my head tormented me. A forgotten nightmare. The fear pulsed within me, palpable, despite no reason behind it. I needed it to stop. I needed to know what I couldn't remember.

The waiting room was dark. A few grubby couches set around a coffee table cluttered with magazines similar in age and use to the ones I'd left behind at my own office. No receptionist greeted me but that made sense since a psychic would know when clients were coming ahead of time. Money saver.

Taking a seat, I rummaged through the magazines looking for something worth my time. Settled on an old black-and-white rag, *The National Intrepid.* I'd never heard of it but the photo on the cover struck my fancy: a very realistic image of a baby with bat wings, giant fangs, and bulging eyes. I imagined the bat baby's eyes were red, like so many eyes seemed to be these days. The title of the article read: *Child Vampire Found Alive.*

Flipping through pages about Chupacabras, UFOs, and government conspiracies, my eye lingered on an article about monsters living beneath the streets of Los Angeles. Why not learn something new about my hometown? Poorly written, it told the story of an ancient race of lizard people who once ruled the planet. The lizards fled underground when the dinosaurs met their demise on the wrong end of an asteroid. Beneath the surface, their civilization flourished away from the prying eyes of us primitive humans.

There were maps scrawled by treasure hunters from the early twentieth century outlining the supposed structure of this ancient and advanced race's city. Evidently, many had scoured beneath the sewers of LA searching for signs of these intricate tunnel systems, sadly to no avail. One city official claimed to have encountered one of the creatures down in the depths of the subways. The artist rendering of that eyewitness account looked like something out of an old sci-fi comic, a cross between a bipedal crocodile and a prehistoric raptor.

A throat clearing drew my attention to a woman dressed in black. The desired effect was flowing robes, but they looked more like pinned-together towels that had seen a few too many washes. Her makeup was caked on thick and white on the cheeks and smudged vibrant blue around the eyes. Streaky black hair cried bad dye job. With all that going on, her age was impossible to guess, but I'd say closer to seventy than anything. She moved quick, disappearing through beads that passed for a door, her towel-robes doing a decent job hiding a frail body.

The site of our would-be séance was a bit of a letdown. We sat across from each other in flimsy red-and-blue beach chairs in a drab, candlelit room. Between us stood a folding table covered by a black sheet with yellow and silver felt stars stapled on it. The ceiling had an active and slow leak that dripped periodically, having turned multiple square panels above us into brown sludge. Everything had a musty smell of mold, which was probably exactly what you'd find hidden in the ducting above.

I checked my watch. Still had twenty minutes before Dillard's opened. This was better than meeting the mayor of the shantytown, so I resolved to stay and see what insight this woman had to offer from the ethereal planes. The next fifteen minutes went by with her reading greasy tarot cards that were far from illuminating. Also, allegedly, Mars was in retrograde—I didn't even know Mars had grades—and that meant a meaningful life event was coming my way. Somewhere around her asking about my father abusing me as a boy, I decided I'd had enough.

"Thanks for the memories," I interrupted, cutting short an explanation about the weakness in my water sign. "How much do I owe you?"

My curt words hurt the psychic's feelings. But I had things to do. This was far less entertaining than anticipated and a waste of my hard-earned, stolen cash.

My medium lowered her gaze, took a deep breath, and regained her composure. But when she looked back at me, her eyes were milky white, pupils completely gone, no longer human. Neat trick. I hadn't even seen her put in the contact lenses.

"Those that are reflected may rule this world," she droned into the flickering darkness of this tiny room of the occult, hollow and flat. "A shadow leads, forged in the fire of war. He desires an empire reborn from the ashes of history. But a Shade possesses untapped strength. A bender of time. Defender of the righteous. Though a broken heart and fragile mind distracts from that destiny. Which mirror prevails? Only time will tell if he brings salvation or destruction."

She shook her head, her eyes clearing. Had she taken out the contacts? I'd missed it again. She was better than I'd given her credit for. Sincerely impressed, I applauded.

"How did you do that thing with your eyes?" I asked.

"Don't lose yourself to him," she gasped.

"Lose myself to who?"

"What was that?"

"You just said, 'don't lose yourself to him'."

"Did I?" She smiled. "How strange. Remember, the pull of Mars is strong for you. Don't make any major relationship choices this month. And be diligent with your finances. But opportunities at work may present room for growth."

"You're a real-deal fortune cookie, aren't you?" I glanced around the sad room. "I can see you've followed your gifts to great success."

She frowned. I'd hit a nerve.

"That'll be twenty-two fifty. Tip not included."

* * *

When Dillard's finally opened, I grabbed a tartan button-down shirt, jeans, blue suit jacket, and a pair of sneakers. All on clearance. The entire ensemble cost about fifty-five dollars, a screaming deal unless you only have two hundred dollars to your name and just spent twenty-five of them on a fortune teller con woman. No way around it. Walking into that bank looking like a hobo was bound to raise eyebrows and alarms.

The drive back to Santa Monica was slow with bad traffic, so I took the opportunity to turn my cell phone on for the first time in days. The old flip phone booted up and immediately showed two voicemails. As the car plodded on, I played them back on speakerphone.

"Message one, received yesterday at 9:45 a.m.: 'Hey, Raines. It's Carla. About last night. You can't just show up like that pretending nothing happened. It's not . . . Look, we should talk. Clear the air. Call me back.'

"Message two, received yesterday at 10:52 p.m.: 'Duster, it's me again. I just had a visit from two FBI agents. You need to call me back.'

"End of new messages."

Not good, Raines. You left her hanging high and dry.

They'd gone after Carla. What was worse, she'd called me Duster. She never called me Duster. Sounded rattled. If they'd hurt her, I'd make them pay.

We'll make them pay, you mean.

Don't think about Madison Andrews. Dead. Her body violated. I swallowed my fear.

But it was me they wanted, and they'd probably guessed Carla was an effective lever to pull. They hoped I'd be dumb enough to stick my neck out. They wouldn't kill her. Not yet, anyway. But there's a lot you can do to a person before they're dead.

The urge to call and make sure she was okay tickled the back of my neck. But I couldn't call her yet. They'd be watching, and I had to take care of my business with the safe deposit box first. Once those FBI agents caught back up with me, getting into the bank would be impossible. This morning, right now, was my only chance. I had to make this happen because I was dead in the water without whatever was in that box. Hopefully I wasn't risking everything for a few strands of Madison's hair and a keepsake high school diary.

My phone vibrated, a text message from a number I didn't recognize: *Cops all over neighborhood. Ask for u. Don't come back.*

The phone vibrated with another text: *This is Juan.*

Knew I'd had a good feeling about that kid. It wasn't news. I'd known they'd be surveilling my building. Though it felt simple of the cops to be asking about me in the neighborhood—they must have a low opinion of my intelligence—because they had to know I wouldn't be going back there. But it was standard procedure, cover all bases, canvass my neighborhood, put my picture out to the public.

Let's pray no one at the bank recognizes you from the morning news.

Taking my eyes off the road, I looked down at the cell and tried to think of the best thing to write back. What would a bright kid like that respond to most? Praise? Solidarity?

What are you doing? Lose the phone now.

Suddenly it occurred to me the FBI could track this phone and triangulate my position—we'd had some nifty tools at the LAPD, and I could only guess what toys the government could deploy—it being off probably saved me from a squad of SWAT storming my motel room last night. And now here I was, listening to my voicemails and texting like a dad on his way to pick up the kids from a soccer game.

Stupid. Stupid. Stupid.

Quickly, I memorized Juan's cell phone number and pulled the battery from the back of my old brick. Broke the flip phone in half. Threw the pieces out the window for good measure. Now I needed to buy a burner. My bankroll wasn't looking so flush anymore.

CHAPTER 10

AT HALF PAST 11 A.M., I ARRIVED AT THE BANK. IT WASN'T anything special. Small brick building, down off Santa Monica's Promenade, surrounded by hundreds of shops, restaurants, and tourists. Wasn't great beach weather but that never stopped anyone from going to the beach. The place was a zoo of pedestrians just generally being a nuisance.

Biding my time, I circled amid the throngs of traffic searching for a meter. Parking at the bank with the stolen car would be a mistake for obvious reasons. I'd already made my one mistake of the day turning on the cell phone. And the day was still young.

Found the perfect space, put two hours in the meter, and walked the three blocks to the bank. Along the way, I purchased a discounted newspaper from a vending machine and folded my revolver in the middle of it, clenching it tight under my arm the rest of the way. Near the bank entrance, there was a decent hiding spot behind a couple of bushes where I left my wrapped-up gun. Didn't need anyone thinking I was robbing the place.

The inside was corporate banality at its finest: brown commercial-grade carpet, manufactured wood desks, uncomfortable-looking blue couches and chairs surrounding circular tables displaying loan brochures. Tellers stood behind glass partitions in front of a roped-off area for the line to form. People in suits patrolled the floor, looking for their next mark. Or as they call them in the industry, preferred clientele.

A young woman in a crisp gray suit with a clipboard had the nicest demeanor of any of the employees on the floor. And based on her age, I assumed she hadn't worked there long. Maybe she'd be a sympathetic ear, and her inexperience would help me circumvent normal banking procedures.

She made eye contact with me and smiled. I belonged. Glad I'd bought the nicer clothes.

"How may I assist you today, sir?"

"Well"—I pulled out the key that Madison had mailed me—"I'd like to open my safe deposit box."

"Of course. We'd be happy to help you with that. Give me a moment to get my manager and he can assist you."

"I don't need a manager." She frowned. I stammered on, "I don't want to be a bother."

"Not at all, sir. Our deposit box clients are one of our highest priorities."

"I'd rather you just helped me. Is that all right?"

She sensed this was off. I could see it in her eyes.

Don't push your luck, Raines. Back off.

"Unfortunately," she said cautiously, "I'm not senior enough to help you. But don't worry, you'll be in the best of hands."

"I'm sure I will, thank you," I said to her back as she left me to wait.

Damn. That could've gone better.

Rubbed my hands together to steady them. Deep breath. Shoved my still-shaking hands in my pockets—thought about whistling but realized how asinine that would be—and paced.

You need to calm down. You're doing fine.

She hadn't recognized me. That was obvious. I had the key to the box. And asking to access my box was completely normal. If Madison weren't dead, I'd never have given this a second thought. But she was dead. The cops were on my tail. And there were hundreds of cameras in the bank and surrounding area that had caught glimpses of me. If anyone was watching . . .

Snap out of it. You're blowing this before it even starts.

The woman hustled into the back, behind the laminated glass, and told her boss I was waiting. He came out immediately. She hadn't been joking about being high on the priority list. He was dressed like everyone else who worked there in a smart blue suit one size too big, clean pressed shirt and tie. He was older, with salt-and-pepper hair and thick reading glasses. He had the air of an accountant, which was fitting since he worked in a bank. It was clear as day he had a trained eye for spotting bullshit, and his glance lingered on me longer than the young woman's had.

But after a brief moment of uncertainty, he smiled and treated me with respect. "Good morning, sir. My name's Mike. I'm the manager of this branch."

"Good to know you."

"If you'll follow me right this way, Mister . . ."

"Raines."

"Mr. Raines. Of course."

He walked me back to a nondescript metal door, scanned a key card. The room behind the locked door was simply adorned with a rickety oak wood desk and two matching chairs—one for clients and a less-comfortable-looking one for the banker. The desk was bare save for an old box computer that belonged in the early aughts. Behind the desk was another locked door, which I assumed led to the vault.

Mike hit some keys on the computer. It took a minute for the old dinosaur to pull up the program he'd requested, during which we sat in awkward silence. No use making small talk. Didn't want to risk saying the wrong thing. The computer finally beeped it was ready. He angled the screen towards me so I could just make out a spreadsheet. "I apologize," he said. "But I don't know your full name."

"Why would you?"

My heart pounded. We locked eyes. He'd remember my face if he'd watched the news. Was that why his gaze had lingered? Had he already triggered an alarm? I was losing control of the situation.

"Oh," the manager breathed uncomfortably. "It's just that I register all the boxes here. I try and make a point to never forget a face." Relief hit me. The banker continued, "May I ask what name the box would be registered under?"

"I believe it's under my wife's maiden name," I said, not missing a beat despite my frayed nerves. "Andrews."

"Oh, yes. Of course. Madison, right? I remember her. Lovely lady. Came in about three months back as I recall. Very kind. You're a lucky man."

"I am lucky."

"Will your wife be joining us this morning?"

"Wasn't planning on it."

Mike frowned, and I knew I had a problem. "Well, I'm very sorry to say this but only those whose names the box is registered under may access it. If you didn't jointly open the box together, then I'm afraid only she may open it. It's a safety precaution. Standard-industry procedure. I'm sure you understand."

"I understand completely." My voice came out even. Couldn't believe I was holding it together. "Would you mind checking my name then? Duster Raines. Who can remember what name anyone uses when you're married." I smiled with genuine warmth and hoped it played.

"Tell me about it." The manager chortled. "Let's see, then. Raines. Raines. Yes, I have it right here. Number 406. I apologize, sir. Seems she opened the box in your name. It's my mistake. I should've remembered. Lots of paperwork when someone does it that way. I must have gotten lost in our conversation."

"She has that effect on people."

"Yes. I'm sure she does. Well, I'll just need a form of identification to confirm and I'll take you right in."

Handed him my driver's license. Leaned back. Felt at ease.

Madison had been one savvy lady. She'd registered the box in my name without even knowing I'd take the case. That took guts. Or it could've just been fear. She knew whatever she'd hidden was valuable enough to kill for. Maybe she'd figured it could stay locked away in that vault for the rest of eternity as long as she was safe. She'd been wrong. Dead wrong.

The manager grabbed a key and led me back into the vault. It was bigger than I'd expected. The walls were lined with deposit boxes of various widths and heights. Each one had two locks: one for the banker's key and one for the customer's. The numbers ran into the thousands. He went to 406, one of the small ones, and unlocked the left lock.

"If you need anything, I'll be right outside." The vault door shut behind him and secured with a thud.

Unlocking the second lock with my key, I pulled the long metal safe out and set it on the table in the middle of the room. Deep breath. Opened it. Inside was a ring with a large stone setting. It was a rock I didn't recognize, sparkling green with hints of yellow that almost seemed alive when the light refracted through it.

Underneath was a glossy picture of Madison Andrews by herself. I swore. Wished Dr. Andrews had been in the picture. Probably manning the camera. She stood in front of a wooden lodge surrounded by mountains and trees capped white with snow. I flipped it over and recognized Madison's perfectly looped cursive: *2007, Angeles Forest.*

The ring had the look of a wedding band. I'd noticed her not wearing hers when I first met her. Maybe this was that ring. But why had she felt the need to hide it? And why make me the only person who could access it? It didn't make sense. She'd seemed flummoxed when I'd mentioned the indentation on her ring finger. I'd been flirting, hoped she'd ditched it for me. But that wasn't the case. The truth was far more menacing.

At the time, I'd thought she was glancing around the bar because of her mental instability. But maybe she'd been scared. Thought whoever took her husband was after her. Granted, she'd fed me the crazy line about aliens but that didn't mean someone hadn't kidnapped Dr. Andrews. And now I knew the FBI agents had been at The Lazy Giant.

But they'd been there before she arrived. Were they after me or her? And why? How did it all fit together?

And how had she known months ago to leave this ring for me? Andrews had only been missing a few days. Nothing was adding up.

It was a dead end. *Damn.*

Should've pushed her harder on the ring. But I hadn't, so there wasn't any point in worrying about it now. At least there was the picture of the lodge. I'd have to find it.

I pocketed the picture and grabbed the wedding band to do the same. When I touched the stone, a slight tug pulled at the back of my belly button like a minor drop on a roller coaster. I felt dizzy for a moment, as if I might vomit. But it passed quickly. I turned to leave and saw standing before me a hazy vision of myself, dressed all in black, but I couldn't make out the details of the attire. The other me smiled and waved before vanishing like a wisp of smoke.

I reached for my gun, ready for a fight, and remembered I'd hidden it outside. I felt like I might faint again and leaned against the nearby safe deposit boxes to keep from falling. I tried to center myself. I could feel panic gripping my chest, pulling me into the abyss.

Deep breaths, Raines.

I'd had visions before. Specters in the night. Tricks of my mind. Dead people from my past. But this had been different. This had been something else . . .

What the hell was that?

I wouldn't worry about it right now if I were you. Focus on the moment.

But . . .

Do you really want to have this argument with yourself in a bank vault?

No.

Didn't think so. Now let's go before the cops show up.

The hustle and bustle of Santa Monica had a brighter, more vibrant feel than when I'd last seen it. Grabbing my gun, I hurried into the tumult of tourists with a slight skip to my step. A lead always made the adrenaline pump. Admittedly it wasn't a very solid one. But something was better than nothing. In this business, all it takes is a little break and suddenly you have the answer you were looking for.

For the first time in a long time, I had purpose. I grabbed on to that high-flying feeling and let the euphoria wash over me.

But it didn't last. I was only about a block from my parked Mercedes when I saw a meter maid running its plates. The entire side of the road I'd parked on was cleared out. I looked up at the posted signs and saw street cleaning was scheduled from noon to two on Wednesdays with no parking. *How long had I been in that vault?* I'd messed up big-time, and any second now that parking enforcement officer was going to see it was a stolen vehicle and call the cops.

Without another thought, I ducked onto a different street and walked as fast as I could away from that car, the bank, the restaurants, the ocean, the Promenade, and all the other places the tourists wanted to be. In LA, you walk a few blocks in any direction, and things can change fast. Santa Monica was no different. Even in this expensive town, the shops quickly became a mixed bag of not-so-nice.

A cruddy electronics store was exactly what I needed. The storefront windows were covered in advertisements for computers, cell phones, iPods, and all sorts of devices that no one wanted anymore or that I'd never heard of in the first place. They also had an ATM, cashed checks, and did payday loans. Smart to diversify.

Twenty dollars of my depleted funds later, I had a disposable cell phone.

Out on Wilshire, I caught one of the Big Blue Buses heading downtown. Once I had a seat, I tore the cell open and activated it.

Dialed Carla.

No answer. That wasn't good.

Dialed the only other number I could think to call and waited for Juan to pick up. When he did, I dove right in. "Juan, it's me. Raines. Did you call that lawyer I gave you?"

"I can't talk right now. I'm at school. I'll get in trouble."

"She's in danger. I need to find her."

He hesitated. He was just a kid, and I was a psychotic middle-aged man calling him at school from an unknown number. I didn't blame him for not trusting me, but I needed his help. Now more than ever.

"Please, Juan. I don't know how else to find her. They'll be watching."

"Okay. We're meeting with her today after school."

"Great. Where?"

"My apartment."

"I can probably make that work. Can you let me in through the back alley or something?"

"Yeah. I gotta go. The bell's ringing. I get off at two." He hung up.

The bus lumbered on.

Hopefully Carla showed up to her meeting because, if she didn't, I wasn't sure where to start looking. Only that morning, I'd thought it unlikely the FBI agents would kill her. But now, I wasn't so sure. Those spooks were as dirty as they came. Maybe I'd just been kidding myself about Carla's safety to justify going to the bank to save my own skin. And now I'd put her at risk. But it wasn't something I could dwell on. Carla had to be okay because that was the only scenario I could control.

There'd be cops looking for me there. No doubt. Couldn't worry about it. Had to try. No matter the consequences. I owed her that much. Back into the lion's den. Exactly what you weren't supposed to do.

You only live once.

I leaned against the dirty bus window, stared out at the slow-moving buildings, and did my best to not throw up.

CHAPTER 11

Hunkered down in the alley behind Juan's apartment complex, between some grimy recycling bins and a fetid dumpster, the realization sank in that coming back had been truly idiotic. I'd been off the bus maybe three minutes before my first run-in with the law. An unmarked police cruiser circled back just as I turned the corner into the alley. Another few seconds and they'd have spotted me. Out here, flapping in the wind, I was overexposed; only a matter of time before I got caught. No way to delude myself. A wanted forty-six-year-old, mustachioed white guy, hiding in broad daylight with Koreatown's trash wasn't exactly inconspicuous.

Hell, from where I hid, I made three undercover cops watching the front door of my building across the street. The dragnet tightened its noose around me.

But I needed to see Carla. Needed to know she was okay. This was the only way I could figure out how to do that.

A calculated risk. On the cliff's edge. But I hadn't jumped yet.

Juan's school schedule made this all a bit more complicated. It was still an hour before his release. All I could do was wait with the rats for Juan to get out of advanced algebra or whatever he was taking last period. Hopefully he understood the urgency and made his way home once that bell rang. At least the kid was in school, you had to give him that.

The back door to Juan's apartment building opened, and a young Latina woman, probably in her late twenties, stuck her head out and scanned the alley with hard eyes that'd seen their share of cruelty from an indifferent world. Those tough eyes fell on me hiding behind piles of rotten food and dirty diapers. For a moment, I thought she might scream and bring the police from all directions. But instead, she smiled. And when she did, a hidden warmth emanated.

"Mr. Raines?" she asked.

"Yeah." Busted, didn't know what else to say.

"Juan called. I'm his mother."

She was too young to be his mom. But age was only a number. I'd seen her nose before and it belonged to Juan. An old soul, her strength flowed out. She'd sacrificed youth for that kid. Part of me fell in love, the struggle of the imaginary life I'd created for her intoxicating. Another bad habit of mine.

"You waiting for someone else?" she asked.

The door slammed shut behind us. Paint peeled from the walls of the dimly lit halls. The air pressed in on me, stuffy and humid, and what little carpet remained on the ground smelled of long-forgotten water damage. We took the stairs up to apartment 4J. It was small, much like my apartment, but the similarities ended there. It was tightly packed with well-kept furniture, every nook and cranny covered with generations of family photos. The walls were painted with different earth-toned accents, giving everything an inviting and tranquil feel. This was a home.

She yelled from the kitchen, wondering if I wanted some tea. I did. She went about boiling the water.

The photos were of weddings, picnics, birthdays, reunions. Every event bursting with forty or more people ranging from great-great-grandparents to infant children. One picture had prime real estate on the mantel next to a statue of the Virgin Mary and a framed painting of a white-robed Jesus haloed against the night sky. This special picture was of Juan's mother holding a younger Juan, maybe seven, in front of this very mantel. Squeezing them both from behind in a massive bear hug was a man in military fatigues with a crew cut. Guessing that was Juan's father.

"Juan likes that photo most."

"Thank you," I said as I took my steaming mug from her. "I'm sorry but I didn't catch your name on the way up."

"Valentina. My friends call me Val."

"Well, thanks, Valentina. I appreciate the help."

"Don't be silly. You call me Val. Juan told me what you did. Getting Miss Carla to help with his cousin's legal troubles. Our family's indebted to you."

Never one for praise, I tried to take it graciously. But I couldn't stand the silence long.

"So, what do you do?" I cringed.

"I'm an RN downtown at Good Samaritan. My next shift's at five. That's why we scheduled this time with Carla."

Nodded. Sipped tea. Waited.

She didn't ask me anything about myself. Uncomfortable. The silence gnawed at me again, burrowing into the back of my skull like a ravenous tick.

"Juan tells me his dad's an Army engineer?"

"That's right. He's in the Rangers. Deployed overseas. Stationed somewhere in the Middle East. They don't tell us much."

The Army Ranger father explained that crew cut Juan wore. Just like Dad.

"Impressive," I said. "I served in Iraq. Air Force. But that was a long time ago."

"I know."

Wondered how she knew. Had Juan told her? What else had he said? I didn't ask.

We drank our tea like old friends with nothing left to talk about because we'd said it all long ago. But that wasn't the truth, and the silence had an empty and forced feeling that made everything tighter and constrained in the home. Nervously, I looked around for something to talk about. But there were only family photos and religious icons. Tended to avoid both subjects lest they lead to talk of my own sordid past or beliefs.

Thankfully, Juan walked in and rescued me. He was laughing, carrying his book bag, a different boy than the one who knocked at my door for rent every month. Coming in behind him, Carla also laughed. Bonding. Nice to see her like that. She saw Val first and was all smiles. When I rose to greet her, that smile disappeared.

"What the hell are you doing here?" she demanded.

"Nice to see you, too."

"I'm not in the mood, Raines. There are cops outside looking for you."

"I got your messages. Had to make sure you were okay."

"Ever hear of a phone?"

"Tried earlier. You didn't answer."

"I've been in court. And I called yesterday."

"Too dangerous to call until I had a burner. They'd be expecting it. Tracking my cell. There's something big going on here. I'm just not sure what."

"They said you killed a woman."

"It's a lie. You have to know that."

"I don't know what I know," she said. "But I have half a mind to call them up here right now."

"No," Juan jumped in. "You can't. I mean . . ." He looked to his mom.

"Juan's right," Val said. "Mr. Raines deserves the benefit of the doubt in this home. Without him, we wouldn't have you."

Carla grimaced, taken aback by the swift rebuke from the family.

"Can I talk to you?" I placed my hand on Carla's shoulder. It stung when she pulled away.

Val caught the hint and took Juan into the kitchen.

Carla and I sat in the living room. I said, "I owe you an apology."

"You really want to do this now?"

Of course not. But it had to be done. "The way I acted the other night. I don't have an excuse."

"You broke your promise. Again."

"I know. I'm trying. I guess it's just . . . I don't know. Hard."

"Life's hard, Raines. For everyone, not just you. I can't keep looking the other way. I can't keep falling back in with you. You know I care but you're not the same man when you've been drinking. And I had plenty of that growing up, believe you me."

"I know. I never meant to hurt you. Just lost my temper."

"That's bullshit. If you didn't mean to, you wouldn't have. Whiskey can't be an excuse for everything."

"Well, I'm not drunk now. And, you know, I'm really sorry. It went too far. I didn't mean what I said."

"Look, Raines. You want to drink yourself into an early grave just like your dad did, that's your business. I don't judge. But just because you can't escape the shadow of your father, doesn't mean I have to date mine."

"We're great together."

"Sure. Sometimes. But most of the time it's nothing but fights and heartache."

Carla glanced over her shoulder into the kitchen where Juan and Val sat. The place was tiny, and they might as well have been in the living room with us. Carla frowned, embarrassed. That was unfair: it was me who'd pulled the Dr. Jekyll routine with a bottle of booze.

I grasped at straws, desperate to make this work. "Remember the first time we met?"

"How could I forget? You were framing a client of mine."

"I wasn't framing him. Dude was guilty as sin."

"Says you. The evidence begged to differ."

"Details. Details."

She snorted, trying to stay angry, but I could see her defenses cracking.

"That's why you're the best," I said. "Got him off that day. And I chased you down the hall to give you a piece of my mind."

"Oh, please," she laughed. "You were coming for one thing and you know it."

"Hey, I resent the implication. I'm a gentleman. I purchased you the finest Los Angeles Superior Court dark roast that money could buy."

"I bought the coffee."

"You did? Huh. You sure? Because that doesn't sound like me at all."

Her smile broadened. I smiled back. I'd done it. I always found a way back into the fold with her. We were meant for one another. But then, her smile vanished.

"Raines, you're a good man when you try. But we can't keep going round and round like this. I'm only getting older."

"Give me another shot. This time can be different. I'm trying to be better."

"It's too late."

"Please don't say that. Look, I messed up. I get it. But I can't stop thinking about you and that's got to count for something. Right? Let's just reset. I'll do better. I know I can be better. I have to be for all our sakes. There're greater things for me just around the corner. I can feel it. You and me can share that together."

I was desperate, rambling, talking too fast.

She'd heard it all before, and the old script wasn't playing. She turned away, no longer listening. I swallowed hard, shut out, the bitter taste of defeat.

Not too sure how I'd imagined this going. Truthfully, I'd tried not to think about it too much. Brushed aside the finer details and focused on the apology. Forget the past and all the baggage that went with it. Just live for the now and focus on damage control. But that's not how life works. All we've got are those moments of the past to make us who we are. At the end of the day, it's hard to argue with reality. And now my apology was going how anyone who knew our story could've predicted, which was badly.

There had to be a way to salvage this. I couldn't live without her. But I had to convince her of that fact.

"Do you think with more time you could find it in your heart to forgive me?"

She never had the chance to answer because the door got kicked in and seven heavily armed police officers took us into custody.

CHAPTER 12

THE COPS DIDN'T TAKE ME FAR.

Dragged across the street into my dilapidated apartment building, we rode that creaky elevator to my floor and swept into my apartment—bastards had already kicked down the door—and bound me with plastic cable ties to a kitchen chair. I strained against the bindings, the plastic strong and taut; no way to break free.

Carla, Val, and Juan were gone. No idea what they'd done with them. It was just five police officers in their riot gear and me, waiting silently for something.

"I want to see my lawyer," I said.

No one moved. They were spread out, guarding the windows and doors. The entire place had been turned upside down. The couch cushions slashed. The barren cabinets opened. My collection of canned foods no longer stacked in the precise manner I liked them kept. These men had been looking for something, and I could guess what it was they wanted.

They'd searched me, too, but only a pat down. Worse was coming soon.

"Look," I said, "if you don't tell me what you want, then how can I help you find it?"

Silence. Statuesque. Barely breathing. The protective glass of the cops' helmets reflected black. Stoic effigies. Faceless enemies.

These guys didn't feel like normal cops—too disciplined and militaristic—more like highly trained mercenaries. This was a crack team, just like the guys who'd stormed Madison Andrews's home last night (probably the same guys for that matter). For the first time something occurred to me that I'd never really considered: maybe they weren't cops.

One of the FBI agents—the ride-share service driver—walked into the room. My guards kowtowed, giving him the lead. He assessed my turned-over apartment, taking in what little there was like a health inspector in a meat factory. Ran his finger over my dusty table. Checked the labels on my once-stacked cans of food. Looked at my patio garden, which hadn't been watered in a week. He did everything except acknowledge me.

Then, with a click of his tongue, he proclaimed, "*Ah-ha!*"

That was it. An annoying eureka like he'd discovered the structure of some unknown molecule. His newfound understanding of my soul in hand, he smiled and nodded to himself frenetically. Excited now, he pulled up a chair and sat very close to my face. His breath smelled of mints and coffee. I hate coffee.

"Well, hello, Duster. Long time no see."

"You know, people just call me Raines."

"Do they now?"

"Wish you'd told me you were coming. I'd have straightened up."

"You search him?" he asked one of the nearby guards.

"Just cursory, sir," one of the soldiers responded. "He didn't have it on his person."

"Don't suppose you'll just tell me where it is. Will you, Duster? Save us all the unpleasantness of having to look a little harder." He wore that same fake smile he'd had the night we met. God, I wanted to punch that baby face and knock out his teeth. But there were factors limiting my ability to do so—namely heavily armed militants and my being tied to a chair. So instead, I went with answering his question with a lie.

"I have no idea what you're talking about."

"Save it. I know Madison gave it to you. And I know now that she gave it to you before you met her. I don't know how she did it right under our noses. But she did."

"Is that why you murdered her?"

"Madison betrayed the Legion. And there's only one penalty for sacrilege."

Swallowed hard. Not much to say to that.

He stared me down for a long while, trying to get my read, running a number of scenarios on how to break me. Torture was the obvious play. Pulling out fingernails and the like. But this kid didn't seem the type. Liked finesse. Thought he was smarter than me and wanted everyone to know it. His mistake was believing it.

To be fair, I was the one tied to a chair.

Damnit, Raines. You played this all wrong, didn't you?

This scenario had occurred to me when I'd come back to the lion's den. Captured and questioned. I'd guessed correctly the contents of the safe deposit box would be a major topic of conversation, although for the life of me I couldn't guess why. I'd memorized Madison's picture and destroyed it. If I ever made it to the Angeles Forest, it'd be no problem spotting that lodge. But there's only so many ways to hide a ring if you don't know you'll be able to go back and retrieve it. So, I'd put that little memento in the last place anyone likes to look. It'd worked so far, though sitting had become uncomfortable.

But if the FBI stooge wanted it bad enough, he'd find it on a full-cavity search. And based on how I'd found Madison's body, that outcome seemed likely.

"Expecting a war?" the former ride-share driver asked, indicating my piles of foodstuffs. "Probably not bad to be prepared. But your choices leave something to be desired. I didn't think it was possible for one man to consume this much junk food." The agent kicked an empty whiskey bottle out from under my chair. It rolled across the floor and shattered against the wall.

Stay cool. He wants you riled up.

"And the alcohol," he continued. "You're killing yourself, Duster. It's sad, really. Believe it or not, your choices matter. If you make the right choices, you live longer. Take instant ramen, really bad for the heart. All that sodium. Or going on the run when you don't understand what you've gotten yourself into. Did you ever consider we could've helped?"

"You play the hand you're dealt," I said. "And when there's a small army after you, then you improvise. And I got to say, I know I'm amazing but all this seems a bit much."

"We know what you're capable of even if you don't. Had to make sure we took you alive."

"That why you framed me, too?"

"Call it added incentive to cooperate. Obviously didn't work. It's my fault. I wanted to have some fun and really see what you're made of. Should've known about the escape hatch. Sloppy. I take full responsibility."

"At least I proved you aren't that smart."

"See, now is that any way to talk to your friend, Duster?"

"I don't even know your name, *friend*."

"Well, since you're going to be dead soon anyway, why not?"

Panic ripped through me. Knew this interrogation was bound to end with me six feet under. But to hear it said, well, that's another thing.

Don't give up, Raines. Fight. Run. Do something. Anything.

But I didn't see any options. I was in a lot of trouble.

"You can call me Jacobs," he said. "My partner goes by Torian."

"Good." My voice came out steady and cold. "I was sick of calling you the driver."

"Very funny, Duster."

"So, where's your girlfriend, then?"

"You know, people always make that assumption about us. But Torian prefers girls. Not that it's any of your business. Anyway, she took your lady friend. What was her name? Carla? Well, she took Carla to one of our more *secure* locations. You know, privacy. Don't worry, though. She's always gentle with her new toys."

Losing what little control I'd been exercising, I lunged out of my chair and tried to get at Jacobs. I envisioned ripping his throat out with my teeth and strained against my bindings to achieve that end. I'd be dead soon but I'd take him with me. Instead, I fell hard to the floor. Writhed against my cinch cords and the cold linoleum, a murderous fury burning within, looking for an outlet, only finding hard plastic to cut up my wrists and ankles.

Jacobs hadn't flinched, just smirked, watching me squirm.

"Anything happens to her," I said from the floor, "I'll kill you both."

"I believe you. Even though you're tied to that chair. Isn't that funny? Beaten, I still see that fire burning in your eyes. That passion in your soul. You used to use it in your youth. Finished what you started. But you let it get muddled. Tried to douse it with alcohol.

"And why?" Jacobs asked. "Because you killed a few people? Who cares? Your conscience? That's weakness. It's beneath you. See, I know what you could be. *Who* you could be. And that's why seeing you like this sickens me. It's pathetic. You don't deserve the blood that runs through your veins."

"What the fuck are you talking about?"

Jacobs got down on the floor so he could look me straight in the eye. His smile vanished and his stare held only malice. "I know you better than you know yourself, Duster. You've made a lot of guesses. About Madison Andrews. Why she died. About us. Who we are. What we're after. I know because I've seen your mind work on a much higher level. But knowing you and the way you think, well that just made manipulating you simpler.

"The gun you spotted on me the night we met, FBI issue, that was my touch. Torian didn't think you'd be smart enough. Thought you were just another drunk. But I knew what the real Duster Raines was capable of. And sure enough, you noticed. Didn't account for those dart throwers. That was unfortunate. But we still ended up right where we were always meant to."

"You're not making any sense." But I'm not sure he heard me because he kept talking.

"Sadly, you're not a man for our cause. There's a revolution coming and only the best will do. We warned you what would happen if you didn't pass our test. In another life, you'd have been invaluable. But here and now, in this reality, you're a liability."

"So, you tricked me. You aren't the FBI. Whoop-de-fucking-doo. Want me to pin a medal on you?"

"Shh. There's no need to get angry."

"Little late for that. You're running your little psychology experiments like I'm a mouse in your maze. No more. I want to know what the fuck this is about."

"I told you. A new society will be born. And only the chosen shall partake."

"Whatever your bullshit little army is about, it doesn't matter. You'll go down like all criminals do. And I promise, I'll be there when it happens."

"We're not criminals, Duster. We're patriots. Your problem is you think you know everything. But you of all people should realize assumptions often lead down the wrong path."

He was right. I'd misread this entire case from the word go and now I was bound in my own apartment with a nut job and his heavily armed mercenary friends. I didn't like where any of this was going. Crazy religious jargon about someone's birthright being wasted usually ended with you dead in a ditch after your blood's been drunk by a cult.

Keep him talking. Buy us more time.

"Maybe you could show me the true path."

"Good guess. Cult line. Chosen one. But you're not that important."

"Please, I want to fulfill my potential."

"This is bigger than you, Duster. There's a war coming. And we're just the first wave." Jacobs stood. Dusted himself off. "I won't lie, I wish I could take you up on your offer. But you're a loser, Duster Raines. Not fit to clean my boots. I'd hoped for the opposite. You could've been a powerful ally." Jacobs took a deep breath, steadying himself for his next words, tears in his eyes. "It breaks my heart knowing you won't see the battles to come. But fear not, our cleansing fire shall burn. The Legion shall rise from the ashes of this corrupt society."

He stroked my hair with a lover's touch and whispered, "May the Eternal Watcher bless you on your journey into the next life, old friend."

That sealed it. Without a shadow of doubt, Jacobs was insane. And I was screwed.

"You two." Jacobs pointed at two of the faceless militants. "Take care of him. Keep it quick. We owe that much to the shadow of the true Duster Raines. And when it's finished, search him properly."

Jacobs marched from the room and three guards followed. The two remaining soldiers dragged my chair up off the ground and set me upright. One of the men aimed his military issue assault rifle square in my face. Couldn't get a good read on the make but it was equipped with a scope and silencer, like something you'd expect to see a Navy SEAL use. The whisper of bullets would alert no one to my demise. Long after this moment, the smell would bring someone to discover my corpse in a pool of hardened blood, a gaping maw burned into my skull where my eyes used to be, no one able to identify me without dental records.

Stop it. Focus. We aren't dead yet.

This looked like the end. But it gave me one small advantage, I had nothing left to lose.

"At least let me die on my feet," I said.

My reflection stared back from the gleaming visor of the soldier with the gun in my face, a broken man. So this was rock bottom. Won't lie, I'd hit the ground harder than expected. Hopefully I survived this to crawl out of my newfound low.

The mercenary turned to his partner, who shrugged and said, "If he wants to do it standing up, then let him."

The smooth glide of metal across leather kissed my eardrums as my executioner drew a combat knife. He knelt behind me and I felt the release of tension as he undid one of my ankles. No way to know if he'd undo my wrists, so I would have to act when my feet were free.

My heart raced but my mind was clear.

The moment the mercenary undid my second ankle, I stomped hard on the ground and sent myself hurtling back into him. Completely off-balance, we fell to the ground and the chair shattered from the impact. One of my wrists came free but the other was still bound to broken wood. With that shard of jagged chair gripped tight in my hand, I flipped over and jabbed it hard at the place where his helmet ended—right beneath the jaw in the meaty part of the neck.

The merc screamed in pain and stabbed me hard in the shoulder with the knife he still held. Wound hurt like hell but I stayed on him, dug my wooden stake deeper into his neck. Blood poured from torn arteries and veins. It only took a couple seconds before the man went limp.

The other guard, stunned by my sudden assault, had wasted valuable time watching me kill his friend. Snapping back into the moment, he ran at me; probably hoped his friend was still alive and didn't want to risk firing his weapon.

The dead mercenary's rifle felt light as I raised it to fire. The other guard realized his mistake and froze dead in his tracks. He raised his weapon. It was a race of who could fire first. The world slowed as adrenaline coursed through my body. The pain in my shoulder subsided and all that existed was this gun and my enemy.

Time stopped. I stood outside reality as I sighted down the scope of the gun right on the soldier's face mask. That protective gear didn't stand a chance against this high-powered rifle.

Had him dead to rights. This was his end. Pulled the trigger.

A burst of silent bullets flew from the rifle and connected deadeye where I'd been aiming. The mask shattered and the bullets ripped the man's face apart. The soldier reflexively pulled the trigger of his own weapon and fired a torrent of bullets in my general direction. Most of them sprayed harmlessly into the wall behind me, but one found a home in the muscle of my upper thigh while another connected low in my gut. The pain excruciating, I collapsed.

My enemy hit the floor, too. But he was as dead as his friend with the chair leg in his neck. His automatic weapon stopped firing. All was still.

I crawled over to the wall, and I propped myself up against it, every breath pure misery. I undid my belt and secured it tight around my thigh. The wound didn't look too bad, but the blood loss would be a problem if I didn't get it stopped soon. Yanked the knife out of my shoulder. It bled and burned like hell, but I still had full mobility. I'd gotten lucky on two counts. But the third wound, the bullet in the abdomen, was going to be the killer. It pumped slow, gurgling my blood out with the rhythm of my heartbeat, the methodical spurts like a Vegas hotel fountain signaling the imminence of my death.

No idea what had been hit but there were plenty of vital organs to get in the bullet's way. I needed a doctor. Ripped my shirt into strands and pushed them into the wound, trying to clot the bleeding. Reached around and checked my back, feeling a hole where the bullet had come out the other end. That was good. Stuffed more torn shirt into my back wound. Thought about pouring some alcohol on all this bloody mess—I certainly had enough to spare. But dying from infection didn't really matter if you'd bled to death three days prior.

Get up. Find help.

Stumbling onto my feet, I steadied myself with the assault rifle. Using the weapon like a cane, I hobbled from the apartment. The elevator rode slower than usual, groaning down for what felt like an eternity. The world started to lose its color as life slipped through my fingers.

There was no one to be found in the monochrome lobby. The soldiers of fortune who'd left me to die were gone, but it looked like they'd taken the entire neighborhood with them. Where was Mr. Kim when you needed him?

Out on the street, I made my way to Juan's building. Hoped the mercs left the kid and his mother there. They weren't important to them. But they were to me. Val was a nurse. She could help.

Clung to that thought for strength. Took another step. Almost there.

The sky still held a beautiful hue of blue amid all this gray. Yesterday's storm had washed away the pollution, cleansing nature and leaving only beauty. White clouds clumped together in impossible shapes—dinosaurs, ninjas, pirates—the dreams of children. I couldn't remember the last time I'd watched the clouds, taken a moment to enjoy what was around me.

A stage play danced before my eyes, a story for the ages.

Those epic cloud heroes kept moving in spite of my admiration, soaring to another place. Escaping. Wished I could escape. If only I could glide out of this world and into another one. A happier one. The one I was meant to live in. But I couldn't.

It occurred to me that I hadn't crossed the street but instead lay in the road watching imaginary sword fights in the sky. Tried to stand but my body wouldn't obey. Hazarded a breath and watched as Pinocchio the cloud took a swig from a whiskey bottle, then passed it to R2-D2.

Wasn't he a real boy now?

He shouldn't be drinking, I thought. He was underage.

Then, everything went black as I slipped away to nothing.

CHAPTER 13

THE IRAQI BOY LIES AT MY FEET, BLEEDING THROUGH HIS
throat. It was a good shot but not a kill shot. Not yet, anyway.

The sand soaks red with more and more blood as the child
gasps. Suffering. He stares wide-eyed at me. I am the Angel of
Death and he knows it. Wish I could tell him different, but it
would be a lie.

I'm a soldier. This is war.

That's my justification. My mantra. Over and over again:
Soldier. War. Soldier. War.

These things happen. Him or me. Kill or be killed.

But it's phony and I know it. I had other choices; didn't
have to kill him to survive. Or maybe I did. I don't know. I
can't see the future. Didn't mean I had to do it, though. But I
made a choice. And this boy dies for my existence. His life ends
for mine.

Should be sadder. I'm a murderer. But I'm oddly detached.
Whatever soul I had before this moment dies a little with every
pathetic gasp that escapes this little boy's lips.

Stare at the kid, watching his endless stream of tears. Wish
I could stop this. Hate him a little for putting me in this

situation. Why didn't you listen to your parents? Stay home. Don't you know there's a war?

Fuck that. It's me I should hate, not the kid.

He says something I don't understand partly because it's in another language and partly because he's choking on his own blood.

Shit. What am I waiting for?

Focus. Make it fast. You're a monster for not doing this sooner.

Raising my gun, I put another bullet in the young boy's head. What a waste. But at least I ended his agony. The only silver lining in this fucked-up moment.

Who am I kidding? There's no redemption here. This desert is the beginning of the end for me, and I know it. Can already feel it in my bones, an empty space opening inside me.

The boy lies still. He feels no pain. But my suffering, I think, has only just begun.

CHAPTER 14

"Hang in there, Duster," said a voice I couldn't quite place.

Tried to open my eyes but it was difficult. So tired. All I wanted to do was stay in that void and never come back.

Maybe I'd get that wish because I couldn't feel my body. I was weightless. Floating consciousness. A state of being. Pretty sure this was what dying felt like. One last pull and I'd be there.

But sadly, I had things to do. A few loose ends to tie up. Death would have to wait.

With a little bit of focus and a heck of a lot of willpower, I got my eyes open. I found myself in the back of an old station wagon sprawled on top of some cardboard boxes and dirty laundry. Guess I still had a body. It was a start.

Out the back window, it was neither day nor night; just a sad, gray concrete that brightened considerably every ten seconds as we passed beneath embedded commercial-grade lights. The car sped through tunnel after tunnel—intricate and vast—military in their design. Looked to be a staging installation, used for heavy equipment storage and quick troop deployment. But I couldn't remember such a base being anywhere near Los Angeles.

Tried to move to get a better look but I was still weightless and my body wasn't doing me any favors. I got my head to roll over and caught a glimpse of the driver, a man with stark white hair. Couldn't see his face. Next to him sat Juan, who was turned around in his seat watching me.

"I think he opened his eyes," Juan said to the driver. I didn't see if the old man turned around because I lost consciousness again.

* * *

Blinding white light. That was it. Nothing but a great white expanse stretched out before me in all directions.

So much for not dying. I stared directly into that pale corona like a little kid daring the sun to blind him; waited for something to change and was a little disappointed when nothing did. I'd hoped death wouldn't be some cliché tunnel with me walking towards God, Eternity, or whatever was on the other side. I wanted no part of it.

And apparently they wanted no part of me. I floated there, suspended in oblivion, unable to move towards the light. Neither welcomed nor shunned. A bitter cold nipped at my extremities. Abandoned, I shivered, feeling truly afraid. Slowly, I became aware of a rhythm, a drumbeat that only took an instant to recognize as the repetitive throb of my heart. All-consuming. I'd expected to leave that pulse of life behind. But it hadn't gone yet. It reverberated and taunted me. An echo of my former existence.

Surprisingly, at least to me, my life didn't flash before my eyes like you always hear about. Rather, only the last few days ran through my mind on an infinite loop. The people I'd let down. Tears streamed down my face, blurring that eternal radiance into a collage of whites. I blinked, tried to clear my vision. Those broken fragments coalesced into an overhead light fixture shining down on me. In that moment, I grasped the truth. I wasn't dead. Again. In fact, I was sprawled out on an uncomfortable gurney in some type of medical facility. Next to me, a heart monitor beeped that incessant rhythm I'd been hearing in my faux everlasting slumber.

No elation gripped me in realizing that I still lived. I'd wanted that death. Would've welcomed the peace of eternal abeyance. But wanting something doesn't make it so.

A web of tubes, suction cups, and other wires monitored my vitals and pumped who knows what into my body. Without hesitation, I pulled the stents and IVs from my veins with immense discomfort. My body felt stiff. Clean bandages were wrapped tightly over my shoulder, thigh, and abdomen. I propped myself up and immediately regretted it as my leg, stomach, and arm all objected to the move. But now I could see where I was. The place appeared sterile but hardly state of the art. The room looked like it had been piecemealed together from hundreds of different hospitals with equipment from every decade since the 1950s.

"Hello," I whispered. Coughed and tried again. "Hello?"

A man came in from another room. He had frantic eyes and messy white hair, but he wasn't geriatric. No, his face and physicality told me he couldn't have been much older than me. Fairly certain he was the man I'd seen driving that station wagon—so that had been real and not some near-death hallucination. The wild-haired man wore jeans and a faded plaid shirt. He had a bit of a mad-scientist quality minus a white lab coat and, as far as I could tell, death rays.

"Whoa there," the mad scientist said. "You lost a lot of blood, fella. Suggest you keep it simple for a while." He smiled a mouth of crooked yellow teeth.

"Where am I?"

"My hospital."

"And where's that?"

"Someplace safe. Underground. Don't you worry yourself about it."

My mind raced with questions and concerns about a crazy tunnel hermit who'd magically appeared to rescue me from bleeding out on the streets of Koreatown. But the guy seemed nice enough. And he also appeared to have saved my life. So that put one in the plus column for giving him a chance.

Went to push myself farther up and couldn't do it, falling back into bed. Dizzy, the world barely stayed in focus. "What gives?" I said more to myself than him.

"That'd be the drugs I'm pumping into you. Strong stuff. Was glad to see it all still worked. You know, you scavenge this junk up above. Break into pharmacies, hospitals, hit the suppliers direct. You'd be amazed how lacking in basic security precautions some of these warehouses are. But it never fails. Some things tend to be past their shelf life. Makes treating people difficult. All guesswork. Hoping for the right outcome. Almost none of these meds have expiration dates on the packaging. You know, like milk. Which I found surprising."

"What're you giving me?"

"Oh, the usual. Morphine mainly. Regular doses of lorazepam to keep you down. I won't bother to name all the antibiotics. But if there's a microbe left in that body of yours, I'd be shocked." He chuckled to himself and came over to check my vitals. When he saw the flat line of my disconnected EKG, he said, "Guess I didn't do such a good job. Looks like you're dead."

"How long have I been here?"

"A good while now. Maybe two weeks."

"Two weeks?"

"Well, you lost a lot of blood. Had to give you a few transfusions. Don't worry. I stole it directly from the blood bank and they're always checking for HIV and the like."

"Was it really necessary to keep me sedated?"

"Well, you may be dangerous. Yet to be seen."

"I'm not dangerous."

"Tetanus."

"What?"

"Tetanus. I gave you a booster. You asked what I gave you. Just want to be thorough."

This fast-talking man's words ran together, too quick for me to keep up. My head swam. Woozy. Unable to focus. And I ached all over. This guy probably wasn't licensed to be administering these medications. The recovery still to come made me nervous. "Well," I managed. "I'd appreciate it if you brought my doses down. I'm having trouble thinking straight."

"Of course. I'm sure you won't mind wearing these, though." Before I could react, he secured handcuffs to my left wrist and latched them to the bed. Instinctively, I tried to grab him and stop what was happening, but he easily overpowered me and locked my other hand to the bed. "At least until I'm sure," he said.

"What the hell?" I meant to yell it but it came out slurred and thick. I pulled hard on the cuffs but the bed was solid metal, bolted to the wall, and would've been near impossible for a healthy person to break free of it. And I was anything but healthy.

"Just relax, Duster. I'll explain it all later. When you're one hundred and ten percent. No more drugs, though. I promise." As he was leaving, he turned back with an apology in his eyes. "Though, I think you're probably going to be wishing that wasn't the case in a few hours. Between the withdrawals and your alcoholism . . . Well, you'll see soon enough. But I wouldn't worry myself too much about it. I've got my money on you being a fighter."

I tried to ask how he knew anything about my drinking habits, but he waved me silent. Suddenly very tired, I let him run the show.

"When you wake up later, we'll talk. I'm sorry I have to treat you like this. But it's the way it is. Until I meet the man you are, I have no choice but to assume you're the man he is."

Tried to ask him what in God's name he was talking about, but I couldn't form the words.

He must've left because I was alone.

Lying back into the bed's tattered pillows, I stared into my white light and marveled at the mess I'd wandered into. My instincts told me to start working on a plan, to find a way out of this disaster, but it was no use. My mind was mud. I let out a sigh, resigned to my fate, and fell into the last deep sleep I'd have for a long while.

CHAPTER 15

No amount of therapy silenced my demons. Alcohol offered my only respite. But it never lasted.

The dead Iraqi boy who haunted my dreams crept into my waking hours. Watching me buy groceries. Watching me type police reports. Watching me take a shower. Watching me jerk off. Maddening. Tried to shake him but he was my constant companion, an elusive shadow at the edge of my vision. I'd spin to catch him but find he'd just escaped. In hindsight, I only wish his mirage had lasted. Because the real nightmare began when he let me see him.

No longer relegated to the dark recesses of my mind, he demanded payment. Blood for blood. Justice. But no matter how hard I worked to earn its pardon, that specter never let me forget. No amount of repentance quenched its thirst. My sins were the eternal-damnation kind and more would always be required.

So, I did more. A clue here. Planted evidence there. Cheated the system. Though I only punished the guilty. I knew who they were. My conscience remained clean because I served the greater good. An instrument of something larger than myself.

Those chumps on the police force were hypocrites. Cut my pay. Buried me at a desk. But they didn't reopen half the cases I'd tweaked. Hell, they reworked the files and hid them from the district attorney because they knew as well as I did that those crooks deserved to rot. Most of those bums wished they'd had the guts to do what I had. I was a hero. But they needed a patsy to take the fall for it. Cowards.

When they stole it all away from me, I took up the bottle harder than ever. No longer to keep the demons at bay. Now I drank to destroy Duster Raines. To silence that inner monologue once and for all. Drown the voices in a sea of peat and barley. Partly because it was a battle worth waging. And partly because I was sick of being me.

But I had little choice in the matter now. Chained to this bed with no way to mask my withdrawals, I entered a world of pain. Unclear how much of that agony was residual alcohol dependency and how much was pure morphine withdrawals. But either way, it felt terrible. The highs of the drugs my strange doctor had been dumping into me came off quicker than I'd thought possible; the only place left to go was towards a sobriety I couldn't handle. My body had learned to live in a constant state of inebriation. The liquor kept me in balance. Allowed me to stay sharp.

That seals it. You're positively delusional if you call what you've been doing sharp.

Dry heaved over the side of the bed. Nothing in my stomach to put out. Kept alive on intravenous food and hydrating solutions.

My white-haired caretaker hadn't spoken to me since our first conversation. He would change my bandages, put a blanket on me, make sure the IV drips were properly inserted into my body, and leave. I assumed he did this like clockwork, but time had lost all meaning for me. Suffering was now my only constant, second after horrible second.

No one ever answered my screams.

All the while, the little Iraqi boy watched with the faintest hint of a smile. Standing unbearably still. Blood soaked. His brown, dull eyes judged me. Perhaps I needed only embrace this child and he would grant me an eternal resting place. Maybe that was what I'd been working towards for so long. I'd always known a price would be paid. I'd thought I'd been earning that pass across the river when I put all those schmucks behind bars. But maybe Fate had called in that marker, and this wretched state was my final payment. I tried to reach out to the child but the handcuffs resisted, keeping me pinned to the bed.

"I'm sorry," I cried. "I know I fought it earlier, but I was wrong. Justice always gets paid. You can take me. I'm ready."

He vanished, as if he'd never been there to begin with. A theater the boy played meant to make me doubt my sanity. But I couldn't be fooled. The kid always came back.

Now the room was quiet and still, the child replaced by boxes of medicine stacked to the ceiling. They cast long shadows that morphed with the time of day, an impossibility because there were no windows in this subterranean prison to allow such things. But they danced around the room all the same. The damned came to me in those shadows. Cackling with their horrific, blood-cooling laughs. Mocking my failures. And there were plenty of those to list.

Rolling from side to side, I tried to get comfortable. Turned over to meet the crimson eyes of the robot I'd destroyed weeks before. Was it weeks? I didn't know. That's what the mad scientist told me. Who knew what to believe? But the eyes were real. They glowed a perfect red like the blood of so many I'd sacrificed.

Closed my eyes. Listened to the roar of the beast. Waited for the final deathblow to end me. Nothing. Opened my eyes. The abominations had gone.

Alone with the boxes, my EKG pulsed fast but not out of the realm of normal. *Deep breath.* The demons would return. That was certain. Only a matter of time before I received my final punishment and met that Maker I kept trying to convince myself I didn't believe in.

* * *

"Feeling better, Duster?" the mad scientist asked.

I'd woken to find him sitting next to my bed, smiling his crooked smile.

How long has he been there? What did you confess in your sleep?

"You know." I coughed, my throat raw from disuse. "People call me Raines."

"What people are those?"

I grunted. He didn't know me, but he had a point.

"You've had quite a rough go. But I think you're through the worst of it. Be thankful for these IVs keeping you hydrated. Probably helped with withdrawals."

"Didn't feel too helpful."

"Well, the next time you battle liver failure, we'll give it a try without the machines and see how you do."

I muttered, "Thanks, I guess."

Truth be told, I felt a lot better. All things considered. He was right, I'd seen the worst of it. My body throbbed all over, weakened by the ordeal. But my mind was crisp, the clearest it'd been in ages.

"Don't mention it," he said.

"What about Juan? Val? Are they all right?"

The man looked perplexed. You'd think I'd asked what he thought of my mannequin girlfriend's new dress. Then he smiled, obviously pleased about something beyond this conversation. "You're full of surprises, Duster Raines. The boy's fine."

"And his mother?"

"They took her and the blonde lady. I couldn't help."

Another person lost, and it was my fault. "I'd like to talk to Juan."

"Oh, he's not here. Moved him someplace safe."

"I thought you said here was safe."

"Used to be. Before you came along and opened Pandora's box."

"What's that supposed to mean?"

My caretaker held up a small plastic specimen cup. Sealed inside was Madison Andrews's wedding ring that, until recently, had resided in my lower intestine.

"Don't worry," he said. "I washed it."

"That was entrusted to me."

"Valuable thing for someone to entrust to anyone. Not a normal stone, you see. Do you know what it is?"

"No."

"Figured as much. I believe it's finding its way home."

"What do you know about that ring that I don't?"

Without answering, he undid the handcuffs securing me to the bed in quick succession and freed me. I rubbed my wrists, which were scraped raw from my battle with ghosts.

"Come on," he said. "I'll give you the nickel tour."

The mad scientist led me from the infirmary into a small hallway of stacked stone. The walls were much like the tunnels under Madison Andrews's home, only they'd been reinforced every thirty feet with what looked to be steel buttresses. There were military-grade industrial lights here, too, which gave everything a stark luminescence. If I hadn't known we were underground, I'd have thought we were in the heart of an old, Soviet-era nuclear power plant.

Carved into the tunnel every hundred feet were alcoves that led to rooms thrown together using poorly installed Sheetrock painted to match the drab gray carpet that creaked with every step. One room housed food storage, nothing of note except it contained enough provisions to feed a small army for months. Next, we passed a large barracks with at least a hundred dust-covered bunk beds lining its leaden walls. The final room was an armory. Racks of guns as far as I could see—these weren't hunting rifles, either—mostly high-powered assault weapons of the automatic variety. Stacked on the back wall were crates of hand grenades. Was that an RPG? I couldn't take a detailed inventory because the mad scientist didn't linger.

"What is this place?" I asked.

"Think of it as an outpost. A first line of defense against the coming storm."

"Did you build all this?"

"Ha. Nope. These are relics of the Prohibition days. You can hide a lot of booze underground when no one's looking. Then came the war. Army moved in and did some upgrades. Place was meant to serve as a forward operating base for a guerrilla insurgency if the Japanese ever made landfall and overran the continent. When the war ended, it got decommissioned and forgotten. City built the subway right on top of it. There's a veritable labyrinth of modern concrete tunnels mixed with these old catacombs. Half of them aren't even mapped. So, we put them to use. Impressive, right?"

"You've got enough firepower here to fight a small war."

"That's the idea."

"Where's the army?"

"It's just me down here. The resistance is diffuse. Spread out. That way we can't get destroyed from one strike. We have these bases all over. Built into office buildings, basements, old storage facilities." He waved his hand grandly. "I've always said this was the most impressive of the old retrofits. But maybe I'm biased. Point being, you name a place, then we're in it. Waiting for that terrible moment we all know is coming. And when it comes, we'll fight."

"What exactly do you think is coming?"

He tittered at my naïveté. Apparently, he thought it normal for a crazy-eyed recluse to be living beneath the city with a weapons cache to battle Armageddon. Maybe if I played my cards right, I'd catch a glimpse of those lizard people I'd read about.

"Each outpost is maintained by a single Watcher," he continued. "Beyond preparedness, a Watcher's role is keeping an eye on the enemy and monitoring certain high-value targets."

"Watchers, huh? You know a friend of mine was praying to an Eternal Watcher right before he ordered my execution. You wouldn't know anything about that, would you?"

"That man's nobody's friend."

No arguing there. And the mad scientist knew about Jacobs. Similarities in their phrasing couldn't be coincidence. But he didn't seem ready to divulge any new information about my faux FBI agents' cult. I'd play it cool for now.

We reached a large metal blast door reminiscent of the one that had guarded Madison Andrews's panic room. My resident Watcher punched in an access code, and the door opened to a much larger and more modern tunnel structure fabricated out of poured concrete and held up by a framework of metal girders. The wood-paneled station wagon that had brought me here sat parked nearby. He led me past the car and ducked into an alcove at the other end of the cavernous space. There stood another metal security door, which he opened with a quick punch of a command code. This door led to a room with twenty or so computer screens monitoring a maze of tunnels.

"This is identical to the panic room in Madison's home," I mumbled to myself.

"That's because Madison is one of us."

"Was," I corrected, forgetting decency.

The man considered my words for a long time before he managed, "I didn't know."

"Happened right before you found me."

"Poor Maddy."

"If you knew Madison, then you must know her husband. Dr. Andrews."

My caretaker didn't hear me, his eyes welling with emotion. He glanced away to hide his tears. It only took him a moment to regain his composure, returning his stoic gaze to me as if nothing had passed between us. Most people wouldn't have noticed the break. I did.

"I'm sorry," I said. "Really. But I need to know. This all started because Torian and Jacobs wanted him found."

"They don't care about finding Dr. Andrews. Only killing him."

"But how do I fit into it?"

"Well, that's the hundred-million-dollar question now, isn't it?"

The mad scientist typed in some commands at a nearby computer terminal. One of the screens snapped to a newsfeed showing a shot of downtown Los Angeles from a helicopter. In fact, this angle showed an entire sky dotted with helicopters, like a swarm of locusts hovering over a burning forest. Smoke rose from various skyscrapers and buildings throughout the downtown area. One of the taller spires—I think it was the U.S. Bank Tower—visibly burned as flames spewed from the windows of its top floors. Fires raged for miles across the metropolitan area. Emblazoned at the bottom of the screen in dramatic red letters, the chyron read, *Terrorist Attacks Continue.*

"Your *friends'* handiwork," the mad scientist said. "Quite honestly, I'm amazed you're alive after meeting those two sociopaths."

Not feeling very well all of a sudden, I took a seat. Torian and Jacobs were loose on my city, and I'd unleashed them. "I don't understand. They didn't feel like terrorists. More like freedom fighters."

"You're not far off the mark. But terrorist isn't, either. This is classic nation destabilization tactics. Hell, you were in the military, the good ole US of A practically wrote the playbook on this during the Cold War."

"Destabilization for what?"

"This is the beginning of the end. The opening attack in a long-awaited war." With grave certainty, he focused on me. "They've infiltrated every corner of this planet. Law enforcement, government, corporations, you name it. They're paving the way for an invasion."

"An invasion from where?" I asked. "China?"

"No, no. China's infiltrated, too. This isn't a country. It's bigger than that. It's about our way of life. Our resources. Things we take for granted. Our very liberty's at stake. We thought we could slow them. Maybe even stop them. But you taking that ring accelerated their plans. They can't allow you to keep it. Too dangerous for them. They'll systematically tear the city apart to find you. It's only a matter of time before they locate this hideout. And if they have a little fun burning down LA along the way, all the better for their endgame. We anticipated this when we extracted you, but it's still unfortunate."

"What could be so important about that ring?"

The recluse ignored me, flipping through different television feeds with no audio. But the images clearly showed neighborhoods all across the city under attack. Fires burned. Buildings collapsed. People fled. One channel displayed shaky camera work from a cell phone of soldiers clad in the same black armor and reflective face masks as the mercenaries who'd attempted to execute me. Armed with assault rifles and flamethrowers, the death squad wreaked havoc against the local police. And the scariest thing about it, they were winning.

The Watcher switched the screens off.

"You may hold the key to saving us, Duster. Technically, I hold it now"—he pulled the specimen cup from his pocket and rattled the ring in it with exaggerated gusto—"but you're helping. That's for darn sure."

"You need to tell me why they want that stone."

At that, a clattering alarm bell, like something out of an old schoolhouse, banged out a warning as emergency lights began to flash red. The screens flickered back on, showing feeds from CCTV cameras throughout the interior of the base. From one TV to the next, crossing multiple cameras, eight heavily armed mercenaries marched lockstep through the tunnels with unrelenting purpose. The fact was not lost on me that each screen they crossed moved them closer to our location. At their feet were three of the robot cheetah attack dogs I'd encountered in the catacombs beneath that mansion in the Hollywood Hills. The machines' eyes glowed a bright crimson like blood and death.

"Nuts," the mad scientist said. "Looks like they found you."

CHAPTER 16

BACK IN THE ARMORY, THE MAD SCIENTIST TOSSED ME AN assault rifle.

Checked it. M16. Newer model. Fully automatic. Looked like it came off Fort Bragg that morning. So what was it doing down here in this outpost?

My caretaker's stories bled together in a devious mix of extremism and zealotry. He feared some imminent threat, apparently linked to *my friends* the mercenaries. And while those guys were dangerous, it certainly didn't feel like they'd overthrow the government any time soon. But here I stood among a stockpile of weapons amassed to fight just such a threat.

The hermit tossed me a duffel bag. "Ammo," he ordered.

I obeyed, grabbing as many magazines as the bag could hold.

With a duffel stuffed with explosives slung over his shoulder, the mad scientist headed for the door.

"Hold up," I yelled. "What about the grenade launcher?"

"We're in a goddamn tunnel system, Duster. You'll probably just kill us. Let's stick to the hand-thrown variety. Deal?" He ran down the hallway.

"Fair enough."

When I came out of the bunker at the parked station wagon, the mad scientist was already at the other end of the tunnel at the computer control room. He tossed one of his grenades into the room and ran back to me. Seconds later, it exploded. Black smoke billowed from the alcove. The enemy wouldn't capture whatever was stored on those hard drives. This Watcher wasn't messing around.

"Get in the back," the mad scientist said. "I'll drive. You can lay down cover fire if we're pursued." He tossed his sack of grenades in the trunk of the station wagon.

"Don't you have anything a little faster?"

"Afraid not. Military vehicles are a little harder to come by."

"Right . . ." I climbed through the back hatch into the recluse's dirty laundry and a pile of discarded boxes for bulk-bought apple juice. "But you could've at least gotten a newer car."

"Don't let old Woody fool ya." The wild-eyed recluse slapped the steering wheel of the 1970s station wagon and attempted to start the wreck's engine with a crank of the ignition. It coughed and moaned as it tried to turn over, crunching metal and gears until finally springing to life. "She's got a few fights in her yet."

Behind us, one of the robot cheetah dogs emerged from a side tunnel. Its red eyes scanned the room, tracking just like the machine I'd encountered weeks before. But up close, in the better lighting, I could see its construction exactly. Its narrow face snarled like a hyena with layered, razor-sharp fangs mimicking a shark's. The contraption's long legs were cat-like and built for speed with a torso reminiscent of a wolf's. All shining, reflective metal. The robot bobbed up and down, seeming to breathe, as it stared at the car. Any moment, this Frankenstein creation would barrel down on us. But instead of attacking, it raised its head and howled. Its horrible wail reverberated off the concrete—a screeching, deafening sound—and reached a decibel I'd never heard. And probably never would again since it felt like my eardrums were about to burst. It took all my will-power to not drop my gun, curl up, and cover my ears.

"Shoot that fucking thing!" the mad scientist shouted over the racket.

I smashed out the back window with the butt of my rifle and unleashed a hail of bullets towards the robot dog. It stopped howling and evaded my shots in fits and starts. I could barely see the blur of metal as it dodged to a new position, and my bullets struck empty ground.

The station wagon's tires squealed as we made our escape. The dog pursued, its legs moving in a blur, faster than anything living with four legs could accomplish. This was an aberration of nature, a hybrid of animals stitched together to create a monstrous hunk of metal. And unfortunately, it had been pro-grammed to eat me for dinner. The robot more than matched our speed, gaining ground fast. Again, I took aim and fired a burst of bullets. They connected but glanced harmlessly off its backside, slowing the creature for a moment before it regained its footing and continued its pursuit.

"The head," the mad scientist snapped. "You gotta shoot its damn head. Only way to take them down."

"I know. I know." I did know. I'd killed one of these metal-lic monstrosities before. Apparently, this was my new normal. Again and again, I fired. And over and over, the robot avoided with perfect agility—its movements a blur of silver—dodging my shots like they were nothing.

How did you kill one of these things?

Dumb luck, I guess.

I decided to make some luck of my own. Grabbing a gre-nade from the duffel, I pulled the pin and counted to three.

The mad scientist caught a glimpse of my intent in the rear-view mirror.

"Wait, don't—" he started. But it was too late.

I lobbed the grenade out the back hatch of the laboring station wagon. It landed near the robot and exploded, caving in some of the tunnel and burying the thing beneath it. The explosion threw the back of the car up, lifting the wheels off the ground and probably singeing some of the wood's paint. The car hammered back down. Tires screeched. Shocks groaned. But otherwise, we were fine.

"That got him," I yelled, feeling the rush of victorious adrenaline.

"Careful, you son of a bitch. You'll bring the whole place down."

The wiry-haired hermit switched gears and turned hard into another passageway. We were flying through this underground maze. The tunnels whirred by, all looking the same, but I knew we were moving farther and farther from our attackers. This was the mad scientist's domain and he knew his way around down here. We were easily getting away.

No sooner had I thought this than two more robot dogs came out of side tunnels and were right on top of us.

"Hang on." The mad scientist downshifted and spun the steering wheel hard. The tires protested as rubber tried to regain grip. I held my breath. Then the wheels caught and the car thundered down another tunnel.

The cheetah dogs were hot on our tail. I fired round after round, hitting their legs and bodies now and then, but the headshot hit was impossible. These creatures knew their weakness and every evasive maneuver protected that vulnerable spot. It really was a marvel of engineering; I couldn't believe these things even existed.

Besides wasting bullets, my suppressive fire did serve a purpose. The force of each connecting shot knocked them down, slowing them and keeping them at bay. But it was only going to last so long. With each passing moment, these monsters gained ground, and no number of bullets could stop it. I shuddered at the thought of being ripped apart by those metal teeth.

My gun clicked empty. Grabbing at the duffel bag, I pulled out another clip, slapped it into the M16 and reloaded the chamber. I turned back to fire just in time to see both dogs leap into the air, something propelling them like rockets up over the car. But there wasn't a flame, just a rippling of air behind them as they hurtled towards us at an incredible speed. The beasts landed with a bone-crushing thud, crumpling the metal roof of the station wagon beneath them. The claws of these animals made quick work of the ruined car top, ripping open a four-foot hole. The two creatures snarled down at me, seeming to enjoy the moment, their glowing red eyes full of malice and apparent hunger.

The robots' programming must have been overwhelmed with catching me. Or perhaps these things just weren't good in close quarters. Because as the dogs came in, I let off a shot and finally connected with one of the beast's malevolent eyes. The robot gave a violent shake, then blew back into the air. An electrical bolt leapt out of its now-defunct head and struck the car, leaping around the entirety of the metal frame in a blue arc like a Tesla coil, eventually grounding through the tires. The carcass of the deactivated beast fell off to the side of the speeding car. The station wagon lurched as we ran over the robot's broken frame with one of the back wheels.

I swung my rifle back to where I guessed the other dog would be. But it was too late. The thing was on top of me and tore the rifle from my grip with its jaws. I grabbed hold of its warm metal torso as it ferociously snapped at me with its razored teeth—again, and again, and again—if it weren't for its stainless-steel outer coating, then I'd have thought a feral animal was trying to take a piece of me. Even the sounds it made were visceral. Primal. An odd choice to go to such lengths to create something so real and then not bother to finish the job on the outside. I tried to throw the thing off me, but it weighed a ton. I struggled, keeping the machine's teeth from sinking into me—but only by an inch.

My heart pounded. I gritted my teeth. The thing was relentless. I was losing this fight. At any moment, it would land a fatal blow.

The car pitched forward as brakes shrieked. The momentum of the abrupt stop sent the beast up into the air and, just as suddenly as it was off me, its head exploded in a rain of sparks and metal.

The mad scientist hadn't even turned around to fire, his M16 rested on the armrest of the front seat blindly pointed back my way. The wild-eyed loner smiled at me in the rearview mirror. "I told you," he said. "Shoot the head. Simple."

I pushed the now-dead robot off me and laughed; the only reaction I could manage after yet another near-death experience. "Thanks," I said. "Next time I'll listen."

"See that you do." He threw his driver's-side door open and stepped out into the tunnel. He was looking up at the ceiling, as if our location were written in the stone, reading an invisible map that only existed in his mind. "Well, this should be fine, I think. Yes. This'll do."

Standing up in the back of the car since there wasn't a roof anymore, I took in where we were. This tunnel looked just like all the others. Frankly, I wasn't sure how the guy knew where we were—maybe he didn't.

"Should do for what?" I asked.

He pulled out a C4 detonator, inserted a key into its side, and turned it on. The red light on top blinked twice, then went to green.

"For this." He pushed the green button.

In the distance, reverberations echoed, then grew louder as explosion after explosion chased the route we'd just driven. Fiery death hurtled towards us, and all I could do was stand and watch. The final explosion blew smoke and concrete from the ceiling not more than four hundred feet from us and collapsed the entire tunnel we were standing in. A deluge of smoke and concrete dust surged past, covering us in a fine film of grayish-white powder.

"Well, if there were any more of those pooches out to get us," the mad scientist said, "then I think we just got them."

Dazed, I could barely hear through the ringing in my head and the dirt caked in my ears. I coughed, trying to catch my breath within the swirling fog of debris, working to contain my fury at nearly being blown to bits on the whim of my caretaker.

"What happened to not bringing down the tunnels?"

"No," the mad scientist corrected me. "I didn't want you to bring down the tunnels on us. I brought the tunnels down on them. You can see the difference."

With a small chuckle, the mad scientist got back in the car and revved the engine.

I stood in the trunk of the station wagon, looking back at the collapsed tunnel through the fog of destruction. My breaths came short and quick. The room spun, and I vomited what little was left in me over the side of the car. Cleaned myself off. Embarrassed. Hadn't realized how worked up I'd been until that very moment.

"The pooches'll do that to you," the mad scientist said. "Don't worry about it. You're a real crack shot with that rifle. We could use a guy like you."

Tried to steady myself. Didn't do a good job of it.

"I'd sit down if I were you. Not all the tunnels are as tall as these. Would hate for you to lose your head, too." He laughed like it was the funniest thing he'd heard in days.

Barely hearing what he was saying, I nodded absentmindedly and sat down in the back of the wooden station wagon next to the decapitated remains of the robot dog. The car took off through the rubble and into the labyrinth of tunnels beneath Los Angeles. I had no idea where we were heading. But at that moment, I didn't really care.

CHAPTER 17

A FEW HOURS LATER, WE CAME OUT OF THE TUNNEL SYSTEM AT the edge of the Angeles National Forest. These woods stretched across miles and miles of untamed land, devoid of humanity save for a few hiking trails and small towns. Behind us, the soft hue of the city lights illuminated the darkening sky, their glow an ominous halo of tranquility around billowing plumes of black smoke that filled the horizon as the city burned.

The sun unceremoniously slid beyond the snowcapped peaks, casting long shadows across the tree-covered hillsides. Here at the mountain's base, the air bit at a stark forty-something degrees. And it grew colder by the minute. My breaths came in fleeting wisps of cloud that disappeared into the bracing night air. With twilight upon us, our need to get a move on felt all the more pressing. The coming darkness would engulf these mountains, and we were ill-equipped to deal with the elements.

Over my repeated objections, the mad scientist decided to ditch the station wagon. We drove down a few back roads—if you could call these rocky and potholed dirt paths roads—moving deeper into the forest. We came to a sharp drop-off on the side of the road. My caretaker threw the car into neutral, pulled a heavy-duty flashlight from the glovebox, and got out.

"You coming or what?" the Watcher said through the shattered back window of the station wagon.

Reluctantly, I joined him. I slung my rifle and pack of ammunition and grenades over my shoulder. My companion did the same. Beyond that, the mad scientist had packed a go bag for exactly this scenario. It contained a few provisions, canteens, a compass, and warm jackets. Smart. But it wasn't much.

We gave the vehicle one solid shove and watched as it careened down the hill. It bucked and yawed, barely avoiding trees and boulders, before coming to a crashing halt at the bottom of the gully.

The grade too steep from that point to hike down, we doubled back and spent the better part of thirty minutes reaching the crash site. The ruined car had smashed into boulders and teetered atop some felled trees, the rear wheels no longer touching the ground. We couldn't have gotten the car out of there if we'd wanted. Finding some loose brush, we covered the vehicle. Threw some dirt on her for good measure. A quick and dirty job, it wouldn't hide the old rattletrap from someone really looking for her. But it would do in concealing the vehicle from the idle passerby who might report it. Hopefully it bought us a little time.

"You're sure this is a good idea?" I asked through gasps of harsh cold air, trying to keep up as he plunged headlong into the forest.

"Those robots are all networked together," he said. "One of them sees something, they all see something. That's how the other pooches found us so fast. The first one brought the pack like a homing beacon."

"You figure they know about the station wagon?"

"Definitely. And with the entire city in disarray, I'm sure there are roadblocks and all sorts of police out. We can't know who's with them and who's not. But I guarantee that if we got stopped, they'd know it. Better to keep off the roads."

"So that rules out stealing another car," I said. "There's got to be a better way than hiking into the woods."

"No time to debate it. Besides, you could use the exercise." He vanished into the forest.

Alone at last, free for the first time in a long time, I considered my next move. I could've gotten the heck out of Dodge right then. Done my best to disappear. Or at least crawled back into a bourbon bottle and forgotten all about the murder of Madison Andrews, the ring she'd sent me, battles with killer machines, and the answers to my questions that hopefully waited at the end of this quest to find Dr. Andrews.

Did I even want those answers anymore?

Did you ever?

Managed to take two steps towards the city before I turned back. That's the problem with a conscience—sometimes it gets you into more trouble than you're worth—because now I couldn't stop thinking about where this Watcher had taken Juan. Poor kid. His mom had been taken to God knew where because of me. He was as alone as I was in this misadventure. My responsibility lay with looking after the boy.

And then there was Carla. She meant more to me than anyone breathing, and I'd let her down. Sad thing was, I hadn't thought about her in weeks. And that cut deep. She was definitely thinking about me, though I knew none of it would be good. I couldn't abandon her to those psychopaths. I had to rescue her. And if I was going to do that, I needed those answers I didn't really want from Dr. Andrews. While I may have had millions of options, I only had one choice.

Hurrying to catch up, I followed the mad scientist into the unrelenting darkness.

A few seconds later, I found him leaning against a tree waiting for me. He smiled and said, "Took you long enough."

"Before we go any farther, I want some answers."

"We negotiating now? Figure you're standing here 'cause you already did the math and this is the only choice you've got."

"Fair enough. But you're gonna tell me everything you know. And how I fit into any of it. Because I don't see it. If not, I walk. Options or no."

"That so?"

"It is."

All my anger and fear boiled up. This case wasn't the type of mystery you read about in some pulp fiction paperback. There'd be no deductions ending with me solving the thing, all wrapped up in a nice little bow. Maybe get the girl. No, every lead led somewhere impossible. There were no clues to uncover. Insanity met me at every turn. My home had come under siege. The former love of my life was being held prisoner by paramilitary gangsters. My world lay in ruins. This was no murder mystery. It was a nightmare.

"And I don't want to hear any of this garbage about a revolution," I said. "I just want the cold, hard facts. Because I've seen a lot of military tech in my day and those robot cheetah attack dogs are impossible."

"You're right. They are."

"So how do you explain them?"

"You're the detective."

"I'm not playing Sherlock Holmes with you. So do us all a favor and answer the fucking question."

"Easy there, Duster. I'm on your side." He considered me in the stark light of his flashlight, measuring his response like one speaking with a child. "They don't seem possible because the technology hasn't been invented yet."

Before I could respond, he walked into the woods as if he'd said all that needed saying.

But I was done playing his games. I sprinted after him, grabbed him by the shoulder, and spun him back around. "What the hell's that supposed to mean?"

"Look, I'm not about to tell the whole damn story here freezing to death by the road. Those robots are real. Those mercs are real. And they're coming for that ring whether we like it or not. So, you can stay here and get killed by those pooches if you like, but I intend to be long gone before they get here."

With that, he peeled my grip from his shirt and disappeared into the frigid mist.

I stared after him for a long while. I didn't know what to think. Hadn't gotten any info, just more bullshit. But Juan was on the other end of this guy's trek. And Carla was still out there. My answers would have to wait.

* * *

We hiked in silence for a few hours.

I'd realized about an hour in that my guide had no idea where he was going. While he'd been so sure in his underground lair, here in the mountains he looked out of his element. The blind leading the blind. And going out into the wilderness with no sense of where we were headed lacked any semblance of a good plan. There'd been plenty of people who'd figured you couldn't get lost in these mountain ranges. The city surrounded them. Millions of people everywhere. Safest place you could be. If you get lost, just pick a direction and walk, the rest would sort itself out. Their dead bodies stood testament to how wrong they'd been. But the recluse had a destination in mind, which was more than you could say for me. So, I sucked it up. Let him be. Stopped with my, as he put it, incessant questions. I just hoped he took me to Dr. Andrews.

We came to the mouth of a cave, and the mad scientist went in. I followed. The darkness consumed me. I could barely see my hand a few inches in front of my face. The light from the hermit's flashlight guided me forward as we plunged into an eerie silence. I listened hard for the breaths of a wild animal. I'd survived one robot animal attack that day and I didn't want to add a real animal to the list. But we reached the back of the shallow cave safely. The place was dark, damp, and stank of mildew, but no creatures lived here.

The mad scientist plopped down against the cave wall and sighed. "We'll camp here tonight."

"Do you have any idea where we are?"

"Give or take. The town's about fifteen miles up the mountain from here. Don't you worry, I'll get us there."

"Don't got much choice now."

He grunted and said nothing else.

After a few moments of silence, I said, "You know, you never gave me your name."

"You just want it all, don't you?" From the spill of the flashlight, I could make out his crooked, yellow smile. "Well, they call me Badger on account of living in the tunnels and all. That's as good a name as any."

"Fair enough, Badger."

"Got to admit," Badger said, "you're a fighter. Was mighty surprised when you staggered out of that apartment. I've been watching Torian and Jacobs a long time, and they don't usually let people escape."

"Yeah, figured I would end up like Madison." He flinched, the mere mention of her name putting him on edge. I moved past it. "You got any idea why she came to me?"

"I've got a few. It wasn't part of the plan, though."

"What was the plan?"

"That's above your pay grade."

"Come on, Badger. We're in the weeds here. Give me something."

"Yeah, suppose you're right. Plan was always the ring. Maddy managed to smuggle it across to us. But Torian and Jacobs must've sniffed her out. That's the only reason I can see that they killed her."

"It was personal," I said. "Roughed her up good looking for that ring. But Madison had already ditched it, put it in a safety deposit box."

"She must've been scared to do that."

"Scared. Maybe a little crazy. She hired me to find her husband, Dr. Andrews. But when I asked her who took him, she didn't say mercenaries. Or Torian and Jacobs. She said aliens."

"That a fact?"

"Why would she say that, Badger?"

He ignored me. "I can't believe they left her to die with those bastards. We were supposed to bring her in a few days after she got the ring out."

"Out of where? What's so damn special about that ring?"

He took a deep breath, seeming unsure where to begin. Finally, he moved over next to me so our legs almost touched and spoke in a hushed tone, as if sitting in a confessional at a crowded church. "You know how you look in a mirror and there's a reflection?"

I waited for him to finish. He waited for me to say something. Apparently, that had not been a rhetorical question. I said, "Yeah, sure."

"Well, imagine that reflection is a living you. Not actually you but a fragment. A shard of a different reality. That's what we're dealing with here."

"I don't follow."

"It's sort of like a game of marbles. You've got a bagful, and you dump them out on the ground. Some of them stay close together and some of them scatter. Well, that's how the universe works. See, because there isn't just one universe, there's a lot of them. Those universes are like a vast web. And it's got lots of strands to it and . . ." He hesitated, struggling for the words. "Those strands sometimes intertwine, wrapping together like two guitar strings that got tangled up before you could string them. And that's when you get a situation like ours. Do you see?"

I thought back to that night in the motel a few weeks back. Seemed like ages ago. I'd been fairly loaded on booze and beef jerky, half-scared out of my wits, but I remembered parts of that science show I'd watched on public broadcasting. There'd been talk of a Mars anomaly. Maybe it was a black hole or maybe a tear in the space-time continuum. No one seemed all that certain. But there had been that woman pitching her theories about alternate realities. Possibly, she'd said, it could prove her theory on the multiverse. Perhaps it was a gateway to the other side. And maybe, it was man-made.

"Are you talking about alternate realities when you say other universes?" I asked.

"That's right," he said. "Good. You get it. Infinite possibilities."

I wouldn't have gone so far as to say I got it. But I'd watched a fair share of TV in my day.

"And what does any of that have to do with Madison?" I asked.

"That's the kicker," he said. "Madison isn't from here. She's from another place entirely. I mean, she's from Earth. Just not this Earth."

"You can't be serious."

"I am. That's why it's funny she told you aliens took Andrews. To Madison, the people of this planet are the aliens."

"You know how that sounds?"

"Hey, you asked."

"So, who took Andrews? Where can I find him?"

"No one took him. He's right where he's always been. With us."

"Then why would Madison say he'd been abducted?"

"I don't know. Only person who could answer that is Maddy, and apparently, she's dead."

I chose my next words carefully. "All right, say for a second I believe you. How does that explain those mercenaries or killer robots? Even if there's another Earth, that tech's still impossible."

"It's not impossible. It's just from the future."

"Oh, so they're time-traveling dogs?" I quipped. "How did I not see that?"

"No, no, no," Badger stammered. "I mean, sort of. Their world evolved completely different from our own. There were no Dark Ages. Rome didn't fall. The Han dynasty of China expanded. The two empires united. No such thing as Eastern or Western cultures as we think of them. Forget everything you know about history because there it's different. They're probably a good three hundred years ahead of us if you can really measure such a thing. Those dogs are just the tip of the iceberg. Wait until they start pulling out the big guns."

"You're telling me that Torian and Jacobs are from the future, and you guys are some sort of resistance because they're going to invade our planet?"

"You're not listening. They're not from the literal future. This isn't some time-travel paradox thing. They're simply from a more advanced alternate reality. It may as well be Mars. They're from a world where countries don't exist. Where factions have risen in place of borders. And a focus on a new prize—*this* Earth—has brought all those warring parties to a head.

"But remember," Badger continued. "Infinite possibilities. Even though things are completely different, sometimes they're exactly the same. There could be a Torian and Jacobs running around this Earth. Maybe different names, but then again, their parents might've made that same choice. It's impossible to know until you compare it all side by side. But from what we've been able to glean, duplication of people is extremely rare. And comes with certain consequences. We call those who exist in both realms Shades."

He talked way too fast, excited to convert me to his truth.

What a bunch of bullshit.

You said it.

Sure, this had been a crazy, mixed-up case—and there were robot cheetah dogs. I couldn't really account for them, but there had to be a more reasonable explanation. I ran through the events of the previous few weeks, and suddenly the night I saw Torian and Jacobs playing darts stormed back into my memory. What if those two really hadn't known me? If what this crazy hermit said had some truth to it, then Torian and Jacobs hadn't been playing the long con at all. They just hadn't known their doubles were at that bar. And my taking extra caution because I'd seen those two before heading to Madison's home had saved my life.

Coincidence. Dumb luck. My calling cards.

"So why the ring?" I asked.

"It's the key. Allows you to pass from one realm to the next."

"How's that supposed to work?"

He shrugged, acted like he didn't know. I didn't buy it. There was more to Badger than met the eye. But clearly my caretaker was a true believer in the cult of the other world. A religion where mirrors were gateways to another dimension, and an army of Shades with murderous robot dogs marched to conquer our Earth.

But I did have to give this outlandish story some credit. It explained away a few of my concerns. Though one thing didn't add up. The question I'd been asking since the beginning.

"Say for a second I buy all that," I said. "Why me? Why'd Madison bring me in?"

"Same reason we were watching you in the first place."

"I thought you were watching Torian and Jacobs."

"No, you've missed the point. Like the ring, you're integral. It couldn't be anyone else. You told me Torian and Jacobs framed you for Maddy's murder. They probably hoped to draw you to their side. Wanted leverage over you so they could exploit your mind."

"Why would they need my mind?"

"That's simple. Same reason Madison believed you could help her. Because you're you and they know your potential even if you don't."

"Jacobs said a similar thing before he ordered me killed."

"You're a danger to them, Duster. Not just because of what you're capable of but because of who your Shade *is*."

"So, I won the twin lottery. What am I, some kind of superhero over there?" Badger's dread-ridden expression wiped the grin off my face.

"No," the Watcher said. "You're no superhero. You're one of the three members of the Directorate. But *member* makes it sound like you have equals. You don't. You're the top of the pyramid. The apex predator. The worst of the lot and that's saying something. I wish I had better news for you but I don't. You're the villain of this story, Duster Raines. Your Shade's the harbinger of our doom."

CHAPTER 18

THIS PLACE FELT LIKE A SHAM. A FRAUD. ALL TOO PERFECT.

No longer in the cave, I rested atop a plush bed in an immaculately kept room ornately decorated with antique wooden furniture and flowered wallpaper. Hundreds of scented candles illuminated the suite with a dim flickering light. Their sickly sweet fragrance burned lilac and jasmine. In bed next to me lay Carla, a kind smile directed at me. Her naked body glistened in the soft glow of candlelight.

The smile confirmed it. This was a dream. But a good one. I'd enjoy it while it lasted.

We kissed, a passion dancing between our lips we hadn't shared in years. She tasted just how I remembered, like toasted almonds and sour candy. Her body pushed into me with a familiarity reserved for few. Maybe none. I pulled her on top of me and ran my hand down her back, her skin smooth save for the gentle fuzz that lingered beneath my touch.

That smile shone again. For some reason, she liked me. And I liked her. Maybe loved? Not sure. Didn't matter.

We made love like that. Taking our time. Enjoying each other. Getting tangled in the sheets. Our bodies pressed together—the only people in the world—our warmth a bulwark against the bitter cold of the truth.

She snored next to me now.

An ancient television pulsed on a dresser in the corner of the room, wrapped in a wooden frame with rabbit-ears antennae and dials and knobs to find channels. There couldn't be many of these left in the world, let alone one that still worked. And that hum. Not sure that sound existed anymore. But that's how the future worked, the leaving behind of something that once held promise for a newer and better model. Progress.

This particular channel showed Badger dressed in a white lab coat like the mad scientist I knew he was. He stood perfectly still against a nondescript gray backdrop, watching me with a glint in his eye. Something sinister hid behind his crooked smile. I saw in his gaze a plan for me I couldn't guess. But if I managed to learn his designs, I knew I wouldn't like them.

I changed the channel.

The next station showed me. Well, sort of, but not really. Harder around the eyes, less gray hair, maybe thinner. His skin shone a healthier shade that had seen the proper amount of sunlight. Perhaps he'd imbibed fewer drinks in his forty-six years. A life lived less hard. And he had no mustache. Nobody's perfect.

My double wore a scowl and talked fast, gesticulating wildly, looked to be giving some type of speech. But I couldn't hear him. I tried to turn up the volume but only the humming increased. This place was a vacuum, devoid of all sound save for that frequency of tube televisions. Progress.

Nothing else in the universe mattered except for these two Dusters. Just this hardened man—who was me but wasn't at the same time—shouting silently at his less impressive self, who sadly was the only me I'd ever known. My double reached some strong point now. Rallying the people. Terrifying and awe-inspiring all at once. I watched that humming, silent speech and felt envious of this powerful man.

I turned the TV off.

Carla had vanished, her place in bed still warm. She must have gotten up while I'd been watching my speech. The candles had gone out and smoke twirled into the air, leaving everything in a haze. The door hung wide open to an unrelenting darkness.

Had Carla gone that way? She must have. Nowhere else to go.

I swallowed nervously, the memory of Carla's kidnapping infecting this magical place.

For what seemed an eternity for such a small room, I made my way towards that gaping doorway and out into the cold. Overhead lights snapped on, reacting to my presence. As the lights sprinted ahead of me, reverberating with the effort of illuminating this place, I saw an unimaginably long hallway stretched out before me with no end. The walls were stark gray, some type of metal I didn't recognize. I'd expected the wall to be cold, just like the hall, but it wasn't. Instead it was warm, like the skin of some animal. When I ran my hands along its surface, it danced with a luminescence unlike anything I'd ever seen. Beautiful hues of silver, blue, and black ran away from my hand like ripples in a lake. The place came to life, every step causing a cascade of colors to stream away from me. The entire hallway pulsed to my existence.

Another step. More ripples. Another step. More ripples. Another step. More . . .

After a while, I lost count. No sense of time or space existed as I made my way deeper into infinity.

I shivered in the oppressive cold, my breath coming out in huffing clouds. I tried to stay close to the colors, to feel the warmth of its living form. But the place wasn't really a place;

the more I searched for the confines of the walls, the more I realized they weren't there. Kneeling down, I reached for where the ground should've been and found nothing but color and air.

Yet there I knelt. Shaking. Had to keep moving or I'd freeze to death.

I stood. Took another step. Onward. How long had it been? I didn't know. Just keep moving.

Rather anticlimactically, the colors coalesced, and the hallway ended at a single, dilapidated door. I touched it. No ripples. Lifeless and unwelcome in this mystical place. This portal had once been painted white, but the paint had peeled and yellowed around rotten wood. In the middle of the door were the remnants of numbers that had been scraped away. It looked like *848*, but I couldn't be certain because they'd been gone an immeasurably long time.

I tried the door handle. Cold brass. Rusted. Very old. Unlocked but stubborn. Eventually it gave way under more force than I thought it could manage.

"Are you sure about this, Mr. Raines?" a friend's voice asked from behind.

Startled, I turned back the way I'd come to face Madison Andrews. She smiled at me, and I saw in her a softness not present when I'd met her in real life.

"But you're dead," I said.

"Yes and no."

"What does that mean?"

"You've met Badger, then?"

"How do you know that?"

"Because you know it."

"And you're me?"

"Yes and no."

"I don't understand."

"We've shared something, you and I. That ring. It does more than bridge the gap between realities, it also—"

She spun around, suddenly afraid of something that wasn't there.

"What does it do, Madison? Please, tell me."

"They're coming," she whispered. The hallway lights behind her snapped off one after the other, racing towards us. Each extinguished light went out with a thudding dread. *Boom. Boom. Boom.* Every reverberation struck at my desperation for Madison to answer. The lights kept going out, those percussive blasts sending shockwaves through my body. I held my breath, anticipating the deafening end to it all. But it didn't come. That final light above Madison lingered longer than the rest. She stood incredibly still in that spotlight, the only thing visible in the impenetrable dark.

"Tread lightly, Duster Raines. Things aren't what they seem." Her voice resonated out into time without end and back again. Before I could ask another question, the light above her went off, and that sickening sound of the coming fury echoed into total darkness. I reached out to catch Madison, keep her safe, but found only empty vacuum.

The door still stood behind me, its outline oddly visible, almost glowing, in this seamless abyss. But what stood on the other side was a mystery, the glowing portal containing only more darkness. Everything in me said not to go through but I had nowhere left to go. So I pushed back the veil and stepped into the void.

Outside now, towers tore into the sky all around me, like the jagged fingers of a dead giant grasping from the grave. The skyscrapers were all uniform onyx, unreflective black spires of misfortune, rising hundreds of stories. An ugly shadow of the city I loved.

I stood on some type of suspension bridge running between two of these impossibly tall buildings. Below me, all I could see were the towers disappearing into gray storm clouds. The bridge was constructed of a clear plastic-like substance with millions of cables and wires running inside it, wrapping around one another like roots of an ancient tree. Reflective black vehicles sped along this network, slashing through the sky like thrown obsidian blades, the red glow of their running lights blurring past like streaks of blood.

Above this bastion, what sky I could see was formed of poisoned-brown clouds, the swirling contaminated mess dotted with blimps hovering between the buildings and roads. The airships gave this black and red city its only other color, bearing neon signs advertising everything from laundry detergent to strip clubs. Zipping between the slow-moving zeppelins were small flying craft, thousands of them, like swarms of gnats dancing between pulsing lights. These drones watched, keeping tabs on everyone and everything.

A symphony of machinery. A discord of dystopia.

Then it appeared before me out of nothing. The television. Plain as day. The same stupid channel of Duster Raines. That speech, over and over. My *Shade*. Me. Screaming. Furious. But only that hum rang in my ears. It called to me. Taunted me. Whispered to me, *This is progress*. I felt this other man's fury as if it were my own. I put my face right up to the screen, felt the static electricity dancing between our noses. We were one.

This version of reality consumed me. Every moment that passed, I felt a piece of myself die—leaving behind a man I did not know. I had to escape. All my determination went into pushing the palms of my hands hard against the screen. But I was stuck there, unable to move, losing myself.

A pulse of blue energy arced through the TV, electrifying my entire body. The pain was intense. I screamed, my mind barely able to hold on to consciousness. This was no dream.

The TV exploded with a bolt of crackling electricity, throwing me to the ground. All around me the world shattered into a million tiny fragments, scattering like a flock of birds heading out to sea. I stared after the fragments as they coalesced into a single impossible point. In that space, I saw millions of Duster Raines looking back at me, seeing this very instant for themselves, as if I were trapped in a labyrinth of mirrors. Infinite possibilities. And then, one reality slammed down upon me, and I saw the way things might be.

Gasping for breath, I gathered myself up off snow-covered ground. No longer in the nightmare Los Angeles, I stood on a vast ice field filled with thousands upon thousands of human beings in tattered clothes. Exhausted eyes stared out from scrawny, malnourished bodies, all shadows of their former selves. Guarding these throngs was a legion of soldiers wearing monstrous bug-eyed masks with an intricate breathing apparatus where the mouth and nose ought to be. Two sleek tubes jutted from their masks and secured tightly at the chest into some type of reflective black body armor. Their eyes pulsed a putrid yellow and the edges of the mask glowed red, giving the faces a devilish quality so horrific that it had to have been by design. They were all armed with sleek rifles that I knew—though I couldn't explain why—fired energy rather than bullets.

The soldiers forced the slaves into reinforced steel caves dug into the snow. It appeared to be some type of mining operation running deep into the ground to allow for so many to enter. Slag piles broiled at countless cave sites across this field of death, but the fires did not melt the arctic snow. A rancid stench rose out of the burning ground in a brown vapor. Above the various mines, a massive ventilation system caught the smoke, pumping the fumes of toxic deluge out of the domed facility.

What was the point of building a dome if not to regulate the temperature?

Freezing to death and desperate, I looked at the structure above, searching for an escape route. Maybe I could get up to those exhaust ports and find a way out. As I scanned the pipes, a hole in the smoke revealed something more shocking than slaves, mining facilities, or doomsday armies. Past the invisible ceiling, behind the clouds of poison smog, wasn't the sky at all. Beyond that smooth glass barrier wasn't the moon or the stars but a mammoth, spinning sphere of gas. A planet that any school-aged kid could name: Jupiter.

Another gust of wind shattered my reality, and everything changed again.

Abruptly, I no longer stood on that frozen tundra of a moon in orbit around Jupiter. Instead, I found myself on the bridge of a war vessel with hundreds of computer stations, larger than any aircraft carrier command deck on our own ocean. But this was no vessel of the sea. Because at the fore of this sizeable command center, a massive viewport opened to outer space, and through it I could make out the distant blue sphere of Earth.

The bridge was made of more of that living metal, beautiful and splendid with colors running all around as hundreds of uniformed men and women made their way to different workstations on the bridge. The pulses of color here seemed less random than the ones I'd encountered before, as if they were the circuits of the computers themselves.

The crew did not wear gas masks like the ground troops and were obviously human, their military tunics simple, tight fitting, and gray. A single red line ran down the center of their coats, and different insignia on their shoulders demarcated rank. Stitched upon the left breast of every uniform was an insignia of Earth with other planets and stars atop a round shield crossed by sword and spear.

These people couldn't see me. I was a ghost.

Unhindered, I moved towards the center of the bridge to a raised platform and a single command chair where a man sat. Looking down, I saw myself sitting there—just as I'd known I would—with stark, intimidating eyes. This me wore a very different uniform than the rest of the crew: a long, black jacket that cut off at mid-thigh and pants to match. They bore no creases or wrinkles. It would have been simple save for the intricately designed epaulets: a circle of golden flowers surrounding a silver lion grasping Earth in its jaws. A similar red thread as the other uniforms ran around the brim of the jacket's high collar and joined at the chest, dropping straight down to a golden belt buckle that bore the same crest as the shoulders.

This other Duster Raines looked past me out a viewport towards the pristine blue planet of Earth below. Unlike the others on the bridge, I knew he could see me. He just didn't care. My existence in this moment not worth his time. That hurt more than I thought possible.

Pathetically, I shouted at him, "Look at me, damn you!"

But he fixated on the blue planet, a hunger in his eye. His entire life had led to this moment. And in that instant, I knew his mind. My Shade intended to rule us all.

CHAPTER 19

How long it had been, I couldn't say. But I woke with a fury from that dark place, lost and unsure of what was real and what was fantasy.

Already the dream swirled away from me, dissipating into the ether. I tried to focus, desperate to remember it clearly. I'd been given a gift. The heart of that reality lurked within me, hidden in the deepest recesses of my mind. But the memories were hazy. Just a jumble of moments. Glimpses of some state of consciousness I couldn't quite understand.

My ears rang with an oppressive hum. *Where had I heard it before?* I grasped for the thought, but it slipped away, like sand through my fingers.

And then it hit me, the taste of burnt almonds and sour candy.

Carla. Remember her?

Like a chain reaction, the memories flooded back. Madison. LA. Hell. Jupiter. That other Raines. Each one like a wave crashing to shore. Vivid. Unlike any dream I'd ever experienced. And in that instant, I knew with certainty—deep down in my core—that those visions had been very, very real.

Badger leaned against the cold stone, waiting for me to gather my wits. How long had he watched me while I slept in this dank cavern?

"You have demons, Duster Raines," Badger said.

"Those weren't my demons." I caught my breath. "That was something else. Insanity."

"What'd you see?"

"What does it matter?"

"Dreams matter. They're a gateway to our inner self. And when you're carrying a stone like the one you've been . . . Well, sometimes you see things that aren't so inner."

"Again with your magic ring?"

"Lots of things seem like magic until they're understood. If I could explain how that ring worked, I would. But sometimes science needs time to catch up with the things we don't understand."

"So, you're telling me you have no idea what you're talking about."

"That's one way of looking at it, to be sure."

"How about you tell me what you do know and I'll reach my own conclusions?"

"Fair enough, Duster." Badger ran his hand along the rough contours of the stone wall, tracing invisible cave drawings left behind by philosophers of the past—if he could only reveal these imaginations, then it would all make sense.

"That stone," he began, "it's one of many. In this realm, it hasn't even been discovered yet. But that other place, *their* world, they've found it. It's not so plentiful here on Earth but out there in the galaxy it's everywhere. Moons, asteroids, planets, all just filled with the stuff. The Shades, they've mined their entire solar system for it, fought wars with one another over it. The material powers their ships, their weapons, those robot pooches."

"I saw a Jupiter mining facility. Human slaves forced to work on some arctic moon." The words spilled out of me before I could stop them. I'd wanted to keep the dream to myself, knowing it proved my own madness.

But his explanation hit close to home. And that couldn't be coincidence. Could it?

No, I didn't think so. And the longer I thought on it, the more I realized I believed his crazy stories. And I wanted more. Needed to belong. I'd entered Wonderland, and it was time to trust my rabbit.

"No. No," Badger muttered. "That's all wrong."

"What do you mean?"

"Well, you're not seeing his world. I mean, not really. You're seeing your Shade's ideas, how he perceives reality and how he wishes that reality would be. It's impossible to know for certain. But that's what makes you so important. Your ability to see into his mind could be invaluable to us."

"I don't want anything to do with that world."

"The stones," Badger continued, ignoring me, "when held in close proximity, can open up the realms between two Shades. It doesn't work with everyone, mind you, because not everyone has a mirror image for the stone to reflect. The two worlds are close in a cosmic sense, but they're nearly unrecognizable when compared side by side. But run those infinite possibilities enough times and you end up with the same answer. An aberration. A seeming impossibility. We don't know exactly how many duplicates there are, but probably less than a millionth of one percent of individuals in this world have an identical in that other world. But that's the ticket. Where the magic happens. When those who have a Shade hold the stones, sometimes they can feel their double's wants and desires. See their hopes and dreams."

"More like nightmare," I said. "A broken world. Los Angeles a hellhole. Futuristic but ruined."

"That's their Earth. His city. The capital. But the Europa Mining Facility hasn't been worked in over a decade. For you to see that would mean—" He stopped so suddenly it gave me a start. I focused in the dim light on Badger's face and saw the gears of his mind working overtime.

"Spit it out, Badger."

"Don't you see?" he asked. "The invasion I've been warning you about. It's not just for this world. It's for the resources of our entire solar system. They mean to come for the stones. Take them right from under us. Or over us, depending on where Jupiter is right now."

"I don't understand. All those people I saw. The dome structures. Why all the fanfare? Couldn't they just use robots to mine the stones?"

"Why would your Shade risk his fancy machinery and the resources to power them when this planet is filled with free and replaceable labor?"

"But surely that's easier than an invasion. We wouldn't even know they were there. They could take it from us without firing a shot."

"Why hide among the masses when they could rule as our masters?"

"So this is just another war for resources, land, and power."

"You're starting to accept the truth."

"Part of me wants to. Probably the part that doesn't want to be crazy."

"You're not crazy." Badger stood and made his way towards the mouth of the cave. "Come on, you can debate your mental health while we head into town. If your dream is right, then your Shade is fixated on his plans to take this world. We should hurry. This war ain't gonna wait forever."

* * *

Forests stretched in every direction for miles. Birds chirped, oblivious of the approaching calamity. No sign of civilization. Though I knew if I could get above the trees I'd be able to see a sprawling metropolis in the distance, ruined and smoldering, spewing black smoke into the sky. The devastation wrought on the city last night had seemed extensive. And if those mercenaries were still at work, then the damage done would be catastrophic. The bug-eyed masks I'd dreamed flashed into memory, followed quickly by those mercenaries hiding behind the reflective gloss of their riot masks. Could they be one and the same? My gut said yes. And I'd gotten back in the habit of listening to my gut.

But the longer we hiked, alone with my thoughts, the more I doubted myself. My previous certainty of an invading force of identical twins from another universe, descending on us from space and enslaving us all to dig up Jupiter moon rocks seemed a lot less likely—especially when I said it like that. No, it seemed more likely that I was delusional, and my unstable companion named Badger was the least qualified to judge my sanity.

But I ignored the thought as best I could. This felt real. Had to be. My dreams had been more than dreams. They were visions. And if that was the case, then I had a role to play in this war for better or worse. I'd be a believer. I'd always known I had a larger destiny than the hand I'd been dealt. I'd rescue Juan and Carla, save the day, and maybe even the world. Hopefully the other Duster Raines didn't beat me to the punch.

After hours of hiking through woods, we came upon a paved road. There were no cars as far as the eye could see, but all the same, we followed it at a safe distance hidden in the trees. Badger felt we couldn't be too cautious, especially so close to our destination. And with all I'd seen last night, I tended to agree.

But nature had other plans. About three miles down road, we reached an impassable canyon. No point in trying to cross without rope and other climbing equipment.

"Is there another way around?" I asked.

"Nope. Ravine runs for miles in both directions. One of the reasons we picked this place as a base. Canyon's a natural chokepoint to the town. Makes defending it easier. I'm afraid we've come as far as cover will allow."

We doubled back and snuck out to where a bridge traversed the chasm. We sat at the edge of the road for a few minutes, listening to the still day's air, not trusting our senses. But silence endured. Our breaths were deafening in their solitude. Not another soul for miles.

"It looks clear," I said.

"Yeah." Badger sighed, then moved onto the road. "Come on. Let's be quick about it."

The ravine dropped down a good eight hundred feet to the bottom. The bridge spanned a distance equal to or greater than the drop itself. Constructed of concrete, it had been sturdy once, but now it appeared old and ill-kept with cracks running along it in all directions. Every thirty feet or so, there were interlocking metal teeth, creating sections of the bridge that were intended to prevent soil movement and earthquakes from breaking the entire thing apart. A good idea if the mechanisms worked properly; unfortunately for us, the teeth obviously needed to be replaced. The concrete could use some patching, too. But even in this sorry state, it would hold the two of us just fine.

Badger kept looking up at the sky as we moved onto the bridge, watching for something. Drones, maybe. But if they had drones meant for reconnaissance, then the odds of us spotting one with our naked eyes were next to none. Still, it probably made him feel better to keep a watch, so I didn't mention it.

About halfway across the ravine, our worst-case scenario came to pass. We heard a car approaching from behind. As it lumbered around the corner and got a clear view of us, it stopped short. Even at this distance, I could just make out the markings of the Los Angeles Sheriff's Department. I'd hoped for locals, or maybe the forest service. I'd gotten neither.

Running was our obvious choice. But even at a full sprint, we were almost a minute from the other end of this bridge. And that car could run us down in no time flat. We had our assault rifles, but they'd be able to radio for help before we could overtake them and stop it from happening. We were in serious trouble.

"Shit," Badger said.

"We don't know they're looking for us." But before the words were out of my mouth, I knew they weren't true.

"Are you with me, Raines?" Badger asked.

I knew he meant right now. In this moment. This fight. But to me, that question held deeper meaning. Everything Badger had told me was true. His war had begun. And for the first time in a long time, I felt like I belonged to something worth fighting for. Seeing that other me in my dream, his ship, the enslaved miners, it had awoken something within me. I'd drunk the Kool-Aid and passed the point of no return.

"Yeah. I'm with you."

The police car crept forward. It had a slow roll to it, and the side doors opened at about thirty yards from us. Two police officers, dressed in khaki sheriff's shirts and brown trousers, their golden badges gleaming in the midday sun, emerged from the vehicle. They were using the doors as shields and allowing the car's momentum in neutral to carry the vehicle forward.

They both aimed rifles directly at us. The weapons were a dark gray metal that, as far as I was concerned, had only ever existed last night in my dream. Their weapons glowed a warm red that I instantly knew meant death.

"Badger," I warned.

"Yeah. I see them."

Without another word, we raised our M16s and opened fire.

The two men lifted their left hands reflexively. They hadn't anticipated our willingness to fight, and perhaps they hadn't known how well armed we were. Those car doors wouldn't protect them from this onslaught. But as our bullets tore into the vehicle and ripped through the doors, they struck an invisible circular barrier centered on the left palm of each man. Torrents of bullets pinged off their force fields with a percussive thud, revealing the invisible shields in bursts of blue and white.

"Personal shield generators," Badger yelled over the weapon fire.

No shit, I thought.

We continued to fire ineffectively until both our guns clicked empty. The car stopped, now a bullet-ridden mess. The engine smoked, and the tires had all been blown out. They were probably twenty-five yards from us, and they weren't getting any closer with the vehicle. Minor victories.

The two sheriff's deputies returned fire. But these guns didn't fire bullets. They let out a ripple of energy that morphed the air around it into a pulsing sphere. Stunned, I watched the two cocoons of death barrel towards us. Badger tackled me, taking us both to the asphalt hard. The energy flew past, narrowly missing. The side of the bridge took a direct impact from the waves, and the guardrails bent and exploded in a rain of metal and concrete.

"They're not using the low settings," Badger said. "They're trying to kill us."

"No shit," I said out loud this time.

We were up on our feet quick, taking cover behind some of the rubble of destroyed bridge that had fallen in our path from the explosions. But based on the last demonstration, this cover would do nothing against those rifles. We hunkered down as wave after wave of blue energy connected with the concrete and metal girders all around us, blowing them to smithereens and raining down destruction on us.

"Fuck me," I said. "How are we going to fight against tech like that?"

"Exactly," Badger said. "We're totally screwed. That's what I've been trying to tell you." He reached into his pack that held the grenades and pulled one out. "Get ready to run."

Before I could object, he pulled the pin, armed the grenade, and dropped it back in the bag. "Fire in the hole!" he yelled and threw the bag over his head in a high arc back towards the police cruiser.

The world stood perfectly still, as if it knew I needed the time to truly comprehend what Badger had just done. My spirit floated above us, looking down at this ramshackle bridge and the two sheriff's deputies armed with personal force fields and ray guns. The bag held frozen in midair, the deputies' faces somewhere between bafflement and fear. Next to my floating essence, a bird hung in flight trying to do what I should be doing, fleeing this death trap. If I could've stayed in that state and escaped, I would have. But it only held for an instant, and just as suddenly as it had frozen, the motion kicked in like a freight train and threw me back into my body in real time.

I gasped, trying to take in what had just happened. But the only thought I could muster screamed, *We're going to die.* There wasn't time to worry about such things because we were already up and running away from the soon-to-be exploding bag. I let my survival instincts carry me; all that mattered now was to reach the other end of the bridge.

Our first moment of luck came when we didn't get shot the instant we stood up. I knew the two cops were wondering what to do about the bag of grenades. Their indecision and brief pause in fire gave us a good ten steps of unmolested movement. And we needed every step we could take.

A second bit of luck came when the bag of grenades exploded. I didn't see where the pack landed, but I'd guess it rolled under the front of the car because the ensuing explosion flipped the patrol vehicle up into the air, sending it crashing back down onto the bridge. The engine ignited in a burst of flame, sending a plume of black smoke into the sky. We couldn't have planned it any better.

Risking another look over my shoulder, I caught a glimpse of our third bit of luck. The two cops dragged themselves away from the burning vehicle, stumbling up onto their feet. Right as they were about to resume firing death balls at us, the burning car's gas tank ignited in a second explosion. The force of the ensuing fireball threw the two deputies into the air like marionettes with tangled strings, flinging them over the railing and down into the ravine below. I listened to their screams, which ended abruptly a few seconds later when they met the ground.

We'd been luckier than anyone had a right to be. I couldn't believe we were alive. But neither Badger nor I took it for granted and kept right on running. And good thing we did because our luck had just run out.

The car explosion had sent a concussive blast rippling across the bridge, causing the entire structure to shudder at the added strain. That shoddy workmanship, which had been so apparent before, began to buckle. The center of the bridge plummeted into the ravine, creating a gap between us and the burning car. After the terrible racket of falling highway impacting the ground below ended, all was still. And it seemed the demolition of our bridge might end there.

But then, a low grumble became a deafening groan. We stumbled mid-run as the entire bridge swayed in the wind like some sort of giant cement hammock. Another crashing boom sent the road beneath the bullet-ridden car into the pit below. Spiderweb cracks splintered in every direction across the asphalt. The fissures ran under our feet, and I kept waiting for my next step to send that piece of road down into the canyon, taking me to a swift death. The bridge convulsed in death spasms, rattling as it sent more and more asphalt hurtling into the ravine.

It was nearly impossible to keep our footing as Badger and I tried to reach the other side. We had no choice but to try, moving as fast as possible. Behind us, section after section of the bridge caved in with increasing speed. We weren't going to make it. We ran anyway. Only thirty feet to go but it was going to be ten feet too many.

Badger tripped. I stopped to help him up, and he pushed me on.

"Go," he said. "You have to survive."

"We're making it together or not at all."

But the heroics didn't matter. We were out of time.

The falling concrete had reached us, unleashing a terrifying roar as it threatened to swallow us whole. I grabbed the mad scientist tight and forced myself to keep my eyes open in this final moment. If this was the end I'd craved for so long, then let it come. But for all my attempts to drink myself to death over the past decade, I now very much wanted to live. Sadly, the universe didn't care about my wants. It'd come to collect. The final payment for my sins past due. I took what I figured would be my final breath and braced myself for the end.

Inexplicably, the bridge stopped falling. I looked down. We had about three inches of concrete between us and a drop that easily would've killed us both. That miraculous three inches was made of one of those interlocking metal teeth systems meant to keep the bridge from collapsing. Obviously almost none of them had worked—as evidenced by the gaping hole that now existed where a bridge had just been—except for the section we'd barely crossed. These little metal teeth had saved our lives.

Below in the ravine, the car wreckage burned next to the broken bodies of the two men who'd had us on the ropes only moments before. Battle was funny like that. Victory never certain. Maybe that should give us hope for winning this unwinnable war.

"Thanks for trying to save me," Badger said. "But it was fucking stupid."

"You're a cranky old hack," I said. "You know that?"

"Hate to break it you, but we're the same age."

We both laughed, relieved to be alive. After we'd taken a few moments to process it all, I said, "How about we get off this damn bridge before anything else tries to kill us?"

CHAPTER 20

THERE WERE NO PEOPLE HERE. NO CARS. THIS PLACE WAS A ghost town.

Badger and I hoofed it up a two-lane road, which ran between two blocks of wooden buildings before disappearing again into the forested mountain ranges. At the center of this so-called town stood a single traffic light that blinked a continuous pulse of red. Most of the buildings were boarded up and abandoned but a few inklings of the former residents remained. A striped barber's pole hung above a shop, dim and faded. Next door, a timeworn sign advertised a market that didn't look like it had electricity, let alone food. A *No Vacancy* sign sputtered pathetically in a hotel lobby window, though it obviously hadn't hosted a patron in quite some time.

"Not that I was expecting a parade, Badger, but this place is pathetic."

"This road used to be a shortcut over the mountain pass back in the early nineteen hundreds," Badger said without looking back. "Before the interstate made going around them faster. The businesses died a slow death as the town got lost on this lonely mountain road. A place that time forgot.

"We took up residency about ten years ago. I can count on my hand the number of people we've had come through this way that we didn't invite."

"Well, that explains how sad it is. But where are all the people? Where's your resistance? Where's Juan?"

"Wouldn't make much sense to be out in the open, now, would it?"

We circled around the back of the hotel to an unmarked door, which opened to a small lodge where a solitary woman tended an empty bar. She was tall—taller than me and I was six-two—gaunt, and the veins in her arms pulsed as she wiped down the counter. I couldn't be sure of her age—if she were thirty, she might as well be sixty. Her winnowed face gave a sense of virility and youth but her countenance nothing but sour vinegar, covering a disappointment that in my experience only comes with old age. She wore a disapproving frown directed squarely at me.

Dead animal heads hung on the walls, giving the lodge a rustic, mountaineering feel. Very authentic. An empty hearth sat in the corner—if you got a fire going in it, the place would be downright festive. If there had been any people to be festive with.

Badger took up one of the stools at the bar, and I followed suit.

"Beer, Badger?" the tall woman at the bar asked, softening ever so slightly.

"Sure. Why not?"

"And you?" she asked me.

"Nothing. Thanks. Trying to cut back." I couldn't believe the words had come out of my mouth. World-saving must quench that eternal thirst.

"Good for you," the bartender said with little empathy.

"You going to introduce us, Badger?"

"Sure," he said with a smile. "Duster Raines, this is Remley. Remley runs the bar in our little town."

"Cut the crap," I said. "I like a drink as much as the next guy. More than the next guy. But there's things need doing. We almost got killed on that bridge. Don't tell me there won't be more of them."

"He's feisty," Remley said.

"Yeah," Badger said. "Got a mouth on him, too."

"I thought I'd be more impressed," she lamented.

"Sorry to disappoint," I snapped. "I'm not your world destroyer. But don't worry, you can meet him soon. He's on his way."

The color rushed from her face. "Then it's true?"

Badger took a long draw on the beer Remley set in front of him. I already regretted not taking one.

"Duster over there," Badger finally said, setting his beer down, "had a dream and all that. But you know how those things can be. Could be on his way now or he could be coming in six years. Hard to say."

"You haven't heard, then?" Remley asked.

"Heard what?" All I could do not to yell.

Remley flicked on a small television nestled in the corner among an eclectic mix of alcohol bottles with off labels I didn't recognize. She spun the dial quickly and found a channel covering the news. An anchor, dressed smartly in a blue suit and tie, shared a split screen with a woman I immediately recognized as the professor from the public access debate about space, anomalies, and the hypothesis of man-made wormholes. The chyron at the bottom of the screen reminded me that she was Dr. Eliza Nielsen of MIT.

"I've seen her on TV before."

"She's been spreading the word about the coming invasion as best she can," Badger said.

"She's one of you?"

"Shh," Remley hissed. "You're missing it."

On the TV, the news anchor continued his interview with Dr. Nielsen. "So, you're saying the odds of this occurring naturally in our solar system is next to none."

"That's right," Dr. Nielsen said.

"But if that's the case," the news anchor said, "then how does it exist?"

"A fair question. And I think if we follow what we know to its logical conclusion, then it will be apparent. Though we may not like the answer.

"As I stated at the top of your show, this is not a naturally occurring phenomenon. The math simply doesn't allow for a singularity of that magnitude to occur so close to a planetary body without destroying it or causing some other dreadful occurrence. So, I propose that something is preventing it from causing that cataclysmic event. Something not of nature is keeping the energy of that anomaly in check and localized to that specific spot.

"If we allow for that," Dr. Nielsen continued, "then we can move on to who is controlling that energy. So, we look at people on our own planet. Other governments. And the obvious conclusion is that the technology to create a rift in space-time such as the one currently present over Mars doesn't exist. We simply don't have the technology or resources to maintain an energy output of that magnitude over a sustained period of time. So that leads us to option three. If it isn't natural and it isn't us, then it must be someone else."

"You mean like aliens," the news anchor said.

"Perhaps aliens. Or maybe, as I have proposed before, other dimensional beings. Not unlike you and me. There is a possibility that another society of humanity has evolved on another

Earth, in another universe, whose technology has advanced well beyond our own capabilities. Perhaps they opened this rift."

"Excuse me for saying so," the news anchor said. "But that doesn't sound like science. It sounds like the pitch to a summer blockbuster."

"I know what I've said sounds improbable. But it isn't impossible."

"To be fair," the news anchor said, "no one in the scientific community agrees with your theories. Am I right?"

"They're wrong," Dr. Nielsen said flatly. "And frankly, there's a higher probability I'm right than this being a random manifestation. My associates just don't like what that means. It makes our little planet less unique. Less special. And the idea of other humans—well, that goes against our ingrained cultural belief structures. It's only natural for people to ignore the facts I've presented."

"Very well, doctor. Thank you for your time today." The news anchor turned back to address the camera directly, obviously flummoxed. "If you're just joining us, NASA has released images captured by one of its Mars rovers, *Curiosity*, early yesterday morning. The image depicts some type of rift that NASA is currently calling an *anomaly*."

The screen flashed to the pictures of the Martian surface. The red alien soil ran out from the base of the rover to a desolate mountain range on the distant horizon. Frozen above those mountains in the still night sky hung a large green and blue ripple. It reminded me of pictures I'd seen of the northern lights up in Alaska. But those lights here on Earth had spread across the night sky, pulling back and forth in a rhythm with the Heavens. Boundless. But these lights above Mars were different. Contained. Like a stitch had been pulled from a wound and torn open, allowing colors of pure energy to bleed from that localized area and chase away the blackness of space.

"It's unclear if the anomaly poses any threat to Mars and what that threat might constitute," the news anchor's voice continued as more images of the void flashed on the screen. "What NASA is willing to say—"

Remley turned the television off.

"Well, shit," Badger said. "Guess we don't have six years after all."

"Was that what I think it was?" I asked.

"That was the Gateway," Remley said.

"They've finally harnessed enough energy for a large-scale invasion," Badger whispered. He looked at me, and his eyes told me all I needed to know. His war had finally come.

CHAPTER 21

BADGER HUSTLED FROM HIS STOOL TO THE HEARTH, ABOVE which a mounted elk head hung. Without a word, he pulled one of the antlers, and it gave way with a click. The fireplace groaned as it rolled away from the wall, revealing a metal blast door. Badger quickly entered a code into a keypad, and the doors whooshed open to a stairwell leading down.

"What is it with you guys and secret passageways?" I asked.

No one answered.

Hidden doors. Mysterious corridors. Otherworldly invasions. Felt like I was in an old weekly comic serial—the kind where everyone wanted the hero dead.

Are you supposed to be the hero in that analogy?

Shut up.

"You coming or what?" Badger demanded. Before my eyes, the calculating, calm man who'd spent the last two days preaching the existence of other universes and the need to fight an unwinnable war had disappeared. In his stead stood a hardened man, resolute in purpose. A leader. And not in the habit of asking twice.

Remley hustled around the bar and followed Badger down the stairwell, neither of them waiting for me. I pursued them both. No choice. Events had taken on a life of their own and momentum now carried me towards their inevitable conclusion. The metal doors whisked shut behind us and sealed tight.

Flickering lights illuminated the rickety metal stairwell as we descended at least five stories. At the landing were four paths that honeycombed deeper into the mountain's bedrock. But these tunnels were nothing like the ones that Badger had nursed back to health beneath the sewers of Los Angeles. That place had been patchworked together with older tunnels and commandeered for the purposes Badger and his resistance required. But these passages were flawlessly hewed from bedrock in the mountain, unlike anything I'd ever seen.

The strobing artificial lights from the stairwell spilled into the cave entrance, but that inhospitable light gave way here to a constant soft green hue. The walls themselves seemed to be alive, pulsing with a bioluminescence of their own, like some radiant sea creature from the depths. I ran my hand along the glowing walls, expecting a cold and inhospitable earth, long hidden beneath the ground from heat and sunlight. But instead, I found a smooth surface covered by a synthetic substance that made it warm to the touch. Come to think of it, the entire place felt warm, a perfect temperature to live in. Yet I saw no signs of human construction. Nothing that indicated these tunnels wouldn't come crashing down at a moment's notice, but here they were. Perfect.

"Damn," I said. "And I thought I'd been impressed by secret elk-head doors."

"The tunnels were created using nanoprobes," Remley whispered. She showed deference to Badger, not wanting to disturb his train of thought. I'd entered the Church of the Rebellion, and Badger was a priest here, or perhaps the Pope. "You program the layout you want and let the little buggers go. They use some type of synthetic acid. Melts away the rock."

"I don't see any vents."

Remley smiled. "Carbon dioxide gets absorbed by the coating on the walls you just touched. It gets purified, then secreted back out as breathable atmosphere. Completely biological and sustainable. Once it's up, there're no computers to maintain it. No wires. Nothing."

"Let me guess. *Their* technology."

"Smuggled out. We have friends on their side. Like any war, there're patriots and spies."

The Europa Mining Facility had hundreds of tunnels dug into the surface of the moon. Had this tech been created to make that job easier?

You know that's wrong.

But why do I know that?

Those tunnels I'd dreamed on that alien moon had been meaner, roughly constructed, held up by metal, lit and warmed with fire. The dome structures hadn't even moderated temperature to a suitable medium, it just made the air breathable. Badger had said the use of human labor was cost effective, but I saw a different purpose. The mines were as much a prison for political dissent as a factory, and comfort was the last thing you gave to a forced labor camp.

Interesting you would reach that conclusion.

What are you getting at?

The voice didn't respond. But I sensed a flippant shrug directed at me.

Something felt wrong about this technology. Something foreign. But I couldn't put my finger on it.

Badger said nothing, taking me deeper into the subterranean labyrinth. We entered a substantial cavern, and I discovered where the town had been hidden. Hundreds of people hustled about, dressed in weathered hunting gear that looked like it'd been raided from an army surplus store thirty years ago. For some reason, I'd expected uniforms, though the expectation made little sense for an underground cell with limited resources. Despite the motley look, everyone worked with precision. Some at desks carved directly from stone, typing furiously at computers that had been jury-rigged into generators. Others talked into headsets to people I imagined were stationed in similar rooms somewhere else in the world. Still more people organized crates likely filled with weapons, foodstuffs, and other wartime supplies. The resistance hummed in full mobilization. A true military operation. Badger's army existed.

"Well, I'll be damned," bellowed a voice from the crowd. A giant of a man, at least six feet eight and built like a fortress, emerged from the throngs of personnel and embraced Badger, lifting him a foot off the ground. The titan's neatly trimmed white hair and goatee popped against his Black skin and faded red flannel shirt. Unlike Badger, the giant's white hair came from age. Easily pushing seventy but with the vitality of a much younger man.

"Good to see you, too, Burke," Badger said.

"When we heard about the tunnel collapse," Burke said, "we assumed the worst."

"I wasn't about to miss this party."

Turning his attention to me, Burke's gap-toothed grin vanished.

"Duster Raines." I extended my hand. "But people call me Raines."

"I know who you are." Burke didn't take my outstretched hand, so I put it back in my pocket. "I still don't like this plan, Badger. We can't trust him."

"What plan is that?"

"You didn't tell him?" Burke asked Badger.

"Not yet," Badger said. "I thought I'd let him decide for himself."

"That'd be all well and good if we had time to coddle him," Burke said. "But we don't. Have you seen the news?"

"I showed him," Remley interjected.

"Then you know we have to use him, whether he likes it or not."

"I'm standing right here, guys." I waved to prove the point. "But I came for two reasons. I want to see Juan. And I want to meet Dr. Andrews. You give me those and we can talk about your plans."

"You didn't tell him shit," Burke laughed. "You're a real son of a bitch, Badger."

"I told him enough. Assemble the Council." Badger put his hand on my shoulder, squeezing a reassurance that was anything but. As he led me away, he whispered, "We have a lot to discuss, my friend."

* * *

The War Council gathered in what I can only describe as a conference room, though the chairs and table were hewn straight from the mountain itself. It all felt surprisingly comfortable despite the fact it was made of rock. Sitting around the stone table with me were five council members. Burke, Remley, and Badger I'd already met. Joining them was a kid in his twenties who fancied himself an engineer. He went by Arvind and spoke with the crisp English accent of someone born abroad and then educated at Cambridge. Nervous sort. Uncomfortable with my presence, though he didn't dare say it to my face. Beside Arvind sat Dr. Eliza Nielsen, the woman I'd seen describe the Gateway twice now on television. She wore her black, frizzy hair up in a tight bun and had changed from the suit she'd worn on TV into the same faded hunting gear as the rest. I'd been wrong, the resistance did have a uniform, just not a very impressive one. She met my eyes straight-on with neither prejudice nor hatred, the only member of this ragtag band not ready to cast me in the same lot as my Shade.

"How much have you told him?" Eliza asked Badger with little fanfare.

"He knows about the other side," Badger said. "He knows his Shade leads an attack on this world. He saw that himself."

"Then you have the stone?" Burke asked.

Badger pulled the specimen cup that held the ring from his jacket pocket and set it in the middle of the table.

Burke exhaled. "Thank God."

"God had nothing to do with it." My outburst surprised everyone. "Madison gave her life for that trinket."

Badger squirmed in his chair. Madison's death always struck a nerve.

"We tried to get her out," Remley told Badger. "But Torian and Jacobs were one step ahead of us. If she'd—"

Badger waved his hand, silencing her. "She knew the stakes."

"At least she got the ring to Duster," Arvind said.

"I go by Raines."

"Beg your pardon?" Arvind asked.

"Never mind. I promised Madison I'd get that ring to her husband. So, where is he? Where's Dr. Andrews?"

Burke laughed. "He's sitting at this table."

I looked Arvind over. The young guy melted in on himself. Madison would've run circles around this kid in her sleep. She wasn't just out of his league, they weren't even on the same planet. I tried not to laugh. "You can't possibly be Dr. Andrews."

"He's not Dr. Andrews," Badger said. "I am."

Badger's gaze bore into me, unwavering. I swallowed hard. Badger was Dr. Andrews. That piece of information fit so perfectly I was angry I'd missed it. Of course he was Andrews. My alarm bells should've gone off the moment I realized he wasn't just some grunt stationed at a recon outpost. I'd known all along Badger knew more than he'd let on. He wasn't that good an actor. But I'd dismissed it. Or gotten caught up in the story of being important. Plus, he'd been devastated by the news of Madison's untimely demise; and while it might be a stretch to say he'd reacted how any husband would, it should've piqued my interest. I'd been blind to the obvious.

"So, you're more than just a lowly Watcher," I said.

"We're all Watchers, Duster."

"Why didn't you tell me?"

"I didn't know if I could trust you at first. And after that, it just never felt like the right time."

"Fuck you. You knew I wanted answers about Madison and you—"

"All right," Burke interrupted. "Now that we've cleared that up, how about we move on to the problem at hand?"

My fury boiled but I remained silent.

Eliza rose from her chair and waved her hand over a wall. As if by magic, the rock became a screen, which displayed an image of the Gateway in low orbit over the dead world of Mars.

Image looked to be in real time. Shouldn't be possible.

Did they have access to their own satellites? Unlikely. Maybe piggybacking a signal? But that didn't account for the inevitable time delay from transmitting over a great distance.

My mind raced. I didn't have answers. But my sudden wherewithal to even ask the questions startled me. Where had that come from?

Eliza had moved on and I didn't have time to ponder. "The anomaly formed thirty-six hours ago. Our readings indicate it's stable. We can only assume they'll start sending ships through in the next day or two."

"And when that happens," Burke said, "we'll be in real shit."

"Fortunately," Eliza said over Burke, "the power required to bring anything sizeable through, such as a dreadnought-class attack cruiser, is astronomical. I anticipate they'll only be able to bring one ship of that size through at a time, with a delay of at least twenty-four hours between each attempt. Otherwise, they risk destabilizing their containment fields and losing control of the energy. But they could send smaller frigates through at more regular intervals of three to four hours."

"One of the big ships will be more than enough," Remley said. "Dreadnought would bring at least ten thousand shock troops, another five thousand operations personnel and pilots. That one ship could do a lot of damage to us before we could take it out."

"Fifteen thousand people?" I asked. "How big are these things?"

"Over two thousand meters long and about five hundred across," Remley said. "Six Nimitz-class aircraft carriers lined up to give you a real-world point of reference. Each ship has a complement of a thousand strike fighters and another three hundred bombers. Its defensive grid boasts seven hundred pulse cannons and ten thousand ion missiles."

"So, really big." No one smiled at my joke. "I'm assuming they've got versions of those handheld shields we ran into on the bridge."

"That's right," Badger said.

"Physics still applies," Remley added. "Enough energy can overpower their defensive grid, but it'd take a lot of firepower. And they'll be ready for any standard attack our governments would throw at them."

"They're flying fortresses," Burke said dryly. "They get a few of those through, some of the support ships, the entire planet will be overrun in a matter of days."

"I can't believe this is happening," I managed. "How do they even know we're here?"

"Same way you knew they were coming," Badger said.

"The stones?"

"They were discovered in that universe about three hundred years ago," Badger said. "An incredible resource. Nearly unlimited power for the masses. National borders collapsed under a more humanistic world. Peace reigned. At least that's what the propaganda machine spun.

"But the mining operations drained the solar system's moons dry. As supplies became more limited, energy was rationed. Then the Great Blight of 1874 came, and grain supplies were wiped out. Food scarcity led to more rationing and even greater unrest. As you might imagine, a hierarchy emerged. The masses realized the eradication of poverty they'd been sold was a myth. The classes that had always existed but were easier to ignore in good times became painfully clear in the bad. Fighting broke out and new factions rose where countries had once stood.

"Literal class warfare. The entire planet engulfed in flames. And war raged for a hundred years. Your Shade was a military officer in the North American Confederation, which had always enjoyed a better seat at the table than most. As the war took a turn for the worse, he managed to wrest control of one of the largest mining conglomerates on the planet. It was his changes to mining practices and refining processes that led to a stabilization of the grid. With his newfound wealth and power, he united some of the other factions under one banner about twenty-five years ago and eventually put down the uprising. He was hailed as a second coming of Julius Caesar."

Badger caught my look. "Yes, they had one of him, too. Though their Brutus wasn't as good with a knife."

I laughed. No one else did. He wasn't joking.

"The other Duster Raines," Badger continued, "unified the planet once again but this time under his personal banner. Your Shade was elected to lead the new order, though calling it an election implies a fair fight. It wasn't. He created the Directorate, a small group of oligarchs charged with the bureaucratic necessities of ruling the world, and put himself in charge. First among equals. In reality, he became an autocrat and ruled with an iron fist.

"But the people saw him as a hero, mostly because he was able to get the bread flowing—a miracle accomplished through population control. The poor were worked to death. And when the bottom fell out, the next class became the lowest rung. The upper echelons saw it as civic duty. While the bottom was so tired from endless war that they simply lost the will to fight. Entire generations had known nothing but battle and death; peace was welcomed, even if it came under the heel of a tyrant.

"Next came the reordering of civilization. The suburbs were emptied and destroyed. Those who met the arbitrary threshold of class were led into the major cities. The rest were murdered, though the Directorate's propaganda called it the Cleansing. The now-empty land was repurposed purely for food supplies for the population that had survived. Containing the population helped with the energy crisis, but your Shade knew it couldn't last forever. He ordered his scientists to begin working on ways to stretch the power of the stones further.

"If you can believe it," Badger said, "in all those years of using the stones, no one who handled one had a double on this side. Well, at least no one who mattered. There'd been reports of nightmares from exposure by the miners, but they were dismissed as a way for them to get out of work. No scientific evidence existed of side effects.

"But when the experiments into stretching the energy threshold began, some of the scientists started having visions of another Earth. More primitive. Like their planet had been before the discovery of the stones. Suddenly people of import were having these nightmares, and the side effects were looked into more thoroughly. Eventually, they realized they weren't hallucinations but visions of another reality. And the study into the multiverse and the transcending of space-time began. They've spent the last fifteen years studying the stones, manipulating them, trying to find a way to enter this realm. About ten years ago, they succeeded in sending a person over. They've been planting people all over this world ever since. All in an attempt to ready themselves for when they could open a Gateway to this universe and begin their mining operations anew."

"Torian and Jacobs," I said.

"That's right," Badger replied with a wry smile. "And the cops on the bridge. They have people all over the planet. But the power consumption is exponential when size increases. Easy to send one person at a time but a ship would deplete a lot of their energy reserves. So, while they have plenty of people here on this world, they can't get to the moons of Jupiter and Saturn to get to the resources. Your Shade's desperate; there's only enough supply to last another twenty years. Then, their entire society will collapse. He's gambling it all on this invasion."

"How do you know all this?" I asked.

"Because." Badger paused, measuring his next words carefully. "I'm one of those scientists. One of the important people who had visions. I was behind the technology that allowed us to come here in the first place. I'm also the traitor who came here to stop the invasion. Organized the resistance. Our world had a chance, and we lost. There's no reason for this world to suffer, too."

"You're a *Shade?*" I stammered.

"Technically, we're the Shades. Some of us, anyway," Arvind said. "It's their term for us. Or at least the doubles on this end; not sure what they call the rest of us. But it's a good descriptor. Makes explaining this to new recruits easier. So, we took it."

"If it weren't for Badger," Eliza said, "we'd have already lost. We've had time to prepare. To plan. To figure out what to do to stop this from happening."

"Lot of good you've done." I indicated the image of the Gateway on the wall.

"We can still stop this invasion from taking place," Burke said. "Since they can only send their fleet through one at a time, we have a small advantage. If we can get to their side and destroy the wormhole from their end, then we stop this invasion before it starts."

"And that's why you needed the ring," I said. "The stone will allow you to open a back door."

"That's right," Badger said. "It was easy to come over because we had the energy supplies for the job. But we've had one of the foremost minds working on the problem on this side."

"The other Dr. Andrews," I guessed. Suddenly, it all made sense.

"Our world's Dr. Andrews has been invaluable to—" Remley stopped short after a harsh look from Badger. There was more to this story of Dr. Andrews and Badger, but he didn't want me to know it.

"How does Madison fit into all of this?" I asked.

"She stayed behind when I left five years ago," Badger said. "Earned back the trust of your Shade. She's been coming back and forth with Torian and Jacobs to find and kill me for years. But she was our double agent. About a week ago, she managed to smuggle the ring through. Torian and Jacobs must have suspected—or someone betrayed her—because she couldn't get anywhere near one of our cells. How she managed to get it to the bank . . . Well, guess we'll never know now."

Everyone in the room shifted uncomfortably. It was clear that Madison's death had deeper meaning to these people beyond the loss of a comrade.

"Why me?" I asked, trying to keep Badger talking.

"Madison believed in the symmetry of the cosmic universe. She didn't ascribe the same negative emotions to you that many of us do. She saw that his strength could be your strength. His brilliance could be yours. But she also knew that we all have choices in life. And she hoped that where he might exploit power, you would choose to help someone in need."

"Well, I'm flattered, I guess. At least I've gotten you what you need so you can stop this."

"You mean *we* can stop this," Burke said.

"Me? I don't think so."

"You're the only chance we have," Eliza said.

"How do you figure?"

"Your Shade is the most important man in their entire power structure," Remley said. "You can get our strike team into places we wouldn't otherwise be able to get."

"They're going to know I'm not him."

"Eventually they'll figure it out," Eliza said. "But that element of surprise might be enough to get us through."

"No way. I saw what that world could do to me. I'd lose myself there. You'll have to find another way."

"I told you," Burke said. "He's selfish just like the other one. I don't know why we expected anything different from the double of a dictator."

"What about Carla?" Badger asked. "They've taken her to that side. The only way for you to save her is to go to their Earth and get her back."

"You don't know they took her there."

"If Torian and Jacobs took her," Burke said, "then she's over there. Those two clock more time on the cosmic interstate than anyone."

Everything in my body told me going was a bad idea. My visions had been all-consuming with an irresistible draw I couldn't explain. It wasn't that I saw my Shade's hopes and dreams. It was as if, in those moments, I'd been him.

You could have that again. Possibly more. Destiny calls.

Maybe . . . But could I survive without forgetting the real me? I didn't know. And frankly, not knowing scared the shit out of me.

Before I could object again, the image on the screen changed. A colossal ship emerged from the Gateway. Beautiful. Its hull glinting a vibrant silver against the black backdrop of space. The dreadnought's hull spiraled in four sections that all wrapped around one another, like pieces of braided rope. The resulting structure flowed together, similar to blown glass. The vessel rotated slowly—creating inertia inside and allowing the ship to maintain artificial gravity—a spiraling corkscrew. It glided through space, a thrown dagger spinning towards our heart, bringing only death.

Emblazoned across the side of the ship was the vessel's name. But I didn't need to read the words to know them: *Liberator.* The irony was not lost on my counterpart from the other side. The ship had no command tower that I could see, the coils of metal perfectly smooth. Instinctively I knew the ship's bridge would be buried deep within her hull, hidden behind miles of that reinforced metal. This ship, for all its elegance, could take a major beating and keep coming back for more without ever compromising its central nervous system. A brilliant design. And well beyond anything we'd even dreamed of on this planet.

Dizziness took me. Processing all this information spinning around my brain trounced my senses. I knew more about that ship than I should have. And I understood, deep in my core, that I knew it because the other Duster Raines did. Somehow, we were connected. And while I couldn't read his mind, I comprehended more about their universe than I had a right to.

Before I could say anything about it, the projection of the ship switched over to my near-mirror image. He sat on the same bridge that I'd seen in my vision, his black uniform crisper and more impressive in reality than it had been in my dream. Draped over his shoulders he wore a crimson stole lined with gold. Upon the left side of the garment, a white and muscular dragon had been embroidered. Stitched on the right was a sinewy black dragon. Both creatures' eyes had been represented in a vibrant emerald green. My double held his chin aloft in a confident and regal manner—his import would be obvious to anyone watching. Part of me envied this stronger, youthful leader, living the destiny I'd always known I deserved.

But for the fates of our different worlds . . .

"Citizens of Earth," my double said, "this transmission will be translated as you hear it in your preferred language. I am First Consul Gaius Octavius, third to hold the name in imperial succession. Leader of the Directorate. Holder of the golden keys to the ancient imperial stronghold of Xi'an. Legate of the true descendants of the legions of Rome. Restorer of the fallen imperial dynasty. Defender of the human race.

"I'm sure by now you have noticed the rift above Mars and that one of my ships, *Liberator*, has just emerged. Do not be afraid I will try and explain what is happening in the simplest of terms. That rift is a portal between our two universes that we call the Gateway. We are, in truth, from a different but nearly identical dimension of space that runs parallel to your own.

"I won't attempt to explain how our presence in this reality is possible in this message, but know that I look human because I am human. We are all human beings but of a different Earth.

You should think of us as your distant cousins. Long lost but finally reunited. We are your brethren come home.

"I wish I did not have to tell you that our power can be used for benevolence or destruction. But we know our own nature all too well, and you have not advanced to the point of world peace as we have. So, know this: Those who treat us as friends will be accorded the same respect. Those who resort to their baser instincts will be treated harshly.

"But do not fear. Soon I hope our two peoples will learn to live in harmony. We intend to share our knowledge with you and help usher in an era of innovation on your planet. Your divisions and borders will disappear. Our purpose is simple: to save human civilization and protect our way of life. We will not allow anyone or anything to stand in our way. We are here to stay. Acceptance of that will be the first step towards an enlightened future.

"I suggest you convene your legislative bodies to discuss this world-changing moment and prepare for our arrival. Things will never be the same again. But know in your heart that this change is good. I will contact you again soon.

"Until then, peace and prosperity be with you. May the Eternal Watcher bless us all. His prophesied return is at hand. Long live the Directorate. Long live humanity."

The image returned to the *Liberator*, slowly twisting through space, hanging in a high orbit above Mars.

"The lying son of a bitch," Remley muttered.

"The silver-tongued charmer that you are," Burke said to me.

"He isn't him," Eliza shot back across the table. "And we need him now more than ever."

"What was that about the Eternal Watcher?" I asked.

"I told you how China and Rome once united on their planet and ushered in unprecedented human advancement for a thousand years," Badger said.

"Sure, what's that got to do with us?"

"The emperor of that union was known as the Eternal Watcher. A living god on Earth. A mantle that was passed down for over a millennium to the strongest in the empire. Some believe the first Eternal Watcher was the true discoverer of the few stones that reside on this planet, thus giving them near supernatural abilities. Though that's more legend than anything else. Your double, the *First Consul*, means to unite the proverbial East and West of our two worlds and become the Eternal Watcher reborn. A true incarnation of the duality the throne always represented. Ruling over two Earths rather than two empires. A prophecy foretold at the end of the empire before the factions sprang up, and our world's demise began."

"There's an actual prophecy about alternate realities from over a thousand years ago?" I scoffed. "I find that hard to believe."

"Adequately vague that enough people will buy in," Badger said. "Isn't that what makes a good prophecy? So now you see why your Shade must be stopped. And I fear without you, we will fail. Your destiny has brought you to this moment. Can we count on you, Duster Raines?"

Good speech. Even brought up our destiny. But he's using us.

I shook the voices away and said, "I'm not doing anything until I see Juan's safe."

"Of course, Duster." Badger's face darkened, a bitter anger I'd never seen in him before. "Like I said, I won't make you do anything you're not comfortable with."

CHAPTER 22

THE CELL I FOUND MYSELF IN BARELY QUALIFIED AS A CAVE.

Prior to my imprisonment, my guard gave me my second nickel tour of the week. With just a wave of her hand and a verbal request, the wall morphed into an alcove, replete with toilet, sink, and shower. But that was the extent of the tour. A seven-by-seven room with a magic rock toilet. I'd been informed I'd be allowed to see Juan soon. Then without so much as a goodbye, my escort left—I may have overvalued that tour—and when the door closed behind her, the seams of it vanished. I ran my hand along where I knew the grooves had been, searching for imperfections in the stone, trying to find the material that had filled those gaps. But it didn't exist.

I waved my hand, asking for a door. But the rock remained. Second attempt. Nothing.

Of course, I had no idea if doors were activated the same way as the bathroom. The rules of this mystical place were still a mystery. Maybe they'd programmed it to specific voices, retinal scans, or even DNA. Or they'd just locked it.

Tried not to panic. Buried alive. The walls were closing in. Trapped beneath miles of impenetrable rock. No one would miss me. And it wouldn't matter if they did because they'd never be able to find me. If Badger and his army forgot me in this jail, I'd die in here. No escaping it. This prison would be my tomb.

A cold sweat chilled me to the bone. I needed a drink. That would put my mind at ease. I could feel those old burdens sneaking up. Shaken. Weak. Anxious. The whispers of the night ever-present. Those insidious thoughts of failure and nagging regret crept back in. This would be the perfect time to chase it away with the bottle. Let my senses numb and those feelings vanish. A drink always made me stronger. Steadied me.

On the stone bed sat my young friend from Iraq. He wouldn't speak. Rarely did. He gazed through me with those dark brown eyes. Judging. Blood pooled out of his forehead, mucking up his features and consuming his eyes in an ocean of red. Then I realized it was no longer that little Iraqi boy but Juan who sat next to me. He bled all over, grotesque, disgusting. But I was the ugly one, not him, my hideous guilt tainting everything it touched.

Kneeling near the toilet, I threw up. Drenched in sweat, I tried to control the shaking of my freezing body. Juan loomed above me, dripping blood. Smiling. Deceitful. No love for me.

Closed my eyes. Tried not to spiral.

He wasn't there. He wasn't real.

Nothing from you but lies, lies, lies.

But I'd been lying to myself for so long, not sure I knew how to do anything else.

When I opened my eyes, the boy had gone. But for how long? My mind screamed at me to take a drink, but I couldn't. And deep down I felt thankful. I needed to stay sober. I needed to save Carla. I needed to protect Juan. That was all that mattered now. The rest were just details.

After a few hours of working on the door problem—there was nothing else to do—I gave up. I couldn't find any indication

there'd ever been a door to begin with. For all intents and purposes, it never existed. Similar to the halls, light emanated from
the walls with no real source, the entire place more magic than
technology.

Unnatural.

When I'd first entered this tunnel system, I'd been struck
by its bizarreness, unlike anything I'd ever seen. And the more
I thought about it, the more uncomfortable I got. Because this
place didn't feel human. The *Liberator* had looked exactly how
you might expect a man-made warship from the future to look.
Age our technology a couple of hundred years, and I could see
the United States putting a vessel like that into space, its origins
unmistakable. But these tunnels and its biotechnology were
otherworldly. No other way to describe it. I didn't care how far
into the future I gazed, I couldn't imagine a person wanting to
live like this, let alone building it. That idea made me nervous
because if the Shades hadn't made this place, then who had?

Time lost any sense of meaning in that tiny cell. I lay in
bed, staring at the ceiling, trying to stay calm and wait for the
opportunity to find my way out. Finally, the seams of the door
returned. It took a minute for my eyes to adjust to the blinding
light from the outside halls. When they did, relief set in at the
sight of Juan being pushed into my prison by another soldier.
This guard said even less than the last one and shut the door
without so much as a nod.

Words escaped me. Unsure if I should rush to the kid
or stay put, I split the difference and took a few tentative
steps forward. Juan did us both a favor and bolted across the
room—ending my awkward shuffle—and leapt into my arms,
squeezing me hard in a hug.

"Whoa, there." Hadn't realized the kid cared all that much.
"Good to see you, too."

Juan pulled away, a little embarrassed. I patted him on the head, not reassuring at all.

"You doing okay?" I asked.

"Yeah. It's been cool."

"Good. I've been worried about you. What about your mom? Where's she?"

Juan shrugged, looked at his feet.

Shit, I forgot. My stomach sank. Those bastards who had Carla had taken his mom, too. Juan and I were both alone. Nice to have something in common. I put my arm around him and pulled him into another hug.

"She's not dead," Juan said.

"I didn't think she was."

"Good." Juan went and sat on the bed. "Because we're going to get her back."

"You bet your ass we will." I sat down next to him. "What have they told you?"

"They thought you were dead. You and that Badger guy. Weren't all that upset. They don't like you much here."

"I have that effect on people."

"I stood up for you. Told them they didn't know you. They said you were a drunk. But I told them you were more than that. That you got my family out of trouble."

"I appreciate it, Juan. But I can fight my own battles." The air went out of the kid's sails. He'd worn his protection of me as a badge of honor, and I'd just ripped it off his chest. For some reason, the kid looked up to me. I tried to get the subject moving again before he realized these people were right about the kind of guy I was. "Have they treated you good? Kept you entertained?"

"For sure," Juan said. "They let me use their computers. Showed me a few things about how the tunnels work."

"You'll be an engineer like your pops one day."

"Yeah. Maybe. I'm good at it, that's for sure. My dad taught me a few things about coding before he left. Came in handy. Helped my cousin earn some street cred before he got arrested. Almost went to jail for it, too."

"You almost went to jail for computers?"

"Drek wanted to rob a convenience store to prove himself in the neighborhood. I didn't want him to get killed. Figured we could steal from an ATM and not use any guns. Drek acts tough but he's not."

"You guys close?"

"He's my cousin."

"Yeah. Sure."

"Anyway, I took a magnetic strip and reset its account number using this program I'd read about online. Then I could make the code whatever I wanted, and the ATM would think it was a legit card. I saw it in a movie once. But I guess it didn't work because we got stopped halfway through by a cop. Got off with a slap on the wrist, some community service. Drek not so much the second time around."

"Were you guys dressed like that when you did this?"

Juan looked down at his baggy jeans and loose-fitting skater T-shirt. Guess nineties grunge was back in style with the teenagers. Maybe it'd never been out of style. I didn't really know. Couldn't blame them either way. The look was classic.

"Yeah. So?" Juan asked.

I patted him on the back. "You're a good kid, Juan. It's lucky you got caught."

"Lucky I met you and Carla."

"Wouldn't count your eggs just yet."

"What's that mean?"

"Nothing. So they told you about the war?" Juan nodded. I waited for him to say something. When he didn't take the hint, I pulled it out of him. "What've they told you?"

"A lot. Shades. Doubles. Twin universes. They're nuts but I went along until I could figure out a way to find my mom." Juan looked at me for reassurance. Guess my face didn't do the job. "You think it's crazy," he said. "Right?"

"It's all true. At least from what I've seen."

Juan pondered that bombshell for a minute, turning over this new reality in his mind. Then he said, "I want to help. I want to fight." He'd accepted it a heck of a lot faster than I had. Guess kids can manage that better than adults.

"Just like your dad." I grinned, hoping I hadn't gone too far. Juan smiled back, proud of the man his father was and the person he'd one day be. At least I got that one right.

"We have to warn him." Juan's smile disappeared. "He could be in danger."

"I'm sure your dad already knows. There's a ship in space. It broadcast a message of peace to the entire world. But there won't be peace. Not with the man who leads them."

"How do you know that?"

"Because their leader's me," I confessed. "And I wouldn't show us mercy."

CHAPTER 23

SHOW NO MERCY . . .

The thought echoed through my mind. Unclear if it belonged to me or my Shade.

Knew I shouldn't have said it the moment it escaped my lips. Our conversation in that cell was definitely monitored. But I couldn't help myself. I wanted these Watchers to know the truth about me—*needed them to know*—that I wasn't so different from a tyrant in a flying death fortress. At least I didn't feel that different from him. Maybe that should've worried me. But in truth, it made me feel important.

My obsessive mission to put right the wrongs I'd done in Iraq had never wholly been for absolution. It proved my mettle. Tempered my blade. I'd always believed a destiny of greatness would be mine. Though the longer I lived this shit life, the less likely that seemed. I'd carried on because that's what you do. Persevere.

But at what point are your actions more delusion than drive?

This double of mine, a man who ruled an empire, gave me hope. Reinvigorated my past beliefs in myself. He'd become the man I'd been born to be.

Sadly, I'd amounted to squat. But now I knew more than one reality existed. And if this universe wouldn't grant me the fate I deserved, then I'd have to take it for myself from another. I would go on this mission of Badger's to stop my Shade. Not for any of them. But for me. I would claim my greatness by destroying the other Duster Raines.

The door abruptly reappeared in the smooth cave wall, and another mute guard hustled us into the tunnels. He escorted us down a few unremarkable corridors, taking us through a large archway and into a perfectly spherical cave that must have been over fifty feet in diameter. Metal grates were installed about a third of the way up the sphere to create a place for us all to walk. Some type of electrical coils spanned the entire perimeter of the room with wires running to the center where a raised platform stood. Atop the platform, two large, steel rings were affixed and appeared to be constructed such that they could spin around one another, passing through gaps in the flooring and whipping back around.

Two soldiers sat at the base of the platform at a cluster of computers and monitoring screens. A few other personnel, led by Badger, hustled around the machine, checking wires, plugs, and connectors. Badger saw Juan and moved to greet us. He smiled, extending his hand to shake mine and I realized this was not the man I knew. His teeth were perfectly straight and white—the complete opposite of Badger's mess of a mouth. I also saw in his eyes a mischievous side that Badger lacked. An opportunist.

"You're the real Dr. Andrews, I presume." I knew it instantly. Badger was Andrews but Madison had sent me to find this man.

"What gave it away?" Andrews asked with obvious disappointment. "The teeth? I keep telling Badger to get his fixed in case we need to impersonate one another."

"That's exactly why I don't fix them." Badger's voice boomed throughout the sphere as he passed beneath the arch with Burke, Remley, Arvind, and Eliza in tow. Badger embraced me as if we were old friends and then cast a wary eye over Andrews.

"Is it ready?" Badger asked. You could hear the bitter taste each word held. He loathed this duplicate of himself. The two men stared one another down, no love lost between them.

"As ready as it'll ever be," Andrews muttered, returning his attention to the contraption. "As you already know, we don't possess the technological capabilities that allowed you to pass into our realm."

"That's why I brought you down here. Your expertise in inferior machines."

Andrews smiled, his contempt for his twin not well hidden. "I've jury-rigged it. Done the best I could based on your schematics. But the bottom line is I don't even know if this thing is going to turn on, let alone open a vortex to another universe."

I stole a glance at the rest of Badger's team but they gave nothing away.

Andrews continued, "I could give you a laundry list of concerns, but I'll stick with the greatest hits. We don't know if the core of the stone you brought back is stable. The only way to test that would be to send something through. And, as we've discussed, if we test it on something nonhuman and it runs out of energy, then we'll be up a proverbial creek without a paddle."

"And that's if he doesn't blow us all up," Arvind added.

"Thanks for stating the obvious." Andrews shrugged. "That's all I've got."

"We'll have to risk it," Badger said.

"Risk what?" I asked.

"A crossover," Badger said. "The ring you brought us should have enough energy to send you and a small strike team to the other side. The Council is in agreement, this is our best chance at cutting the head off the dragon."

"You keep talking like you know I'm going," I said.

"We do know," Burke chided. He wanted me to refuse the mission, itching for the chance to make me go.

"Lucky for you," I said to Burke, "I have some unfinished business with a couple of sociopaths from the other side."

"Like you had a choice," Burke muttered.

"I'm glad you've come around, Duster," Badger said. "I didn't want to force you into this. And we've never been interested in why anyone fights for us. Just the results."

"It's Raines," I sighed. "No one calls me Duster."

Badger smirked. He already knew that.

"I'm going, too," Juan said. Resolute. Brave. Sadly, his moment didn't last.

"Afraid not, kid," Burke said.

"They took my mother." Juan turned to Badger. "You promised me if I worked for you that we'd get her back."

"And we will get her back," Badger said. "But Burke's right. You're too young. Safer for you here."

"When that ship gets here," Eliza said, "nowhere on this planet will be safe."

"I've made my decision," Badger said. "We're already short on power."

I put my hand on Juan's back. "Don't worry. I'll bring your mom home safe."

Juan nodded and sulked off to the side.

"All right," Badger said. "Do you think you can chance sending us all through at once?"

"I wouldn't recommend it," Andrews said. "I really have no idea of the energy requirements to accomplish this. I'm building this thing in the dark, and most of my work so far has been theoretical."

"I'm not interested in the limitations," Badger said. "Only the results."

"I'd say no more than four at a time. Even that might be pushing it. If we have a successful first attempt, we can send more through."

"And the equipment?" Burke asked. "The guns?"

"Lowest priority," Badger said.

"Guns are the lowest priority?" I asked. "You must be joking."

"Raines is right," Remley said. "Lot of gusto to go in unarmed, considering what we're about to attempt."

"There'll be plenty of weapons on the other side. My concern is people," Badger said. "Burke, me, and Remley will take Raines through first. Eliza, you and Arvind will follow with the equipment."

"Don't you think I should go through first?" Eliza asked. "After all, I have the greatest understanding about how the Gateway works."

"Doesn't take a lot of know-how to drop a bomb on it," Burke said.

Eliza squirmed at the thought of being left out. "There's the angle of entry, the force of the explosion, and you have to account for time distillation when passing back through the anomaly. It's all very complicated, Burke."

"So make it a big bomb," Burke said. "Got it."

Eliza went to object again, but Badger stopped her. "I'm afraid brawn trumps brains in this endeavor, Eliza. This is essentially a military operation now, and I need my most experienced soldiers if we have any hope of successfully commandeering a ship to drop that big bomb."

"Besides," Arvind interjected, "this could all be academic. We may have enough power to send everyone through."

"Kid's right," Burke said. "Now let's stop pissing into the wind and get this show on the road." He walked up onto the platform and waited for the rest of us to join him. When we didn't, he barked, "Move! The apocalypse ain't waiting for us to feel good about it."

Badger grabbed a small satchel and walked up onto the platform. Remley joined him. He pulled three mud-brown cloaks from the pack and handed them out. They quickly fastened the cloaks around their necks and tight around their heads, all of them the spitting image of the bug-eyed troops I'd seen in my vision. I guess cloaks were back in fashion in the future—or was it the present? I couldn't keep track anymore.

"You know," I said to Dr. Andrews, "I've been looking for you."

"I've heard. Badger told me about Maddy. Thank you for finishing what she started. She, uh . . . She would've respected that."

"I thought when I found you, I'd get some answers."

"Life is full of disappointments." Andrews clutched my hand, pulled me into a tight embrace, and whispered, "There's no time. Watch your back. Look for a friend on the other side. Things aren't what they seem." He released my hand, smiled with his perfectly straight teeth, then hurried over to the computer station that ran this massive spherical apparatus.

Things aren't what they seem. Exactly what Madison had told me in my vision. That couldn't be another coincidence. Could it?

Badger cleared his throat, drawing my attention up to the platform where my cloaked compatriots watched me expectantly. I looked towards the archway where three armed guards stood—the illusion of choice—and I begrudgingly joined the team beneath the rings. Badger tossed me a cloak, which I quickly put on, then he threw the bag off the platform.

"All right," Andrews said. "Hope this doesn't kill us." He pushed a button on a computer panel, and the large steel rings began to spin around the platform in opposite directions, creating a blurred wall of motion. Andrews punched a few more commands into his board, and the pace of the rings sped up to the point where the blur became nearly invisible between the blinking of the eye. As the rings spun, the air between us and the room began to morph. We were inside a giant bubble of green energy, a phased version of whatever stone that ring held. The energy bubble pulsed in and out, faster and faster with each spin of the rings. The space inside the rings seemed to shrink together as we all moved away from reality and down to whatever hell awaited us. The demarcations between our bodies, the objects in the room, and even the molecules of air disappeared. We were all one thing but at the same time an infinite number of other things. This space within the bubble no longer obeyed the rules of physics we'd grown accustomed to.

The events in the real world all unfolded in miniature before me. I could see Andrews through the phasing bubble, growing smaller and smaller, working frantically at the keyboard to keep this machine running. And I saw Juan, moving absurdly slow, but actually running with everything he had for the platform and those spinning rings. Arvind attempted to grab Juan but missed, falling flat on his face in the attempt. Andrews cried out but I had no idea what he said because no sound penetrated this place, just a solitary whistle like an approaching train. Bewildered, Eliza watched helplessly as the boy ran to his death. Arvind scrabbled onto his knees to grab at Juan again, but I knew no one would be able to stop that kid from his suicidal run. I held my breath as Juan reached for the bubble and jumped.

Impossibly, the two spinning rings didn't crush him. Instead, he hurtled between the rings and into the bubble, falling into my arms. But when he'd passed into the sphere, he'd gone from slow motion to full speed; unready for the shift in time, he slammed into me. I staggered back, falling out towards the spinning rings and partially leaving the bubble. I shoved Juan back into the sphere. This was the end. But I never reached those chomping rings because I froze mid-fall, suspended at a forty-five-degree angle, my head mere inches from the vise. This position would've been impossible except for some new force now present within the bubble. It felt as if the gravity of that place had shrunk, becoming impossibly strong, focused into a tiny point the size of a pinhead at the center of the platform. My body began to tear asunder as that infinitesimal point pulled me down, and the outside world tried to rip me out. My atoms frayed. The molecules in my body unable to handle the strain. A peculiar sensation over-whelmed me as the building blocks of my essence phased out of reality and readied to be shot through this portal to God knew where. And suddenly, I flung back into the bubble like an overstretched rubber band being released.

What should've taken seconds felt like minutes. I never reached the platform. I just kept falling. And with every passing second, I felt my pace increasing to an impossible speed—as if I were the one shrinking as I traveled a greater distance than the bubble had within it.

I fell for miles. And miles. And miles.

The others in the bubble had vanished. It was only me and an eternal fall towards the steel floor. At this rate, I would splatter across the ground into unrecognizable goo. My mind howled, incapable of comprehending the experience. Any moment I would go into shock from the strain of disbelief.

A loud crack tore at my eardrums, like an ancient tree collapsing in the forest. And then an explosion of green fire erupted across my skin. I screamed but no sound came out. I tried to put out the flames, but I had no hands to do it with because my body no longer existed. But I still felt the pain of my atoms disintegrating.

No more lab. No more rings. No more people. Only my mind and a tunnel of green energy warping into a black abyss of nothing. I hoped that the eternal nothing would take me soon, and I would never feel pain again.

Not yet, Raines. Not yet. We've got things to do.

Those survival instincts refused to let go. I tried to breathe but couldn't. It made sense I couldn't since I didn't have a body anymore. But try telling yourself that as you suffocate.

I finally hit the ground, but only with the force of a small tumble. An explosion of energy mushroomed around me, leaving a large black circle scorched on the dirt. My lungs burned as I tried to suck in air. I was alone.

The sky above shone a perfect crisp blue. The bluest sky I'd ever seen. I'd materialized on top of the mountain range that Badger and I had hiked over only a couple of days before. The shapes of those peaks were unmistakable. But the forest that should've been here didn't exist. Instead, the ground stretched out before me, flat and repurposed to grow some type of brownish crop that I'd never seen before on my Earth. From this vantage point, the plant looked dead and inedible but there was too much of it for that to be true—a labyrinth of food production that stretched out in every direction nearly as far as the eye could see.

In the distance, beyond the swaying crop fields, I could make out that vile metropolis I'd dreamed about. It covered over one hundred square miles and reached thousands of feet into the sky as if attempting to break into space and leave this world behind. While the sky wasn't the putrid poison I'd dreamed, the buildings were as I remembered them: onyx, not reflective but opaque, sucking all life and light into them and giving nothing back. A fortress-like wall encircled the city, stretching hundreds of feet into the air, only dwarfed by the skyscrapers it defended.

What could the builders of such frightening towers possibly fear to build a wall like that?

My voices didn't answer.

This place felt wrong. Twisted. Its beauty a lie, hiding something terrible.

I dragged myself up onto my feet, resisting the urge to lie down and die. My body ached, my skin still tingling from the green fire that had burned through every cell in my being. But my body seemed to have reassembled itself with everything in the proper place. If I'd had time, I would've worried about the fact I'd come out on the other end alone. But I didn't get the chance because another deafening bang erupted out of thin air, sending powerful reverberations through my weakened body. The ground kicked up, and a pulse of energy exploded in a violent wave of emerald energy, which threw me to the ground again. When the dust settled, I saw the rest of my party had arrived, Juan included. They all sucked in air in a panic as I had, then slowly regained their wits and sat up to assess their surroundings.

Burke acted first, hurrying to his feet and grabbing Juan by the nape of his neck. He spun the boy around like a rag doll and held him close to his face. Juan's feet dangled a good two feet off the ground.

"You could've fucking killed us," Burke snarled, an ugly fury contorting his face.

"Put him down, Burke," Badger ordered.

"This kid risked the mission. He's guilty of treason and there's only one punishment for—"

I didn't wait for Burke to finish, struggling up onto my feet and running at him full bore. I tackled him from behind before he knew what hit him. We both fell to the ground, rolling in the dirt. He lost his grip on Juan, and the boy scampered away. I straddled Burke. The surprise of the impact had stunned him and gave me the precious seconds I needed to seize the advantage. I pummeled him with my fists, smashing his face over and over again. Once he got back on his feet, I knew I'd lose, so I threw everything I had into each punch. Blood splattered everywhere as my fists struck this giant of a man. Burke took a terrible beating, my knuckles throbbed in agony from the effort, but it probably wouldn't be enough.

And I was right, it wasn't enough.

Burke kicked his knees up into my back and thrust me into the air. The pressure off his body, he got his hands up and secured them tightly around my neck. He stood, keeping me in that stranglehold, and squeezed the air from my lungs. He was strong. Stronger than anyone I'd ever fought. I slammed his shoulders with my fists, but his grip only tightened. I kept hitting him—I wasn't going down without a fight—though the blows did little to faze him.

My eyes felt like they were about to burst from my head. My vision dimmed, darkness creeping in at the edges. I wheezed out what I figured would be my last breath.

Burke gazed at me with detached curiosity as I died. Reddened pus covered his face, blood seeping from his broken nose and cracked lips, staining his once-white goatee. He looked like a prizefighter who'd barely lasted through the twelve-round bout to win by decision. He swayed slightly, trying to hold himself upright. Then, he laughed. An ugly rotten laugh since his face was starting to swell beyond recognition. Droplets of spittle and blood flew from his mouth, splattering my face.

Just as suddenly as it had appeared, Burke's rage disappeared, and he dropped me to the ground. He plopped down in the dirt next to me, catching his breath. "You're a crazy son of a bitch, Raines. I'll give you that."

"Thanks," I coughed. "You touch the kid again, and I'll kill you."

Burke slapped me on the back. "I'd expect nothing less." Then he gave Juan a stern look, made even more insane because his eyes were hidden beneath a face little more than blood and swollen flesh. "You follow orders, or I leave you behind. Clear?"

Juan nodded.

Burke wiped his face with his cloak. He looked awful. But apparently, he felt no pain. Or simply didn't care.

"Now that you boys are done flexing your muscles and wasting our time," Remley said, "how about we discuss the fact the kid probably screwed us with the rest of our equipment?"

"It is what it is." Badger motioned towards that menacing and unending city on the horizon. "Besides, there's plenty of guns to go around in that hellhole."

"How do you propose we get in there?" Burke asked.

"Simple," Badger said. "We walk through the front gate."

CHAPTER 24

I NEVER WANTED KIDS.

Even once I'd met Carla and fallen for her—told her my secrets and she'd absolved me of my sins—I didn't want them. I owed her better. But no matter how hard I tried to convince myself, I couldn't let her have the family she deserved.

She'd said it was all right. That she didn't need children to be happy. But I spotted her dishonesty a mile off. I wanted to believe she'd lied because she loved me. That she'd forgiven me for the murder of the Iraqi boy because deep down she knew it broke me. But how could I trust anything she said if deceit came so naturally to her? Our entire relationship could be a sham. I needed to be certain.

So, I poisoned the well. Thought I'd find the truth in the smoldering ruins of our broken relationship. I didn't. Lay that blame at my feet. I'm guilty. I've never said any different. There was no coming back from where I'd taken us. The things I'd said. The hurt I'd caused. She'd made it abundantly clear: I'd used my last get-out-of-jail-free card. That should've been it between us. We were through.

But no one accounts for the world coming to an end.

Kids. If Carla hadn't wanted them, it would've been fine. My psychiatrist always thought I'd created this scenario out of guilt. You know, kill a boy in a war and punish yourself by denying happiness with the woman you loved. Then, blame the entire debacle on future unborn children. Saying it now, it made a lot of sense. But at the time, I'd been pissed I'd paid for that drivel.

Now's the part when I blame my upbringing. Hate to disappoint. I loved my parents. Mom more than Dad. But that's natural, isn't it? My shrink always called that deflecting. But how can it be deflecting when it's true? Sure, I'd had a hard time of it growing up. But who doesn't? The bruises and broken bones made me stronger.

I will say this much: my mom was weak-willed, and my dad was a drinker. Those two things don't add up to anything but sadness when you're a twelve-year-old boy.

I know. I'm a big cliché. Repeating history. Drinking myself into an early grave like the old man. But at least I knew where I stood. My childhood taught me the inherent selfishness of parenthood. All the best intentions tend to amount to little more than an hourly fee at an analyst's office talking about your feelings and being told you're doing things like deflecting.

All that said, this Juan kid had turned me upside down. I didn't owe him a thing but that hadn't stopped me from feeling like I did. And after I'd just stood up for him—maybe saved his life—he hung close, nipping at my heels, nearly tripping me a couple of times with this long and dramatic cloak I now wore. Truth be told, it made me feel important because, if he stumbled, I'd be there to pick him back up.

Maybe that was what having a kid was all about. A sense of self-worth.

You don't believe that bullshit.

Fair. Bottom line, people don't want to die. And kids were the best way human beings had figured to live forever. That spark of yours gets passed on, and then you spend the rest of your life making sure those little bastards remember you for the rest of theirs. My dad had been dead over fifteen years and I still conjured up his spirit to torment me on lonely nights. I didn't need that kind of immortality.

I caught a glimpse of Juan out of the corner of my eye. He was staring. Probably been waiting for me to look at him for a while. A smile flashed across his face, and he rushed to my side. Seemed excited. Might even be enjoying all this alternate-reality war crap. Kids were funny like that.

I forced a smile. It felt jilted and weak, but he took it. Probably knew it was the best he'd get from me.

With every step our small band made towards that cursed city, I could feel the presence of my Shade grow. An emptiness clutched my soul, feelings that weren't my own. Foreign thoughts slipped into my consciousness. Memories I hadn't lived. It was all I could do to keep from drowning in a sea of confusion.

Juan. Hold on to him. An anchor to your own unique reality.

Good idea. I cared about the boy, and that feeling belonged to me. His presence grounded me. Might keep the pull of my Shade at bay. Lucky for me, Juan had risked killing us all to come along for the ride. A stupid move. But he was young and probably figured he couldn't die.

Bad news, kid. You can.

Above us, the scorching sun beat down through that too-crisp blue sky. We marched through rows upon rows of that mystery crop I'd seen from up on the mountaintop. The plant stood well over eight feet tall and, once we were down in it, obscured our vision in any direction to no more than a few feet. Something about this endless crop supply gave me the jitters. The plant was an odd brownish gray that resembled decaying flesh more than grain. And there weren't any obvious husks or blooms that would indicate food. They were simply tall stalks, like rotted-out bamboo, that reached for the sky around a dark citadel that our universe called Los Angeles.

There was a stillness here. A dead space. A tightening of the air. I breathed it in just fine, but it tasted stale and lonesome.

I heard it first. The low drone of an approaching aircraft. Unmistakable.

"I think we've got company," I said.

"I hear it," Burke confirmed. "Everyone, down."

We hunkered among the crops as three drones flew by overhead. Things were bigger than I'd expected, probably twelve feet across, shaped like arrowheads, the same color as those obsidian towers. They weren't trying to hide; they wanted us to know they were here. They swooped down, buzzed the crops, searching. That tug of this world pulled at me, my twin wanted to find me. And it was all I could do to not light a flare for him. I buried it down deep and tried to ignore it.

"My Shade knows we're here," I said. "I can feel him calling to me."

"Those drones aren't looking for us," Badger said.

"Then who—" But before I could finish the thought, a guttural bark emanated from somewhere in the warren of dead flesh plants. I saw a shadow dart between the stalks. Two cloudy green eyes flashed from the shadows, but they were gone just as fast as they'd appeared, and I couldn't be sure I hadn't imagined them. Then we heard a rustling from behind and spun on our heels to face the threat. But there was nothing there except plants and silence. We were being hunted.

"Run!" Remley shouted.

I grabbed Juan by the arm, and we took off into the tangle of crops, sprinting for our lives. I could hear the huffing of some animal behind us. This was no robot dog. This was a living, breathing creature. Massive. Strong. And it gained on us.

Juan tripped, falling to the ground. I turned back to help him but Badger grabbed me at the elbow, stopping me in my tracks. "Leave him. You're too important."

"Go to hell." I ripped myself free of his grip.

Sprinting to Juan, I slid in the dirt and grabbed him by the back of his shirt, yanking him onto his feet. We stumbled forward, trying to get our bearings. But all I saw in any direction was a maze of plants. We were alone. Our friends had disappeared into the crop fields, leaving us to our fates.

Cowards.

Takes one to know one.

"I got you. We need to—" Juan put a finger to his lips, silencing me.

Then I saw them. Two narrow green eyes with ashen pupils like some sort of mutant cat. They blinked quick, first up and down and then side to side from a secondary set of eyelids. The creature emerged slowly from the shadows, bobbing as it moved towards us on its hind legs. The beast had a long snout like a crocodile and a tail to match. But its skin wasn't leathery scales, rather a rough patchwork of dusty stone covered in a moss-like substance. The thing stood about seven feet tall and had arms like a primate. Its eyes locked on mine, their green clouds swirling in a storm of fury, mirroring the energy held deep within the stone that had brought us here. Within those ashen pupils burned an intelligence I hadn't anticipated. Unexpectedly, the beast smiled at me.

This chance encounter ended just as suddenly as it began. The creature's head snapped up towards the sky. I heard it, too, the drones returning for another pass. The beast disappeared into the darkness of the crops. Juan and I didn't wait, either;

we were up on our feet and running in the opposite direction of the creature.

The rumble of the drones grew to a roar as the ships whipped by overhead. A whistle lingered on the air for a moment and then I felt the warmth. The concussive force of the bomb caught up to us the next instant and threw us to the ground. Disoriented, I face-planted hard into the dirt—no air in my lungs and my ears rang with a piercing tone—I could feel the heat overhead but I felt no pain, everything a daze.

As my head cleared and I got my bearings, I saw the destruction. A large swath of the crops had been blown away by the explosion, leaving a crater of ash and fire. Next to me, Juan sat up and took in the view. We were at the edge of a charred pit at least fifty feet deep and twice that across. No sign of the drones in the sky. Apparently, they thought they'd hit their mark. Not a surprising assumption. I couldn't believe we'd survived. But if we'd made it, then I'd bet money so had the reptile.

"What was that thing?" Juan asked.

"No idea."

We sat in silence, staring at each other, dumbfounded. Evidently this Earth still had dinosaurs. Dr. Andrews and Madison's words rang in my head: *Things are not what they seem.* There was more to this story than I'd been told.

The echoes of our strike team shouting our names broke my train of thought. "Come on," I said. "I don't think we should wait around for that thing to come back."

Moments later, we found Badger, Burke, and Remley on the outskirts of the explosion.

"Did you see it?" Badger asked.

Juan went to answer but I gently placed my hand on his shoulder, stopping him. "We saw it. And I think you owe us an explanation."

"All right," Badger said reluctantly. "But on the move. Don't want to be here if those drones take another pass."

We started moving double time towards the city. Danger waited on both ends of this journey, but I got the sense from my compatriots that the evil empire was a safer bet than the giant rock lizard we'd met. It didn't take Badger long to get his thoughts in order. He wouldn't tell me the whole truth—that wasn't his style—he'd give me just enough to keep me on the hook. But it didn't matter either way and he knew it because I was stuck in another universe with no way back but the plan we'd laid out.

"We call them Stone Tails," Badger said. "They're a subterranean species."

I remembered the trash tabloid I'd read in the psychic's waiting room a lifetime ago. "You're telling me this planet has underground lizard people. Like those quack urban legends about creatures beneath Los Angeles?"

"Well, yes and no. They're not really from here."

"Aliens?" I asked, a little stunned. "Don't tell me Madison had that right, too."

"I told you how this world went out in search of sources of energy. Digging up stones on moons and asteroids. We even started working on ways to harness their energy to bend space-time and allow travel beyond our galaxy. That research was the beginning of the tech that eventually created the Gateway, allowing us to travel between our two parallel universes."

"And what? You traveled too far and found lizard people?"

"No. They're all around us. Those quack stories you mentioned, they're probably true. These beings aren't of any universe that we'd recognize. Think of them like travelers: they move between the space that resides between space."

"Space between space? What the hell does that even mean?"

"They're capable of traversing the void between universes. Just as we did moments ago. The rest of their technology is built on those principles. Very impressive. Well beyond anything we have. But thankfully they've tended to be a peaceful race and aren't advanced in weaponry. Otherwise, we'd already be dead."

"So, what're they doing here?"

"They were here long before our species could even walk upright. We don't know if they came here as explorers or evolved on Earth prior to transcending space and time. But one thing we do know for sure is they still take on corporeal form to mate and lay their eggs."

And suddenly I knew—the green swirls within their eyes, the innate ability to traverse the space between universes—the energy that had brought us here was their own. "The stones are their eggs," I stammered. "You're telling me you started a war with an advanced species because you wiped out their unborn children?"

"Yes," Badger said. "Unknowingly. But try and tell that to the Stone Tails. And that's the real reason your Shade leads the invasion on your universe. He means to take the stones from there and use their power to turn the tide of war, in the process wiping out another generation of Stone Tails. Complete and utter genocide. Now you see why our resistance is so important. It's not just about humanity."

"Is there anything else you've left out?"

"It's complicated." Badger trekked ahead and didn't look back.

"Don't look so glib," Burke said. "At least you're on the right side of history."

"I don't say it often," Remley said. "But Burke's right."

"Whatever helps you sleep at night," I said.

Remley and Burke followed Badger.

Juan looked to me for guidance. I shrugged. "Don't got much choice. Do we?"

"No," Juan said. "Story of my life."

"Most people's story, kid. Don't worry, I'll keep you safe."

Juan nodded. He believed me. I hoped I could prove him right.

* * *

Our group trudged through the crops for a long while in silence. Just one step after another through this gray tangle, making our way inevitably towards that gate and what I feared might be our death. Eventually, we came to a clearing of burnt, lifeless soil—the remnants of a war fought over many generations. The ruined ground ran for at least a mile towards the city, creating a no-man's-land of death between us and the great wall. We set out across that final stretch, each step a struggle, with our boots sinking into the muck, like slogging through a bog.

Every moment I spent in this rotten place left me in greater despair. But Badger showed no fear, not worried about the ruined ground, the imposing wall, or the nightmare troops that guarded it in their bug-eyed gas masks armed with high-powered energy weapons. Least of all, he harbored no fear of death. And that worried me most.

As we approached the defensive barrier, it became clear the wall had not been built out of some advanced metal alloy yet to be discovered on our planet. Instead, it had been made piecemeal from rusted scrap you might find at any junkyard back home. All of it appeared to be hastily cobbled together, as if the builders had desperately scoured garbage bins for supplies with no plan except to build up. Unlike the black onyx towers, which menacingly loomed above us in an impressive display of engineering precision, this wall was a jury-rigged mess.

The eerie essence of this land had gnawed at me since my arrival. Close to the city, the why of it dawned on me. That hive of ships flying above those towers, the vehicles whipping along tracks between buildings, the millions and millions of people that must inhabit this dark citadel, for all that density within the walls, no sound existed out here. And not just the discord of machinery and people went unheard. No birds chirped. No wind blew. This land beyond the walls of that city existed in a vacuum, devoid of all sound. Impossibly quiet.

We came around a bend in the wall and face-to-face with the gate. The colossal doors were open, creating an entry as tall as a ten-story building and easily as wide. A cadre of cloaked, gas-masked troops stood guard along the perimeter. Atop two watchtowers, which flanked the entry, two massive gun batteries had been erected. I knew intuitively that these weapons were meant to stop heavy assault vehicles, an unruly mob, or to send a menacing Stone Tail back to whatever hell it came from. But the guns sat quiet, mostly unnecessary bluster on this abandoned plain, not even turned outward to face us. But despite that, this gate appeared to be the only entry point to an impregnable fortress.

We walked towards the guards. This was the moment I'd feared since I'd been told of this plan. Even if we'd been well disguised, the checkpoints had scared me. But we weren't disguised. Juan had crashed this invasion and was still dressed like he was hitting the skate park with his high school pals. The rest of us wore the cloaks, which did a fine job hiding our otherworldly possessions. But Juan stood out like a sore thumb. When we were stopped and questioned about his strange attire, the guards would recognize me. And then we'd see what a mistake my coming along had been.

But to my surprise, the guards didn't make a move. They were completely uninterested in us. No customs. No ID screening. Nothing. All this firepower was apparently just for show.

We took that first step through the gate into the fortress, and the bubble burst. The sounds of the city, which had receded away like the tide, came crashing down upon us. Sensory overload. Shaken, I gasped and tried to remain calm in the sudden cacophony. There must have been some type of invisible force field insulating the city from the outside world. But if there was a force field, why build a wall?

To keep the monsters out. Or the prisoners in.

The sky above barely showed blue anymore, dominated by those magnificent ebony towers. But beyond the gateway, here at the base of those twisted spires, the streets were anything but impressive. The advanced civilization above had been built upon the wasted remains of the original city. Old skyscraper fronts like back on our own Earth had been repurposed into a marketplace of clothing shops, trinket stalls, food stands, and communal living spaces. Droves of people swarmed between the rotted-out buildings, haggling, arguing, trying to survive. People on top of people. Complete bedlam, like some sort of ancient bazaar.

As we forced our way through the throngs of people, I glanced back at the gate. The guards just watched, waiting for all this anarchy to go too far before they swooped in and enacted their own form of arbitrary justice. Some of the bug-eyed soldiers up on the wall, who moments before had paid us no mind, now seemed to be taking note of our little expedition.

Badger put his arm around my shoulder, turning me back to the city, and whispered, "The last thing we want is the Legion's attention."

They were the first words any of us had spoken in hours.

We disappeared into the crowds, turning down different alleys packed with more people than the streets could safely hold. The mass of bodies throbbed like a gelatinous creature, barely giving room for us to move through. Homeless overflowed from dilapidated brownstones, camping out on the streets and sidewalks, forcing us to climb over them at every turn. Fires burned in metal barrels despite the oppressive heat of the city. People huddled around the flames, cooking some type of skewered rodent that barely looked edible. The air felt tight down here, not enough for all of these people to breathe. Everything stank, a cesspool of charred meat, smoke, sweat, urine, and who knew what else. All of this disorder built within the crumbling remnants of a forgotten society that I suspected had once resembled our own.

The walls of these lower-level buildings were graffitied concrete covered almost completely over by a diseased lichen, which grew directly out of the sewage that flowed like a canal down the middle of the roadways. The sky above was dominated from every angle by the majestic towers. From what I could see, the higher you went, the nicer the spires got with sparkling reflective windows, neon signage, and increased vehicle traffic. The lower high-rise levels, not covered by the rot of weeds, were alive with movement. People hung out of windows to do business with flying barges that stopped momentarily to offer their wares, like the floating river markets on the Mekong Delta, except this economy stretched into the sky.

A drunkard stumbled towards us, her steely eyes unmistakable to a man with my experience. I pushed past the vagrant, heard her grumble a few slurred swear words, and felt her clothes crunch beneath my touch, barely held together anymore by thread or elastic. I watched her disappear into the crowds, no one paying her a second thought, lost forever. Even here at the bottom, there was a clear hierarchy to the sewage dwellers, mostly driven by how clean they were. Though everyone down here was covered in some amount of filth from the streets.

Hidden beneath the grime, people's outfits were a mess of patterns and styles. Some were recognizable from our own planet, a menagerie of cultures from oxford button-downs, burkas, and ball caps to windbreakers, kurtas, and overalls. Some seemed pulled from history: leather vestments, fezzes, robes cinched tight by rope, woven coolie hats, and canvas boots. While others were from some future we hadn't reached: VR-type goggles that glowed in the dim alleyway, plastic-covered fluorescent pantaloons, absurdly colored Velcro sneakers that would've sold well at the pop-up shops of LA and New York back home. Then, there were simply the indescribable, like they'd come from another world entirely.

No wonder they hadn't stopped Juan at the gate.

Our cloaks hid our own outfits and seemed to demarcate us as belonging to a higher rung of this society. Though that garnered us little respect save for a few averted gazes as we forced our way deeper into the bowels of the city's underbelly. There were no street signs, but it was clear we'd passed into the red-light district. The storefronts that weren't boarded up had become bars, gambling halls, and brothels with scantily clad prostitutes of every persuasion working hard to sell their services. Even in this futuristic hellhole, the language of vice was one I understood all too well.

Every so often, I caught sight of a small squad of troops marching down a street. Showing force. Maintaining order. But otherwise, it seemed no rules applied down here. This was the Wild West. Kill or be killed.

"What's the point of a wall if we just walked through it like it wasn't there?" Juan asked. His words startled me. I'd almost forgotten him as we passed through this charnel house masquerading as a city. I wished I could unsee this terror for him.

"The wall hasn't kept a human being out since the war ended decades ago. Now it serves a very different purpose," Badger said. "It keeps people in."

"But why LA?" Juan asked. "Thought you said this was some sort of Roman-Chinese superpower from ancient times."

"That civilization fell a long time ago. Most of what you'd call the old world was laid waste in the intervening wars of the last few centuries. This is what remains. One of the last bastions of humanity. Duster's Shade set up shop here because it's one of the few known sources of Stone Tail eggs on Earth. Though that mine was cleared out long ago."

"An ancient race of underground lizard people," I mumbled, quoting the tabloid I'd read at the mall, "who flourished beneath the surface of our world away from the prying eyes of primitive humans."

"Enough talk," Remley snapped. She pointed up at the flying ships above. "Don't think this place doesn't have ears."

We made our way down more alleyways, and with each turn our sense of vulnerability grew. Other than the occasional drug dealer, people here no longer wanted to sell you things. Those on their feet hurried past, minding their own business. It was clear you didn't linger here if you were smart. Those not on their feet were a mix of junkies, beggars, and corpses. The patrols had dwindled, too. The troops didn't venture here, either by agreement or because the ensuing battle wouldn't be worth the trouble. We were entering the criminal underworld of this already delinquent society. But this wasn't just a city. It was a prison. And the worst among prisoners were always the most treacherous. Whoever Badger was taking us to see, they'd be dangerous. I'd have to be on guard.

We came to a narrow alley that would barely allow for two people to walk abreast. There were no people here, no storefronts, only a dead end at a single door. Above the door, an old-fashioned light bulb (old-fashioned on our planet so I wasn't sure what you'd call it on this one) hung from a chain giving the only light. It swung back and forth, though no wind blew to make it move. Our nervous breaths and the buzzing electricity powering that out-of-place light were the only sounds.

As we approached the doorway, I realized it was the same one from my dream. I'd accepted my vision of this city as truth and had mostly been met by what I'd seen. But the long hallway of cascading colors, a door hanging in an infinite void of nothing, I'd always chalked that part up to imagination. But here stood that door. Real. Just as I remembered.

Paint peeled from the rotten wood—the decrepit barrier didn't look like it would keep much out—and on it, the number *848* hung in rusted bronze numbers. I touched the numbers; they were cold, though the air swam with heat, balmy and humid. In my dream, the numbers had been faded. But here they remained. Was there significance to 848? I didn't know. But this door held significance. Of that, I felt certain.

"I've seen this door before," I said.

"Have you?" Badger asked, amused. "How strange."

He wasn't surprised at all. Burke and Remley cast their eyes down, keeping their hoods tight and their faces hidden from me. I caught Juan's gaze out of the corner of my eye. He looked frightened; he knew something felt off.

"What are we doing here, Badger?" I asked.

Badger didn't answer.

Instead, he rapped on the door three times and waited. After a few moments, the door creaked open. The light bulb overhead continued to sway, casting long shadows down this dark street. I strained to see past the shadowed doorway but couldn't make out anything beyond it. The light of the bulb seemed incapable of passing through this portal into the next room.

"You made it," said a rasp of a voice that I instantly recognized, though I couldn't believe it to be true.

The owner of the voice stepped into the alley to let us pass, and I saw what I knew I'd heard. Madison Andrews. Sadder in her countenance than last I'd seen her but with a new sense of confidence. She stared at Badger with the loathing I'd grown accustomed to receiving from people who knew my Shade.

Butterflies swarmed in my gut as I waited for her to look at me. The last time I'd seen this woman, I'd held her lifeless body in my arms. The way I felt now was hard to explain. Elated to see her but also angry. I'd taken her death harder than I wished to admit and now it was like it had never happened. Somehow that trick cheapened all I'd endured.

This isn't the woman you held. It's her Shade.

But was this the woman I'd shared a drink with or an imposter?

I opened my mouth to ask but didn't get the chance because Madison slapped Badger hard across the face. Then she looked at me with those wild eyes I remembered all too well from our first meeting over cocktails at The Lazy Giant.

"It's good to see you, Raines," she said with a smile. "Did you find my husband?"

Before I could respond, she walked back through the doorway into darkness.

CHAPTER 25

"I FELT HER DIE." MADISON TOOK A LONG SIP OF TEA AND LET her words hang out there in the open. Waiting for someone to respond. Daring them to do it. No one moved. Breaths were held. The room frozen in fear.

We'd been led back through a few tight hallways to a drab kitchen. The home had fallen into disrepair long ago, everything smelling of mold and decay. Each step creaked and moaned, demanding we leave. What furniture still passed as such had not stood the test of time. But it had once been plush, displaying rich colors and exuberant patterns. Precisely what I'd imagined Madison's home should've been the night I found her dead. It had her touch. And its age and disrepair reflected the sadness I knew permeated her being.

We crammed into the kitchen around an old, handcrafted wooden table. Pungent mugs of the same tea steamed in front of us all. The brew was unrecognizable, made of a bitter root that tasted mostly of dirt. The appliances were antiques—even for our timeline, maybe the 50s, though I couldn't place them for certain—needless to say, it all felt alien in this world. I wondered if they were native to this universe or had been brought over from ours. Perhaps early experiments in the testing of Dr.

Andrews's machine hidden in the basement of their mansion in the Hollywood Hills.

Madison gave Badger a forlorn stare across the table. When it became clear he wasn't going to budge, she spoke again. "Did you know?"

Badger shifted uncomfortably. His chair objected to the move, groaning under his weight. He tasted the sludge we were calling tea and, judging by the look on his face, immediately regretted it.

"I heard," Badger finally said. "From Duster, in fact."

"That's not what I meant. I want to know if your dirty little war took her from me." Madison's voice barely registered above a whisper. "Did you order her killed?"

"Come on now, Mad," Remley jumped in. "You know we'd never hurt one of our own. Especially your Shade. We tried to pull her out, but Torian and Jacobs were a step ahead of us all. Including you."

Madison looked at me with sadness. When we'd met, I thought her insane. But now I understood the truth. Her connection to the dead Madison had run far deeper than any bond a normal person could understand. That link pushed her mind to places she could barely comprehend. Changed her. With it severed, she'd been set adrift. A piece of her soul lost forever.

Just like her, the errant thoughts of another man skipped at the edges of my mind. They called to me, becoming one with my core. I saw a Stone Tail slashing at my chest. I saw the bridge of *his* spaceship. And I felt the desperate need to find those green stones. At first, I'd dismissed them as imagination run amok. But the longer it lasted, the more I realized these thoughts belonged to the other Duster Raines. If this pull continued to grow stronger with time, then I could only imagine what Madison felt now. Alone for the first time in forever.

Imagine? You should understand her completely. We need to be careful never to—

Save it. We're busy.

How long until my eyes danced with crazy? Maybe they already did.

Shook my head. Shut him out. Focused on the now.

Madison directed her next question at me, and I had to strain to hear the words. "Were you with her when she died?"

"No," I blurted. "I found her body in that panic room beneath her house. Or your house. I'm not really clear who's who anymore. Sorry . . ." I took a steadying breath. "She'd been roughed up. *Searched*. They were looking for that ring, though I didn't know it at the time."

"It was her idea to send it to you," Madison said. "She was the one who thought you might be of some use to us. Imagine, turning the Shade of Duster Raines. I went to meet you that night. Maddy wanted to come but with my defection they'd begun to suspect her. Maybe their mole really was too good to be true. That night you found her, they'd come for me. She bought me the time to escape through the prototype."

I'd found the spherical room in Madison's home. It had obviously been some type of experiment. An experiment I now understood to be passing objects and people between two separate but similar universes. Madison came here with that machine just as I'd come here with her husband's more advanced invention.

"There was only enough energy left in the system to transport one person," Madison continued. "If only I hadn't hidden the ring. Then we'd still be alive. But I wasn't worried when I left her. She was so certain she'd be able to talk her way out of it. I mean, we were certain. Because there's really no difference in the two. Guess we were wrong."

"I don't know what happened," Badger said. "But my gut tells me she was playing both sides. How do you think they found Duster so quickly that night you met with him? She gave him up. And they killed her for the trouble. She was a traitor to the cause."

"You don't know that," Madison said.

"But you do," Badger said. Madison looked away, unable to meet his eyes. "That's what I thought. I loved her but she got what she deserved. If I'd had the chance, I'd have killed her myself."

"You're a real son of a bitch."

"Watch yourself. I know your loyalty only goes as far as the safety of your husband. But just because I'm here, don't think our agreement has changed."

"You're half the man he is." Madison stormed out before anyone could stop her.

"Well, that was awkward," Remley said.

"Do you think we can still trust her?" Burke asked.

"She'd never risk her husband's life," Badger said. "And she thinks I'll do anything. You saw it. She thinks I had something to do with Maddy's death, for Caesar's sake. Besides, she knows these buildings better than anyone. Without her, our access to the upper levels of the city will be slowed."

"I'm confused," I said. "Isn't that your Madison, Badger? I mean, she's from this universe like you."

"That's right."

"But you loved the Madison of my world?"

"The woman you know from your meeting at the bar, the woman here tonight, was a brilliant scientist. Maybe she still is," Badger said more to himself than me, "but who can tell anymore with the way she acts? We worked together on the Gateway. She was the one who made the final leaps of discovery that allowed us to pass living tissue across the threshold of our two universes.

"But neither one of us agreed with the Directorate's plans. I recruited her, and she helped me plan my grand escape. She agreed to stay behind. We knew that the stones allowed our Shades to communicate with us on a very basic level through dreams. We thought I could use Madison's Shade to coordinate our plans across the rift.

"I found Maddy on your side. She was just as brilliant as the woman I'd left behind, though more understanding of some of my eccentricities. The fruits of that collaboration across space and time are in motion before you now. A decade of work. But things happen. Maddy and I fell in love. The Madison you know began smuggling items back and forth across the brink. She worked with my Shade, the man you know as Dr. Andrews, to build the sphere prototype out of inferior technology. It didn't take long before they fell in love."

"Poetic irony they call that," Burke grumbled, his disapproval not well hidden.

"I'd never have thought my Maddy would betray us," Badger said. "But she did."

"You don't know that's what happened," Remley said.

"It doesn't matter," Badger snapped. "Maddy's gone. All that matters now is stopping the First Consul from becoming the Eternal Watcher."

"Excuse me," Juan interjected. He'd been sitting so quietly that I'd once again forgotten he was there. "But does anyone not have a Shade?"

Remley and Burke raised their hands. Juan laughed.

Oh, I like him.

Yeah, the kid's got nerve.

Badger eyed Juan dubiously. "Count your blessings."

"Come on, Badger. Being in love with me couldn't have been all bad." Madison leaned against the hall door—unclear how much she'd overheard—with a stoic resolution burning in her eyes. Moments before, she'd been an emotional basket case. Now, she looked like she could take on the world. Her sudden about-face concerned me but it was hard to know what was normal for her.

"You've sorted yourself out, then, Madison?" Badger asked.

"I have."

Remley joined Madison, placing a reassuring hand on her shoulder with a warmth I hadn't thought Remley capable of. The two were obviously friends. "So, what's the plan, Mad?"

Madison glided to the ancient metal refrigerator and opened it. The inside had been cleared away and a small hole carved into the wall behind it. We gathered at the fridge. The hole opened into what appeared to be an access shaft. Cables and wires were all bunched on the walls, which ran straight up into what I could only guess were the upper levels of the skyscraper above this house. It'd be tight, but we could get into the shaft one at a time.

"This access point runs all the way to the four-hundredth floor," Madison said. "This section of the city has been marked undesirable, and the troops don't patrol it much. All the defenses have been turned over to automation. I've been working with jetpacks and cables to bypass security. We should be able to access the upper floors. And then, it's all on Raines."

Before I could ask what everyone thought I was going to be able to do, the entire room shuddered as a major explosion ripped through the home.

"They found us," Burke yelled over the racket as we took cover. More explosions reverberated from the front of the home, and I waited for the ceiling to collapse. When it didn't, I got up off the floor. As dust and smoke filled the kitchen, I imagined those bug-eyed warriors marching over the debris of the entryway. We were out of time.

Madison didn't hesitate, going straight to one of the cabinets and pulling out a pair of pistols. She tossed one to Burke and the other to Remley. "Stall them."

Madison stepped through the refrigerator and into the shaft, pulling me in by the collar of my shirt. I grabbed Juan and pushed him into her arms. "Kid goes first."

She wanted to object—even she believed I was the most valuable asset in this situation—but I had the authority to dictate terms. She relented. Madison and Badger hated each other, but I sensed they viewed my role in this little plan the same. War makes strange bedfellows.

She secured Juan into the cable system she'd constructed, which looked a lot like a mountain-climbing harness save for the small detail that strapped onto Juan's back was a rocket. Madison didn't waste time explaining how it all worked. Once she had Juan in the harness, she slapped a button in the middle of his chest and his jet pack ignited. In an instantaneous whoosh of heat and compressed air, he disappeared up into the darkness of the shaft. I thought I heard the faint echo of a scream, but it didn't linger.

Back in the kitchen, Remley and Burke fired their pistols up the hallway towards the front door. Badger knelt with them, though he had no weapon to use himself.

Madison placed her hand on my shoulder, and time stood still. The battle in the kitchen froze like the battle on the bridge had. I looked back to Madison, the two of us moving in normal time, the only people existing in this phase of reality.

"I only have a moment," she said. "Badger isn't the man he used to be. He's lost his way. He's allowed my husband to be a prisoner of that lizard scum for nearly three years. Whatever you do, do not trust him."

"I've seen your husband, Madison. He's not with the Stone Tails."

"Oh, Raines," she said with pity. "I told you when I met you, aliens don't leave notes. And they sure as hell aren't telling you a damn thing." She giggled, that manic energy of hers slipping out. She shook her head, as if clearing out the cobwebs of insanity. But that loss of mental focus was all it took, and time cracked back to the present with a thunderous roar of weapon fire.

"What was that?" I managed, out of breath.

"Badger, let's go," Madison yelled, ignoring me.

Badger tapped Burke on the shoulder and indicated the refrigerator. Burke continued laying down cover fire as they made a slow retreat across the kitchen. The house burned as energy balls slammed into the walls and blew chunks away. Some of the wall didn't even get to explode, simply disintegrating in a fiery ball of energy.

Badger hustled into the access shaft. Not wasting any time, he strapped himself into the cables. His anger erupted when he saw I wasn't wearing a jet pack. "What're you doing? Get in the goddamn harness."

I grabbed one of the packs and began strapping it to my shoulders.

Remley came next, sprinting across the kitchen and taking a sliding dive through the refrigerator. Burke was still at the hallway, firing suppressive shots back towards the front door. "There's gotta be at least fifty of them," Remley huffed. "They must be trying to take us alive."

"Why would you think that?" I demanded.

"Because we'd already be dead if they weren't." Remley chuckled, then she shouted over the energy explosions that would bring this house down on us at any moment, "Burke! Move it!"

Burke obeyed. But he only got a step towards the refriger-ator before one of those energy balls caught the place he'd just left and blew the entire doorway to kingdom come. He took the brunt of the blast and flew across the kitchen, slamming hard into the wooden table, which splintered under the force of the fall.

Burke lay still. I felt the collective breath go out of the team. For all their differences, they were soldiers in the same army, and they'd just seen their man go down. Instinct took me. I threw myself back out of the refrigerator and closed the gap on Burke. I heard Badger shout at me to get back there but I ignored him. In no time flat, I got to Burke and had him over my shoulder in a Herculean effort that surprised even me. I'd worry about it later. I ran back to the refrigerator, carry-ing this giant of a man as I went. But our movements seemed slow—even accounting for the dead weight—like an eternity passed in each tick of the clock. With every step, the kitchen exploded around us as the bug-eyed soldiers unleashed fury.

Remley and I had different interpretations of what it means to be taken alive.

Madison's trick would have come in handy right then, but I had no idea how to control time. I'd have to do it the old-fashioned way.

In reality, it only took a few seconds for me to get Burke back to the refrigerator. I heaved him through the opening in the wall to the outstretched arms of Remley, knocking her back a step under his weight. "He's still breathing," I gasped.

But those few seconds were too many.

Behind me, I heard the unmistakable clinking of a gre-nade bouncing across the floor. I looked towards the destroyed doorway just in time to catch sight of one of the gas-masked mercenaries ducking into the hallway for cover. I looked down and saw the polished metal sphere bounce twice and stop right by my feet. It had a blinking red light that sped up with every second. And I guessed that when that light went solid, I'd want to be somewhere else.

"Grenade," I shouted, kicking the explosive back towards the door. I ducked, balling up as best I could. Mid-flight, the grenade light went solid red and let out a high-pitched wail that nearly caused me to lose consciousness from the pain in my ears. The sound sapped my strength. Debilitating. I willed myself to reach up and grab the refrigerator door. The last thing I saw before I slammed the fridge shut was Badger scowling at me as he hit the button on his harness and launched into the upper reaches of that skyscraper.

The door had barely sealed when the grenade erupted in a burst of blue energy that looked like a jellyfish expanding out from the center of the orb. Blinded by the flash, I felt my body slump to the ground.

I don't remember anything from Madison's kitchen after that.

CHAPTER 26

"Well, well. Duster Raines in the flesh," said a filtered and mechanical rasp of a voice.

I opened my eyes to a blinding white light, which had become a regular occurrence in my life these days, and a splitting headache. They must have used some type of stun grenade. Nonlethal, though just barely. My entire body throbbed. It was all I could do to keep from throwing up.

As my eyes adjusted to the lighting, I saw that two people stood over me. They both wore the bug-eyed gas masks of the Legion, the military faction in this universe, and stared down at me with those ominously pulsating yellow eyes. I tried to strike the closest one, but my arm wouldn't move. Both my wrists were tightly secured to a metallic gurney by some type of smooth steel restraints—another common occurrence these days—with no visible creases or breaks existing in the material. The restraints were part of the table and certainly wouldn't give from any force I could muster.

One of the bug-eyed soldiers pushed a button, and the entire apparatus I lay on angled up to a forty-five-degree incline, suspended beneath a series of overhead lights. As my eyes continued to adjust, I saw I was in some type of medical facility strapped to an operating table. The entire lab was sterile and bland, constructed of a glinting, polished white material like porcelain. Computer screens and other machines whirred, blinked, and beeped all around me. The white room had high ceilings with a semicircle of windowed viewing portals above, like an old surgical theater.

Through one of the windows, an older woman, flanked by two more bug-eyed guards, stared down on me. She was maybe sixty with crisp green eyes that shone with authority even from a distance, and limp black hair streaked with white. She was Asian, if such a descriptor made sense in this universe, possibly descended from that Chinese lineage their fallen empire held so dear. She wore a similar uniform to the one I'd seen my Shade wear, solid black pants and a tunic adorned at the shoulders by gold epaulets.

We locked eyes. She waved at me with a tight-lipped smile, enjoying my predicament, and a shiver ran down my spine. This woman terrified me, though I had no basis for the fear coursing through my veins. I knew beyond a shadow of a doubt that she was more dangerous than anyone in this alternate reality, even my Shade. But the more I looked inward, the more the idea seemed alien. Were these my insecurities? Or were they the doubts and worries of my Shade? Any sense of what belonged to me and what belonged to *him* had begun to slip away. Perhaps no real difference existed anymore.

"How've you been, Duster?" one of the robot-voiced bug people asked, breaking my train of thought.

"Just peachy." It hurt to talk. Everything hurt. "But how many times do I have to tell you kids to call me Raines?"

"Always a sense of humor," one of my masked captors said. "I did like that about you."

"I'm still here for you to like it."

"For now," the other one said.

They both removed their helmets, releasing a clasp on top that depressurized with a whisper of escaping air. I didn't need to wait for them to take off the masks. I already knew I'd fallen back into the hands of Torian and Jacobs.

Their insect faces off, the two seemed older than I remembered. Their youthful exuberance, which had led me to believe they were head of their class at the FBI Academy, was replaced with a somber and more intimidating demeanor. Maybe their sheer black body armor with tubes running to bug-eyed terror masks gave them a bit more clout in the danger category. But more than likely the charade had ended, and there were no more games to play about helping them find Dr. Andrews. Come to think of it, the game had ended a while ago. After all, the last time I saw Jacobs, he'd ordered me executed. I'd gotten lucky that day. Now, I was living on borrowed time.

"Bet you hoped to never see us again," Torian said. She smiled venom, her scar pulled taut, distorting her face into an ugly guise. If only the blade that had left that wound had done its job a little better.

"That's not true," I said. "We have unfinished business."

"That a fact?" Jacobs asked.

"It is. I still have to kill you both."

They laughed. I laughed, too. It was funny. Me pinned down on this slab of pristine metal that probably hadn't been invented in my universe, threatening two elite soldiers who'd had it out for me since the moment I met them. Oh yeah, and lizard people. Did I mention the lizard people? But I meant it. Ending these two was at the top of my to-do list, and I planned to make good on the threat.

"You killed two of my men." Jacobs's eyes glassed over as he spoke, wiping away any trace of humanity. These two were stone-cold killers. Sociopaths. True believers. "I underestimated you," Jacobs droned on. "It won't happen again."

"I came for Carla."

"Of course you did," Torian said. "I've had the pleasure of really getting to know her these past few weeks. You know, a little girl talk. She has a few choice words to say about you."

I said nothing because there was nothing to say.

Jacobs hit a button on his control panel, and a large device swung over the top of me. It looked like a cannon crossed with an X-ray machine at the dentist's office—that is, if the dentist owned a clandestine death ray and plotted to destroy the world between cavity fillings. Knowing what this machine did ranked low as a priority of mine. But I had the sinking suspicion I'd find out anyway.

"You guys sure do know how to put on a show," I said. "Don't suppose I could convince you to just kill me the old-fashioned way."

"Soon enough, Duster," Torian cooed. "Soon enough. But first, we need you to help us with a little side project of ours."

"Like for extra credit?" I asked glibly.

"You could say that," Jacobs said. He patted the death ray floating above my head. "This is all experimental. Very hush-hush. In fact, we didn't even know it existed when we decided to kill you last month. What a waste that would've been. But now we know your double had this hidden away. And here we are. Truth be told, it's the only reason you're still breathing."

"Lucky me," I said. "Has anyone ever told you that you talk too much, Jacobs?"

"Every. Single. Day," Torian said.

Jacobs licked his lips. "I'll cut to the chase. We want to see into that little brain of yours, and this machine is going to make that happen."

"More specifically"—Torian leaned in close and tapped my forehead—"we want to see what's going on in that bigger and smarter brain of your double."

"I thought he was the big enchilada here. So, what—the benefits suck? No dental?"

"Shut up," Torian snapped. "We told you before. We're patriots."

"We're Legionnaires," Jacobs said. "Through and through." He pounded his chest plate with a fist in a sort of draconian salute. "The Directorate, your double—the so-called *First Consul*—well, it's lost its way. We plan to use you to get to him. And when we seize power, we'll establish a new order. Two worlds united under our banner."

The crackle of a speaker interrupted us. "Enough chitchat," the female voice snapped. "Get this done."

Torian and Jacobs both turned to the woman in black behind the glass above. They snapped to attention and brought their fists to their chest in the same salute as before.

"For the Eternal Empire," they said in unison. "For the Eternal Watcher!"

The older woman bowed, a shallow thing, more custom than respect.

"Aren't you going to introduce me to your new boss?"

"She's your worst nightmare," Torian said. "A living goddess. A direct descendant of the first Eternal Watcher. And the true leader of our glorious institutions."

"First Consul Octavius will regret the day he crossed his better," Jacobs intoned. "The one true Empress. Consul Livia Wu Zetian."

"Scripture holds the Eternal Watcher shall rise again from the ashes of—"

"Blah. Blah. Blah," I said. "First you guys had some sort of Directorate. Now you've got an empire? Make up your minds."

Torian laughed. "Look at us. Boring our guest with the politics of a world he doesn't even know."

"He'll understand it all soon enough," Jacobs said.

"I doubt he'll live that long."

"True. True."

"Still right here, kids," I reminded them.

Torian gave Jacobs a curt nod. Jacobs hit a few command codes into a keypad at the base of my gurney. The cannon moved into position directly above my head. Before I could say another word, a laser beam flashed from the device and struck my head. An intense burning sensation centered in the middle of my forehead and slowly spread out through every nerve in my body.

I knew only pain.

And then, I no longer inhabited my body. I raced across space and time, making my way to somewhere that didn't exist in reality but in the link my Shade and I shared.

The elevator doors swung open on the seventh floor of my crap apartment building back in Los Angeles. The colors of the hallway were all tinted a bit gray though, as if the memory of the place had faded away and this was all I could grab on to. I made my way down this lifeless hall to the main door of my studio. Inside, the chair was still splintered in the corner where Jacobs had left me to die with his mercenaries. My two would-be executioners were still there, too, and also still corpses. But other than a lack of color, it looked just how I'd left it, save for the fact that my Shade sat in the middle of my couch. He'd taken the liberty of pouring himself a beverage from one of the few liquor bottles that still had anything left to pour. He smiled when he saw me, rose to his feet, and raised the glass of warm whiskey in a toast.

"Finally," he said. "Duster Raines."

"The one and only," I said. "Sort of."

"It does get a bit confusing at times. But I'll grow on you, I'm sure."

"Doesn't seem like we've got much of a choice."

My Shade motioned for me to join him. I obeyed. Though this was my apartment, so it should've been me inviting him. But this duplicate of mine always took charge. I could see that now more than ever. And while I'd expected it to be like looking into a mirror, it was anything but. This man looked younger than me but beyond the simple explanation of he took better care of himself. There existed something deeper to his youth. Something unnatural.

"Make yourself at home," I said as I sat by him. "Please."

My Shade pursed his lips, seemingly amused, the spitting image of my father. As a teenager, my old man would always smirk that arrogant superiority when I tried to make a point. Father knows best or some other crock of shit. The more he drank, the more often I saw that look. And sometimes, he'd bare those teeth with a belt in his hand while he taught me another life lesson.

Did I look like that? Smug. A know-it-all. A total bastard. Probably. Fucking genetics.

Hating my dad growing up had been easy. The hard part was knowing people in the community liked him. They thought he was a stand-up guy. A real respectable son of a bitch, they'd say at the corner stores. He could've been mayor of our small town if he weren't an abusive drunk. Everything about him was phony and couldn't stand the light of day. So, our family hid behind the walls of our home and protected that wild man who terrorized my childhood. If only people had known the truth. But then, most people's impressions of those they barely know are false. Why go to the trouble of learning the uncomfortable bits? People call that being polite. Minding their own business. Wouldn't want to muddy their hands with someone who physically and emotionally assaults his wife and child. That would get messy.

Intimidation was my father's weapon of choice. Silence his greatest asset.

I remembered months of emptiness in our home as no one dared speak a word for fear of reprisal. My mom would whisper that my dad was alone in his thoughts and we needed to respect his privacy. We'd tiptoe around him, trying not to upset the applecart any more than we already had to trigger this episode in the first place. The older I got, the less cautious I became. Call it willful disobedience. A beating was never too far from reality in those festering, silent months. He'd make my mom or me watch while he took care of the other. All the while, wearing that detached grin.

I never stood up to him—even when I was strong enough to protect us—never hit him back. Just bided my time until I was old enough to move out. And then I disappeared. Abandoned my mom to that hell. Doomed her to spend the rest of her good years alone with that man. What does that say about me?

The apple hadn't fallen too far from the tree in this reality. My Shade was our father. Had his been like mine?

"Yes," my Shade said. "My dad was a piece of work, too."

"You can hear my thoughts?"

"Can't you hear mine?"

"Sometimes, I guess."

"It's a strange sensation, being this close to one another. How did we end up here?"

"Torian. Jacobs."

"Ah . . ." My Shade exhaled with a sadness I hadn't expected. "They have you, then?"

"Yes. I'm on some gurney in a lab on your planet."

"They found the experiment. Only a matter of time, I suppose. What a shame. I would've liked to have found you first.

Imagine what we could do together. But then those traitors forced my hand. Don't worry. I'll liberate you. If they don't kill you first."

"That's real big of you."

"So, they want to see how I think?"

"That's the gist of it."

"Pathetic. They don't see the true potential in having you. You're probably lucky in that sense but unlucky that they may toss you aside like garbage because they don't know your true value."

"I seem to be in high demand on a few fronts these days."

"You mean Badger?" He shook his head in disgust. "God, I hate that stupid fucking nickname."

He hadn't guessed it. He'd heard it through our link. I cleared my mind. Tried not to think on too many details because any advantage this man had put me in real trouble.

My Shade stared at me, waiting, hoping for a glimpse I refused to give.

"What if I told you that Badger and I are one and the same? The top of the food chain if you will."

"I'd say, tell me more."

"I know you already know a few things about my world. The Directorate, our government, there were always three of us. Fashioned in the form of the ancient triumvirate that strengthened Rome from a mindless republic into an empire. Three equals."

"Livia?"

"You've seen her, then? I always knew she had the Legion in her pocket. I didn't realize to what extent until Torian and Jacobs betrayed me. That was my mistake."

"So, who's your third glorious member?"

"You already know the answer to that."

"Badger?" I asked. But he was right, it wasn't really a question because I already knew.

"My very own Brutus."

"That's not how he tells it."

"Well, we all have a right to our opinions."

"I met one of those lizards—a Stone Tail—Badger told me what you did to their kind. What this war is really all about."

"What I did?" My Shade laughed. "Be careful who you trust, Raines. We've all been lying to one another for so long that it really does become second nature."

"Enlighten me, then."

He took a sip of his whiskey and scowled at the taste—he was used to better—and set the glass down. "Badger, Livia, and I ruled our world. Restored order and glory to our once great empire. Rebuilt the ruins of endless war. But complete restoration was never really possible."

I saw it all in a flash. The ruined supply lines. The wasted soil. The out-of-control climate change. A world altered by nuclear war and other weapons we've yet to imagine. They'd won a war for nothing except to await death in peace rather than battle. That fragile balance was now falling apart. I could feel the helpless desperation clenching at my chest. A need to survive. And then, as if the heavens had opened up and given them an answer, they found our universe.

"Did you get all that?" my Shade asked.

I gasped. The flow of information had been intense. I managed to say, "The stones were how the three of you maintained power."

"Of course, but that's overly simplistic. Our technology leapt ahead with endless power. We consumed it en masse. Like any other fuel. That's human nature, right? But this wasn't oil. If only the stones were as plentiful as that finite resource. They don't even exist on this planet anymore. We worked our moon,

Jupiter's moons, anywhere cold enough and isolated enough to keep the stones. Only later did we learn they were isolated for safety, to protect the young of the Stone Tails. But by then it was too late."

"You know now," I said.

My Shade shrugged. "We're at a crossroads for our kind. We've only discovered two universes where our people flourish. Yours and mine. For all we know, we're all that's left in the cosmic multiverse. The Stone Tails stand between the unification of our great people. If they will not coexist with us, then they will be destroyed."

"Just like that."

"I do this for the betterment of our people. Livia agrees with me but desires power above all. Fancies herself a direct descendant of the first Eternal Watcher. As if knowing such a thing were even possible. But you have to hand it to her, it's a stroke of genius on the propaganda front. Probably how she got the troops to betray me in the first place. Wish I'd thought of it."

"And Badger?"

"Badger is the worst of us. He serves a polluted vision of the universe. The power of the stones has driven him mad. He worships those lizards and their abilities. He's sold out our race to a bunch of aliens."

"You can't possibly think he'd side with them over humanity."

"He already has. You've seen his tunnels. I see them in your mind. Where do you suppose he got the means to construct them?"

I thought about Badger's base, how everyone had ascribed it to technology of this world. But it had always seemed alien to me. An unnatural choice for a human to build perfect cave ecosystems. But for the Stone Tails, laying their eggs deep beneath the cores of abandoned moons, it made complete sense.

"You see it," he said. "We've reached an impasse. There can be only war. But we waste precious time fighting each other when the true enemy is clear."

Now I saw this went far deeper than simply a resistance against a greater power.

And perhaps you aren't on the right side after all.

I chased the idea away. Not my thought but *his.* I needed to keep my bearings or risk losing my sanity to this man.

"I serve the greater good," my Shade continued. "Livia serves herself. And Badger, some distorted vision of evolution. A future where we transcend space and time to become more like the Stone Tails. It's a perversion. Blasphemous. I won't allow it."

My Shade tilted his head to the side as if listening to someone invisible whisper in his ear. He nodded then spread his arms out to me for a warm embrace. "Thank you, Raines. You've done a great service for the restored empire this day."

"What do you mean?"

"You bought me time."

Instantly, I knew. *His* loyal troops and Livia's battled in the skyscraper where my body still resided at that very moment. My Shade intended to reclaim what he'd lost when they'd betrayed him. Torian and Jacobs had never stood a chance at gaining a glimpse of his plans. This meeting was a distraction. He'd known those two would find the experimental cannon and use it on me. In fact, he'd counted on it. My Shade was one step ahead. I couldn't help but admire the move.

"I'm sorry I'm unable to help you more," he said. "But I know you. You're a survivor. So, go beat the odds, and we'll meet again in victory." He snapped to attention and saluted me with his fist to his chest. "For the Eternal Empire. For humanity."

Then he hugged me like we were family. "May the Eternal Watcher guide you."

"I thought that was supposed to be you now."

My Shade shrugged with a sly grin tugging at his cheeks.

The next instant, he winked out of existence. But the echoes of his thoughts stayed with me for a moment after he'd gone. I felt his strength but also his uncertainty. Badger could win this war. Livia could win this war. He could see his paths to victory dwindling, and it scared him. My Shade had not intended for me to have access to these thoughts, and he pushed back against me from across the rift. But before he could close his mind to me completely, I saw his greatest threat. The thing he feared above all else. *Me.*

And then, he was gone.

CHAPTER 27

The alarm klaxons blared.

My eyes snapped open. Black smoke billowed all around me, but I was still in the science lab. My captors were nowhere to be seen, and the ray gun that had sent me on my little excursion across space-time appeared to have gone with them, though that last part was hard to know for certain because most of the lab's equipment was on fire. I lay on the ground, my restraints released, next to my now-ruined gurney. The walls were singed, and shattered glass littered the floor. A disaster. I felt lucky the explosions that had reaped all this destruction hadn't taken any of my limbs with them.

The windows above had sealed with reinforced steel—probably because of the fire—so I wouldn't be getting out that way. I hustled for the main blast door and hit the emergency release button on its control panel. Nothing happened. I tried again, but it was dead.

In a rush of euphoria, I felt my awareness expand as everything around me came into perfect clarity. I knew that the power to the unit had been cut. I could see the relays of this station, the schematics, the flow of power coursing through the walls. I staggered back, dizzy, as a stream of information flowed through my mind. Somehow, I knew I needed to reroute the main circuit breaker to bypass the fire safety protocols and open the door. A quick glance around the room told me that any useful equipment I might use to accomplish that goal had been destroyed.

But how did I know all that?

As if from nowhere, the answer came to me. The link that had just been severed with my Shade had given me more than a brief history lesson of another universe. It had also acted as a kind of information download. Incredibly, I understood more about this realm in a few seconds than would have been possible with years of study. The previous glimpses I'd experienced of *his* thoughts, or a stray understanding of *their* advanced technology, had been small potatoes compared to this full-on linkup to my Shade's mind. That's why Badger had brought me—he must've known about the experiment—and he'd guessed, correctly, that he could use me to get to that other Duster Raines.

But not even Badger could've anticipated this level of comprehension.

My gut told me I'd received more than that experimental machine could extract on its own. And I knew it had occurred because my Shade had allowed it to happen. I had no idea what he'd gleaned from my mind, but this two-way street of a mind meld was bound to pay off more for me than my double.

Then why do it? Did he see me as an ally?

No, he wasn't the sort to think he needed one. Maybe the answer was simple: I made an easy distraction to his foes. Their obsession with beating him made me an obvious foil.

Had he left the experimental ray gun behind with this end in mind?

The answer came instantly—rooted in *his* past experiences, not my own—he'd laid a trap. I knew it without a doubt. And I'd served as both bait and snare.

Foreign thoughts moonlighted as my own. An unpleasant sensation. Disconcerting. Someone could lose their mind in this mess. And maybe that told me everything I needed to know about Madison Andrews. If I ever saw her again, I'd have to ask her how she managed to keep it all straight.

But why had my Shade risked giving me this insight?

If Torian and Jacobs still had me, they would've had access to the inner workings of their enemy's mind. I didn't understand the calculus in that. He could've let the machine try to take what it wanted, blocked me as I had instinctively blocked him, and then launched his attack on the tower with his distraction still intact. But instead, he'd given me this gift. Perhaps he felt a kinship to his double and wanted to give me a better than fighting chance.

But the more I looked inward, the more I saw gaps in what I knew. I had codes and understood detailed systems of their technology, sure, but I knew nothing of his current plans. It was impossible to know what else I lacked because I didn't know what to look for. That other Duster Raines had cherry-picked my education. Those blind spots in my mind represented a weakness he could exploit.

And hadn't I sensed fear in him? A fear of his double. Perhaps those gaps were another trap. This time laid for me.

Ideas of what to do swirled in my head. Two minds mingling together. Paralysis set in. Confusion. I could feel myself distracted, not making a choice for fear of making a mistake. Obsessing over what ideas were mine and what were *his*.

There's only us now.

Had that been his plan? Madness. To neutralize his Shade before I could be a threat. No certain answer came to me. He'd denied me that relief.

Don't forget about Carla.

Quiet. I need to focus.

Sure, Raines. Whatever you say.

I ran through my new memories, like checking the filing cards at an old library, sifting through the muddled thoughts. A fog of information swirled in my head, no clear strands existing from point to point. Exhaustion overwhelmed me. I needed to lie down—having a lifetime of knowledge branded to your mind will do that to you—but I kept on looking for a path forward. Then, I found what I was looking for: Carla. If I could get out of here, the prison block was one floor up. That would be where they were keeping her and hopefully Juan's mom. Of course, to use that tidbit of information, I'd have to get out of this room before I suffocated to death from smoke inhalation.

Sadly, I already knew I couldn't escape. The main door's lack of power, the automated lockdown procedures embedded in the fire safety protocols, and the complete destruction of anything useful in the lab meant that the door could only be opened manually from the outside. I ran every scenario again but ended up right back where I'd started. I couldn't see a way out. Untold knowledge coursed through my brain, but I couldn't fix this door. I didn't need a link to another person to know I was screwed.

Barely able to breathe, I coughed, choked on more smoke, felt dizzy. The room was getting darker, but not from the smoke. I was fading away. It wouldn't be long now. I sat down to wait for the end, but I hadn't even had a chance to feel sorry for myself before the door whooshed open behind me.

Outside in the hall, with a computer tablet hooked into the door terminal, stood Juan with Burke at his side. Burke kept his attention down the hall, covering the boy's back with a futuristic rifle he'd commandeered from this universe. Juan grinned his big goofy smile my way.

"Juan?" I coughed. "What are you doing?"

"Saving you. What does it look like?"

Smug and a genius. I loved this kid. And, for some reason, he was on my side.

Burke looked like shit. Burns on his face and hands. Clothes charred from the blast that had nearly killed him. But still breathing.

I stated the obvious. "You're alive."

"Thanks to you, I heard."

"Guess you owe me one."

"Why do you think I'm here?"

I nodded my thanks. "Where's Badger? Remley?"

Burke hesitated. Juan didn't. "Badger changed the plan. Started rambling about a shield generator. I'm not sure he ever intended to knock out the wormhole."

"What does the city's shield matter? I thought he said it kept people in." I searched my mind for the information about the shield but it wasn't there.

"The shield doesn't keep people in," Burke said. "It keeps the Stone Tails out."

"Son of a bitch lied to us." I looked to Burke. "Did you know?"

"No," he said. "I'm here for our world. This alternate reality shit is for the birds. But Remley's with Badger one hundred. We can't trust her to help us."

"What about Madison?"

Burke shrugged. "She's a kook. Disappeared when Badger started to go off the rails."

She'd made her escape. I found solace in that. Wondered if I'd ever see her again.

"I think your mom and Carla are being held one level above us," I told Juan. I pointed down the hall to the right. "There's an emergency access hatch two halls that way. Better to stay off the lifts and out of sight as much as we can. But we've got to hurry; they're going to bring this entire tower down trying to kill each other."

"How do you know—"

"Trust me."

Juan nodded; he did.

"What about the plan?" Burke asked. "Badger may have lost his marbles, but I haven't. I mean to finish the mission."

"We save Carla and Val," I said. "Then we'll steal a ship and take out the Gateway. We need to isolate my Shade from this side. Otherwise, he'll be unstoppable."

"Glad we see eye to eye on that." Burke didn't like the delay that the rescue added—another unknown variable that could threaten the mission—but getting Carla and Juan's mom were nonnegotiable for me. Besides, he wasn't really in a position to argue. He needed me to steal a ship—not to mention fly it—and he knew that. He was stuck with me.

We hustled down a corridor constructed of metal, more like the inside of a submarine than the halls of a skyscraper. There were no windows, and the metal felt smooth, no bolts or obvious workmanship holding any of it together. Also, there was no sign of any troops. The fighting had moved beyond this level.

But Burke took his time, clearing each hall before allowing us to proceed. His training was obvious—you didn't become a soldier of that quality without years of experience—I'd guess he'd been a grunt, probably Special Forces. And based on his age, most likely served in Vietnam. I couldn't stand the guy but was glad he'd decided to fight with us.

We reached an access hatch without encountering another soul. For all intents and purposes, this place was deserted. I quickly entered an emergency command code I knew by heart. The pad beeped twice, then turned green. A loud thud echoed through the empty halls as the locking mechanism turned over.

It had worked; the jumble of information coursing through my mind became clearer and clearer with each passing moment.

"How did you know that code?" Juan asked.

"Because my Shade knows it."

"I don't understand."

"Not sure I really do, either."

I could see Juan's hesitation. The kid had stuck by me despite the terrors we'd encountered at every turn. Maybe he had no choice, but it still meant a lot to me—the loyalty, I mean—however, explaining my seemingly telepathic connection to an identical me from another reality would probably be one bridge too far for my little sidekick. But we'd save that bridge for another day.

Burke said, "So, it's true. You're him."

I shook my head. "I wouldn't say that. I know things he knows. But not all of it. I didn't know about the shield."

"Hell, if you know half of what he does . . ." Burke trailed off, thinking of the possibilities. "We may actually have a shot at winning this thing."

His confidence made me uncomfortable. No one had ever put much faith in my abilities. Well, no one except Carla. But that hadn't ended so well for either of us. I desperately wanted his belief in me to be well-placed. The responsibility of command pressed on me. I'd been promoted. Burke would follow me now. I knew that to be an absolute. My first soldier.

I pulled the hatch back and stepped through onto a small platform in an industrial-sized elevator shaft. It dropped off below us hundreds of stories and ran all the way up the other way to the top floor. The walls in here were different, no longer the smooth and perfect metal of the hallways, but rather a patchwork of millions of tiny microchips, each no larger than a pea. This place was the central nervous system of the entire city's computer mainframe. Each chip contained more processing power than the most advanced computer back in our reality. The innumerous collection of octagonal chips shimmered in every direction like a silver mosaic. But their silver gleam held no pattern, instead lighting up at random in a cascade of the entire color spectrum.

Another waterfall of color coruscated before my eyes, sucking me into a trance, bringing me back to my vision of a hallway outside that perfect bedroom where I'd lost Carla. That black nothing had shifted mystically to my touch, showing me a rainbow of possibilities. But now I realized that dream had been of a system much like the one I now stood within.

Not a dream but a memory of an idea from my Shade.

The connection we now shared so readily had begun to rear its menacing head in that first vision. The banishing of Madison Andrews. The attack of the Legion when I'd infiltrated his city. I just hadn't realized the meaning of those defenses at the time—it was his mind pushing back—a security system. But this computer mainframe was not the same hallway of cascading colors that dream had represented. That place, wherever it was, or would be, held more importance to my double. But I didn't know why. He would never give me that information willingly.

No shit. You really think he'd just hand you the keys to the kingdom? Thought we were smarter than that.

Don't get testy. But what's so important about that memory? What am I missing?

No answer.

A gust of freezing air blew up through the grating, nearly knocking me over and bringing me back to the reality of the now. A moment later, the gust came running back down. That cold wind kept the billions of processors in here from overheating. One blast from Burke's gun could raise havoc since this system ran every facet of the city. But I didn't want havoc.

I wanted to blend in. Besides, I currently had working access codes, so why ruin a good thing?

No, I'd come for a simple metal ladder used for maintenance.

This mainframe would normally be highly guarded and off-limits. The battle raging elsewhere in the building had drawn away the guards and left it undefended, save for the automated systems. My Shade's clearance code had taken care of those. With no guards and the security protocols bypassed, the maintenance ladder allowed us to move unseen between levels.

I helped Juan through the hatch. He stared at the incandescent silver light, broken up as more energy transferred along the walls in swirls of color. Another cold burst of air blew past us.

"Are those computer processors?" Juan asked.

"Actually, the processors you can't see. Each of those tiny octagons contain about a million nanoprocessors. But a computer isn't really the best way to imagine it. This operates more like neurons in your brain than what you'd think of as a computer chip." I frowned, unsettled by my expertise.

"So, you're telling me the power consumption is negligible unless in use. Brilliant." Juan's eyes danced with boyish glee as he considered the possibilities. "But if you actually used this entire room at once, you'd have incredible power demands. Not to mention heat." Another gust of wind blew past us. "Guess that's what the wind tunnel is all about."

The light shimmered across the silver tiles again, and Juan spun on his heels, watching it flash along the wall. "Wait, is this system built on an exchange of information via light rather than electricity? I've read the papers online but it's still experimental at best."

I reminded him, "You're not in our reality anymore."

Juan took that in, trying to make sense of our situation. He'd already known what I said was true. But knowing something and accepting it were different things.

"How do you understand any of this, kid?" Burke asked.

Juan started to answer but I cut him off, "Sorry, bud. We don't have time. With the attack on, they may change my command codes. That would be standard procedure at least."

Burke clicked his tongue. "Makes sense."

Juan wanted to talk computers. Kid was even smarter than I'd realized, and we'd entered his area of expertise. But he wanted to save his mom more so he kept his mouth shut.

I took the lead, climbing the thirty feet up to the next platform. Once there, I entered the emergency access code into the hatch's security panel. It beeped three times, then the board went solid green.

"Sloppy." I shook my head in disgust. The feeling not really mine. *His.* I took a deep breath and tried not to lose myself to the confusion.

"Maybe the attack is distracting them," Juan said.

"Sort of defeats the point of having protocols."

"Unless they want us to have access," Burke said.

The hatch popped open to a silent floor. Another ghost town.

Burke's words hung in the air like an omen. But we couldn't worry about traps now. Carla and Val were imprisoned on this level somewhere, and this skyscraper may not survive the day's battle. We only had one choice. So, we plunged ahead.

CHAPTER 28

WE HUSTLED DOWN THE CORRIDOR, THIS ONE JUST AS abandoned as the ones we'd left below.

The defense of the tower was a complete fiasco. No guards. Protocols collapsing. I didn't even want to think about the vulnerability of the city's power core in a situation like this. And if the fighting took down the central cooling system for the mainframe, then the chain reaction caused by that system overheating would vaporize most of this building. There were safeguards, of course; however, they assumed a unified defense from within. But a civil war in which both sides had access to critical points of infrastructure represented a scenario unaccounted for in the contingencies. The outcome could be disastrous. And if Badger got the shields down, I had no way of knowing what the Stone Tails might do.

How do inter-dimensional beings retaliate for genocide?

If they were anything like humans, it would be ugly. I suspected revenge was a universal trait. Though that might be my human bias showing.

So many ideas. All racing. My mind attempting to keep up. Losing.

My breaths labored in and out, clipped and shallow, as we hurried down the halls. Panicked. My brain all cobwebs. Tried to focus. Disappearing in the chaos. My Shade and me becoming one and the same.

His thoughts. *His* worries. *His* desires.

But what about me?

We keep telling you, it's us now.

The hallway swirled all around me as I plummeted down a well of confusion. I grabbed on to the only life preserver I had in this sea of misinformation—the last vestige of my real self—Carla. She was the reason I'd come to this twisted echo of a universe. But I was getting lost in the reflections of the funhouse mirrors. A labyrinth of thoughts and possible futures. I shook my head, clearing it away. *Focus, Raines.* Phantom thoughts be damned. Concentrate on the mission at hand. Survive the day. Save the girl. That was all that mattered.

"You okay, Duster?" Juan took my hand, helping me up from the wall I hadn't realized I'd slumped against.

Juan. My other beacon. A lighthouse bringing me back to shore. I didn't even mind him using my first name. He'd earned that right.

I nodded yes. He spotted the lie. Intuitive kid. But there wasn't time.

We made our way down three abandoned hallways to the door that would lead to the detention cells. I entered another command code, but the console turned red, giving back an error message. I tried the code again. An angry sound chirped. More red. Another error.

"Damn," I muttered.

"Let me try." Juan brushed me aside and plugged his tablet into the computer terminal. His hands flew across the controls, inputting commands that, for all my recent leaps in knowledge, were beyond me.

"How do you know how to do this?" I asked.

"The computers are incredibly advanced. I mean, billions upon billions of cell-sized processors running like a human brain. All working at the speed of light. It's freaking bananas. Can you imagine the computing potential? Are they even called processors here? Sorry, that doesn't matter right now." Juan kept talking a million miles an hour while he typed just as fast. "But, for all that advanced tech, at the end of the day, binary doesn't change. Coding is coding. Plus, I got a bit of a crash course from Badger and Dr. Andrews before we came over."

"I didn't know you were a programmer."

"I told you how I got arrested."

"This all seems a bit more complicated than ripping off an ATM."

He smiled. "Tip of the iceberg."

"This is all really touching," Burke said. "And while I'm glad you two are bonding, let's let the kid do his job. We're sitting ducks out here."

Juan went back to work. A few minutes later, he looked to Burke. "You ready?"

Burke returned his attention from down the hallway to the prison door, moving off to the side for cover. Juan and I did the same. Burke readied his rifle and gave the order: "Do it."

Juan punched in a command, and the metal entry split in half with a lethargic groan. Beyond the door stood a large circular room with thirty or so jail cells all facing inwards to a central guard station. For all of Burke's concerns, we hadn't seen any sign of Livia or my Shade's troops. Even the guards that should've been posted here were gone. Maybe they'd been called away to help wage the battle elsewhere or maybe we were being set up. Impossible to know. The only thing to do was rescue Carla and Val and deal with the fallout later.

We hustled to the central guard desk that held the computer terminal for the cellblock. The cells were what you'd expect, cot on the wall, toilet in the corner, all cold metal. Not very inviting. There were only two prisoners, Val and Carla, and they were right next to each other. Blue force fields hummed at the entry to each cell, preventing them from leaving an otherwise open room.

Val saw us first and jumped up from her small cot. "Juan!"

Juan rushed to his mother, not minding the nearly invisible barriers.

"Don't touch the blue," she snapped.

Juan almost fell over, stopping just before he would've slammed into the force field.

Val laughed. "It won't kill you, but it gives a serious burn."

Carla rose gingerly to her feet, pain evident in her gait. Her hair was a disheveled mess, her face bruised and swollen, and she had bags under her eyes from sleep deprivation. They'd been harder on her than I'd imagined. She wore some type of gray jumpsuit, so did Val, must've been what passed for prison garb in this universe.

My command codes danced off my fingers into the computer at the central station, but the result was the same as the door.

"Juan," I said, "work your magic."

The kid hustled to my side and began punching in orders to drop the force fields. I moved to Carla's cell. Felt a smile creep across my face, more nerves than happiness.

"So you came," she said.

"Of course."

"She said you would."

"Torian? She'll pay for this."

"I've had worse." Her voice sounded hollow and dead. She blamed me. We'd had something special once, a relationship worth fighting for, a life worth living, and I'd ruined it. There was nothing but bitterness for me here. I don't know what I'd expected to be different. But the realization of the calamity of our broken bond cut deep.

The force fields powered down, and Juan ran to his mother, jumping into her arms.

"I'm sorry," I said to Carla.

"I know." She hesitated, her next words bitter in her mouth. "Thank you for coming after us."

I grimaced, unsure of what to say.

"But don't think this means I forgive you," she said.

"I know."

"Because I don't."

"I don't know what else to say but I'm sorry."

Carla walked past me without another word and gave Juan a pat on the back. He gave her a hug nearly as big as the one he'd given his mom. She laughed, touched by his affection. She'd always been good with kids. That hurt most of all—the what might have been. Her lack of empathy for me left a hole inside. None of this was what I'd dreamed. But no one can undo the past. All the spiteful things said to one another in the heat of the moment, they start to add up. And all the heartfelt apologies and pleas for forgiveness can't erase their wicked memory. They seep into everything, a cancer on the soul. I'd taken from her something I could never give back: her trust and misplaced love in me. Bitter feelings were only the beginning.

Without warning, the room's lights all turned red. A new alarm began to pulse. Different than the fire alarm—less about warning you to escape and more about announcing your imminent demise, its oscillation low and threatening.

"Did we trip something?" Burke demanded.

"No," Juan said. "I was careful."

"The shield," I said. "Badger must've gotten it down."

"Fuck." Burke shifted his rifle from hand to hand, a nervous tick.

"What shield?" Carla asked.

"I'll explain later," I said. "We've got to move."

We ran out of the cellblock and back to the hatch, our pace quickened, driven by the ominous, blinking red lights flashing in the halls. We still hadn't seen any guards, but the alarm added a sense that any moment could be our last.

Once through the hatch, everyone started the long ascent up the ladder. It was thirty-two stories to the hangar bay access point, which would have been a difficult climb even without Val and Carla slowing us down. They were both weak from their poor treatment at the hands of the Legion and needed to catch their breath every few minutes. So, while they rested, gusts of icy wind punished our bodies while we clung tight to the freezing metal ladder rungs as they burned our hands. All that cold meant to prevent a computer based in light from overheating and killing us in a ball of flame.

But eventually, we reached the top.

My codes worthless, it was on Juan to get us into the hangar. And he didn't wait to be told, immediately plugging into the hatch access port. We huddled together as he worked, trying to stay warm and ready for whatever awaited us on the other side of this door. Val beamed as her son worked, proud of his abilities. I felt the same pride for the kid, though I'd had very little to do with his impressive skills. In fact, I'd had nothing to do with them.

"This one may take a bit longer," Juan said. "The security seems to have intensified since the shield went down."

"*What* shield?" Carla asked again, out of breath from our interminable climb.

"How much do you know?" I asked.

"I know I'm in some sort of military installation. That's about it."

I filled her in on all the details: my feud with Torian and Jacobs, the parallel universe, the sprawling city beneath us, the Shades, Legionnaires, our plan to collapse a wormhole by hijacking a spaceship and detonating a bomb inside it, and finally, the shield meant to keep out lizard people that surrounded this black citadel in the wastes of what we'd call Los Angeles.

Carla took it all in, processing the extent of my madness. She looked to Burke for confirmation of my insanity but he simply shrugged. Carla indicated Burke's rifle. "Guess that explains where the big guy's ray gun came from."

I laughed. And, despite herself, Carla laughed, too. And in that laugh, I hung on to an insignificant inkling of hope for our future.

Before I could say more, the hatch unsealed. But unlike the levels below, this one opened to the roar of battle, men and women shouting over the concussive forces of grenades and blaster fire. We'd just found the troops. And of course, they were standing between us and the ship we needed to steal in order to blow this Popsicle stand.

"What do we do now?" Juan asked.

"Improvise." Burke checked his rifle, then moved through the hatch. Everyone followed, taking cover behind a metal bulkhead.

Massive, the hangar bay stretched hundreds of meters in all directions. The floor was reflective black, with red running lights demarcating zones for ships to land and the runways for them to take off through an immense set of sliding bay doors. But the doors weren't there anymore—having been destroyed by an explosion—only a gaping hole that opened to the night sky beyond remained. Outside, drones, transportation vehicles, and larger warships—ranging from sleek aerodynamic fuse-lages to bulky quadrangular monstrosities that defied logic in how they remained aloft—flew around one another in a swarm of battle like fireflies that lit up the sky in bursts of flame when destroyed. Many of the ships in the hangar that had tried to join the aerial combat had been turned to smoking husks and were now little more than cover for the ground forces.

We found ourselves at the far edge of the hangar, opposite where the bay door used to be, with most of the firefight happening near the center. Unfortunately, that's where most of the ships were, too. The nearest vessels to us were all old cargo ships, cumbersome boxes that, even if we could get airborne and past the battle outside, wouldn't have the maneuverability for the bombing mission we had in mind. Nearer us, I spotted a large troop transport, unwieldy but faster than the other options. Far from perfect but it would do.

But no sooner had I seen the troop transport then an explosion erupted from within it, consuming the vehicle in a fiery inferno. Three bug-eyed troopers, their armor awash in flame ran from the burning ship. I imagined they were screaming, trying to douse the fire that covered them from head to toe, though I couldn't hear their cries of terror over the tumult of rampant battle all around us. The burning troops died in agony moments later.

"What's our best option, Raines?" Burke snapped.

"The one that just blew up."

"That's going to be a tough one to fly."

"Yeah, yeah. I'm on it."

I scoured the hangar for another ship. There were maybe a hundred armor-clad soldiers shooting at each other with energy weapons and hurling explosives. Most of the vessels had been destroyed or badly damaged in the fighting. I'd started to lose hope when I saw our ticket out of there. An old Nebula-class attack cruiser from the end of the last war. More elegant than the frigate that had just blown up, long and sleek, reminding me of a larger version of the jet fighters I used to fly in our own universe. Thing was a relic now, nearly thirty years old, but it had clearly been retrofitted. Not surprising, those old ships were workhorses. Could take a beating in battle and stand toe to toe with the larger ships in the fleet. The cruiser had a crew capacity of fifteen, living quarters, and was capable of traveling from Earth to Jupiter in three days. Translation, she was fast as hell and could outrun the larger battleship my Shade had brought with him to the other side. The only problem, she sat parked on the far side of the hangar bay with all the turmoil in between.

"That one." I pointed to the impossible-to-get-to cruiser.

"Figures." Burke assessed the situation, made a split-second decision on the course to be taken, and proceeded with confidence. Tough not to like that about him. "All right, everyone. Listen up. Stay close. Keep your head down. If you see a rifle along the way, grab it. Keep an eye on each other. I've never left a soldier behind, and I don't intend to start today."

Burke led us along the wall that would get us to our ship the fastest. Tediously slow-moving, we trudged ahead, forced repeatedly to hide behind crates and other equipment to avoid detection. Fortunately for us, these soldiers were more concerned with killing each other than with escaping prisoners. Juan, Carla, Val, and I procured rifles like Burke's from dead troops along the way. If our luck held, though, we wouldn't need to use them. Despite a few close calls, we'd managed to avoid detection and were already halfway around the bay to our escape from this death trap.

But then, everything went to hell.

A group of four soldiers, eyes glowing that putrid yellow from their bug helmets, came running out of one of the ships about fifty feet from us. They ran like their lives depended on it, straight for the stacked crates we hid behind. The reason for their haste became clear a few seconds later when the vessel they'd just disembarked blew up. The explosion was contained but immense, tearing a hole in the hangar bay floor and taking three unsuspecting enemy soldiers with it to the floors below. The gaping hole in the floor blazed as the ship's unspent fuel ignited. This building would only take so many explosions like that before the support structures collapsed, and it all came tumbling down.

The four Legionnaires hadn't seen us yet because we were well-hidden. If I had to guess, they were my Shade's troops. Taking out ships to prevent Livia from launching any incursions through the Gateway. That other Duster Raines didn't control this hangar, so he ordered his troops to eliminate the threat. Made sense. I'd have done the same thing—*or would I have?*—impossible to know the answer to that, now that our two minds were mixed together in this bizarre soufflé.

Juan took aim with his rifle, using the crate as cover. The kid handled the weapon well. I thought of his dad, serving overseas. He'd probably shot plenty of times with the old man. But before Juan could fire the gun, Burke placed a steadying hand on his shoulder.

"Easy, fella," Burke whispered. "Wait 'til you can see those ugly yellow eyes up close before you make a move."

Juan nodded. Let out a nervous breath.

The soldiers stopped about ten feet from us, exhausted from their sprint but exuberant about what they'd just done. While they slapped backs and congratulated one another, our team remained concealed. The battle thundered all around us, and these four wouldn't wait long to rejoin the fray. When they did, our path to the ship would be wide open.

We bided our time, hoping to go unseen.

But one soldier's gaze lingered on our hiding spot longer than it should have. They looked to one of their allies, got their attention, and pointed at our crates. Busted. The four of them creeped towards our spot, readying their rifles.

Burke held up three fingers to our group. He gave a silent nod. Once. Twice. And on the third nod we all stepped out from cover and opened fire. Three of the bug-eyed soldiers went down in our first barrage. But bad luck allowed the fourth trooper to escape their death. They darted behind debris from one of the destroyed freighters and out of sight.

In that instant, the world slowed as it had in so many of my battles these past few months. I floated above it all. From here, I saw the bug-eyed survivor talking into their wrist, calling for reinforcements. No time left. I needed to act now.

Clambering out from behind the safety of the crates, I took off full tilt. My movements seemed to take forever, like sprinting underwater, but I knew I ran faster than I ever had before. With one giant leap, I landed on top of the detritus directly above the surviving soldier before they'd even realized I'd started running. They raised their gun to fire at me, but I moved lightning quick, vaporizing them with a close-range blast from my rifle.

Time returned to normal.

Burke and the others hustled to my side. "How did you do that?" he asked.

"I'm not sure."

"I've never seen anyone move that fast," Juan said.

"It has something to do with the stones," I said. "But I can't find the thought."

"We'll worry about it later," Burke said. "We've got company."

From the center of the battle, two robot dogs and three soldiers dashed straight at us. The reinforcements. I hadn't been fast enough.

"Run," I yelled.

We sprinted across the deck for the frigate. But we were still a couple of hundred yards from it, and those robot dogs would close this gap long before we made it there. I fired shot after shot back towards the dogs, trying to slow their advance. But, as they had in the tunnels, the robots dodged the projectiles with ease. I waited for the world to slow again, allowing me to hit these monstrous would-be killers, but it never did. I had no control over this newfound power, and everything continued happening in real time.

You may be the sorriest excuse for a superhero ever.

We kept moving. Burke, Val, Carla, Juan, and I all fired shots over our shoulders to cover the retreat.

Juan tripped. It happened fast.

Carla and I were next to each other. My focus had been devoted to keeping her safe. That distraction cost me. When I turned back to fire another shot, I saw the kid sprawled on the ground, a good thirty feet back the way we'd come, struggling to get back to his feet in his panicked haste.

"Keep going," I said to Carla.

"Raines, wait," she yelled after me. But I was already gone.

Val hadn't lost track of her son and was right there with him as incoming fire slammed into the ground all around them, sending chunks of black fiberglass and metal into the air in bursts of smoke and flame. She helped Juan back onto his feet. They turned and hustled towards me, away from danger.

I ran as fast as I could—which wasn't that fast considering what I'd accomplished moments before—firing shot after shot over their heads towards our pursuers, trying to give the boy and his mother a fighting chance. But the dogs and soldiers had gained ground and fired their own bubbles of death with far greater accuracy. The floor all around me exploded, vanishing in scorching glares. I nearly took one of the crackling blue spheres to the chest and was forced to hit the deck hard to avoid it.

Behind me, Burke and Carla took cover behind some equipment. They returned fired from that position back at our pursuers, but they were too far out of range to be any help.

Juan and his mother ran with everything they had. I knew I could get them to safety, I just had to reach them. If they could hold on a few more seconds, then we'd be safe. I got up on my knees and laid down covering fire. One of the dogs took a direct hit to its head and erupted in a rain of fiery metal.

They were almost to me. They were going to make it.

Then, the world slowed again.

One of the soldiers fired a shot directly at Juan. No doubt it would hit him.

Scrambling back to my feet, I ran for Juan, reached out to grab him. He was maybe ten feet away—I'd cover the distance in a fraction of a second but the pulsing orb was faster and would reach Juan before me. I shouted for Juan to look out, but it would be too late. I couldn't save him. This was the end.

But Val saw the wave of energy, too. She threw herself into her son and shoved him to the side. Juan fell to the ground. Safe. But Val took a glancing blow in the back of the shoulder from the phasing energy blast. She screamed in anguish and crumpled next to her son.

Time returned to normal as I reached them. Juan helped his mother flip onto her back. The burn on her shoulder looked nasty, charring her skin and slowly melting it away. The acrid smell of scorched flesh permeated the air, pungent and nauseating. The shot hadn't been direct, which was the only reason she hadn't been vaporized the instant it hit her. But these weapons were made to kill, and in a matter of moments, the energy would take its course.

"Mama," Juan said. "Are you okay?"

"Shh," Val said, placing her hand on Juan's cheek. "Don't you worry."

Tears streamed down Juan's face. He saw now what I already knew: the wound had continued spreading, the odor of it awful and obviously of death.

"You have to be okay," Juan pleaded.

Val looked at me. "Promise me you'll protect him, Mr. Raines."

"I swear it." I could feel the tears in my eyes now. Juan's mother had sacrificed herself for her son. No greater love. And I could feel the weight of responsibility she'd placed on me. Val's request bound me to the boy. I would defend her sacrifice until the day I died.

"Please don't leave me," Juan begged.

"I'll always be with you."

Juan buried his face in his mother's chest and sobbed. Val hugged him hard, not wanting to leave her son. "I love you, *mijo*. Be strong. We'll be together again one day." She died then, silently holding in her agony, protecting her son from this gruesome moment as she turned to dust in his arms.

Only the memory of her remained.

Juan lay there in the space where his mother had been, whimpering like a wounded bird. His breaths came quicker and quicker as something welled up within him, a primal hatred with nowhere to escape. Then, he screamed a savage fury and grabbed his rifle, whirling to fight his mother's killers. But the three soldiers and the robot dog were only a few steps away with their weapons trained on us.

"Drop it, kid," a garbled voice of one of the masked soldiers demanded. "Or so help me."

I grabbed Juan from behind, putting him in a bear hug and holding him tight, preventing him from firing the rifle. They hadn't killed us yet, and prolonging their decision to capture us was our only chance to survive.

"Let me go," Juan seethed. When I didn't, he turned his fury on the three soldiers, spitting his words at them like daggers. "Murderers! I'll fucking kill you!"

The soldier who had spared our lives brought her hand to her ear, listening to a radio voice we couldn't hear, then she spoke into her wrist, "Bring them over."

Three more soldiers escorted Burke and Carla to us. Our weapons were unceremoniously confiscated. I tried to hold on to Juan, who used every muscle in his body to get away from me. I kept him close—wanting to make it better but knowing I couldn't—I'd promised I'd keep him safe. But, looking at our current predicament, I wasn't so sure it was a promise I'd be able to keep. I had to try.

From behind, one of the soldiers struck me hard in the back of the head and yanked us apart. My vision blurred, nearly going out, but I managed to stay on my feet. Juan resisted his new captor, kicking, thrashing, spitting, screaming, but he wouldn't be able to free himself as the soldier dragged him away from me.

Then, I noticed it. The silence. In all the chaos of trying to save Juan, watching his mother die, I hadn't realized the battle had ended.

"Duster Raines," the lead soldier said in the raspy tin the masks gave their voices. "The First Consul will be pleased to know you survived."

"You killed one of my friends. Nearly killed me. If the goal was to take us alive, then you fucked up." I clenched my fists and tried to stay calm, but I could feel my ire boiling over.

"It wasn't the mission," the soldier said. "But objectives change. Consider yourself lucky. You're to accompany us to secure the Gateway."

"And my friends?"

The other soldiers corralled Juan, Carla, and Burke away from me, their rifles trained on them, ready to shoot.

"I'm afraid we don't have room."

I heard the rifles powering up for the shots that would kill everyone. I had no options.

"Please don't," I pleaded.

"Fire," the lead soldier ordered.

But the shots never came.

A low rumble, like a predator's growl, filled the hangar bay. Before my mind had fully processed what I'd heard, an explosion of bright green light erupted all around us, blinding me. Then, I heard the screams. When my vision returned, I saw two dead soldiers on the floor. But no sign of their assailants.

Suddenly, in another flash of radiance, three Stone Tails appeared out of thin air, though I knew they'd actually come from another reality. The other soldiers tried to fire at the lizards, but they vanished and reappeared faster than they could shoot. One of the reptiles materialized right behind the lead soldier and ripped her head off with its powerful jaws. The creature vanished again before the dead trooper's body hit the ground in a pool of her own blood.

The robot dog spun around and unleashed a high-pitched howl at the empty space from where one of the lizards had just vanished. The Stone Tail reappeared, phasing in and out of existence, stuck between both realities, obviously in pain. Then, the robot unleashed two quick bursts of blaster fire from its mouth and killed the Stone Tail. But its body didn't vaporize. Instead, the weapon had the opposite effect, bringing the Stone Tail over from that realm and solidifying it here with us.

So that was what the dogs were for; they were designed to fight Stone Tails. No sooner had I thought it than three more Stone Tails appeared around the robot dog and ripped it to shreds with their teeth and claws. These creatures were impressively fast and strong—no wonder they hadn't developed conventional weapons; their bodies were weapon enough.

The battle ended in less than thirty seconds. The six soldiers that had held us prisoner were dead. For now, Juan, Carla, Burke, and I had been spared.

Two of the Stone Tails went to their fallen comrade's side, placed their claws on the corpse and vanished in a flash of emerald light. A single Stone Tail stayed behind. This lizard-like creature stood taller than the rest, nearly eight feet, its body a swirling granite of black and gray rock covered in yellow moss, with eyes that glowed the same green as the mystical stone I had carried. He walked forward—at least, I think it was a he—all the while appraising me. Their awesome power having just been demonstrated, I tried to control my fear. If this thing had wanted to kill me, I'd be dead already.

Still, it was hard not to feel intimidated by this giant beast.

Immediately, I regretted the thought. Calling them a beast was wrong. This was a sentient being. Not a monster. Hatred of the Stone Tails pulsed through my blood, but I knew that malice belonged to my Shade. I tried to keep an open mind.

"Not of this place," the Stone Tail said, pointing one of its claws squarely at me.

"No," I said, a little shaken but gaining confidence. "We're not."

"You are a Dream Walker, then?"

"I don't know what that means."

"Apology is mine. We do not often inhabit this space in time. This corporeal form rusty. And your many spoken languages always elude. But rejoice, you are ascended. You travel between the realms as we. Hearing the songs of the Fates and knowing the myriad possibilities always to choose."

"Only because of machines," I said. "And not of our own free will."

"Clarity," the Stone Tail said. "All blurs. The appropriate moment not reached. But one day. Though maybe never."

"I'm sorry. I'm not following."

"Not in this place of time to know."

"What should I call you?"

"You could not pronounce." The Stone Tail laughed, a guttural thing almost like a bark, but there was no mistaking its intent. "But in the here and now, call this one Varnok. I lead for present."

"I'm Duster Raines." I extended my hand to shake. A dumb thing to do but I did it out of habit. Varnok, to my surprise, took my hand in its claws. His palm was made of coarser stone than the rest of him but was warm to the touch. He pulled me in close, stared into my eyes. Green clouds swirled arounds its ashen pupils.

"You have carried our young," Varnok hissed.

I swallowed my fear. "I have."

The Stone Tail bared its teeth. And while not completely up-to-date on my alien reptile body language, I got the sense this represented anger. But then he said, "If you are not of this realm, then battle is not with you. Go in peace."

"Wait," I said. "What about Badger?"

"Badger? Ah, the helper. He is of us now."

"And what about my world? This universe means to take your young from ours."

"Yes. We know. Sadness of war inevitable. Humanity always leads to death. My kind knows all too well. It has been. And will be. Many streams, similar outcomes."

And before I could ask what any of that meant, Varnok vanished in a flash of green energy.

Burke placed his hand on my shoulder, startling me; I'd forgotten he was there. I hadn't realized how lost I'd been in the conversation with Varnok.

I looked back to Carla for assurance. But she couldn't care less about me. She held Juan, who looked as if he could barely stand, stroking his hair and whispering to him softly. The boy stared past us all, his eyes glassy with tears, possibly in shock.

"Well, shit," Burke said. "That was unexpected."

CHAPTER 29

THE INFINITE VOID OF SPACE SPREAD OUT BEFORE ME, AN uncompromising sea of the unknown. All those stars pulsed with the light of ancient eons, a glimpse of the past, their spark long since lost to oblivion. The breadth of the infinite was awe-inspiring, the magnitude of time an incomprehensible eternity, its emptiness all-consuming. I'd dreamed it often enough, longed for some embrace of death that would make me one with that nothingness. But being in the cockpit of our recently acquired Nebula-class frigate, I experienced something else entirely. With only the thinnest of protections keeping that abyss from swallowing me whole, I existed at the edge of the void. Death surrounded me, but for the first time in a long time, I felt alive.

I sat at the helm of our new vessel. The captain. In control.

Truth be told, it hadn't been the smoothest of takeoffs. Barreled over a few crates. Lurched into a wall. Probably scratched the paint. But it's like riding a bike. Just needed to knock off some of that rust. After all, I'd been an ace pilot once. One of the best. I certainly didn't need a telepathic uplink with my Shade to know how to fly. Though my sudden understanding of their technology probably helped with the learning curve. Score one in the win column for my splintered mind.

No need to explain yourself to us.

At least stealing our ship from the hangar had been a song after the Stone Tails had chased away any sort of resistance we might have encountered. And with our enemies locked in a life-and-death struggle elsewhere in the tower, we'd slipped right out with a few of my Shade's command codes. Of course, they'd been out of date with the rules of engagement finally followed—*better late than never*—but Juan had simply manipulated them, opened a backdoor into their mainframe, and overridden the security protocols.

Simple for him at least.

Brilliant Juan. Poor Juan. We'd almost pulled off the impossible.

But the boy's mother . . .

A wretched casualty that never should have been.

The first of many when this war reaches our home.

Now, the kid slept. Carla had tucked him into one of the cots in the back of the ship after he'd helped me hack into the planetary defense systems so we could escape undetected. You had to give him credit; he knew when to mourn and when to fight. A soldier, like his father. And only fifteen years old. Impressive. Val and her husband—I didn't even know his name—had raised a good kid.

Our vessel hurtled through the cosmos towards Mars at an unbelievable clip.

We were twenty hours out of Earth's orbit and, according to my instruments, another twelve hours from the wormhole. I'd run multiple system diagnostics to find any flaws in our stolen spacecraft. But, as far as I could tell, the ship hadn't been damaged in the fighting. Our frigate was in pristine condition—except for the paint—and all systems were operational. We were ready for the mission ahead.

But I was alone.

Unfortunately, the ship's cockpit required a complement of four to function at peak efficiency. My chair obviously controlled flight, as well as primary blasters and short-range missiles. A copilot chair sat next to mine, mostly redundant systems to the pilot—meant to alleviate strain—optimal but unnecessary. Two other stations sat aft. One controlled secondary weapons and defenses, such as mines and anti-missile flares. While the other dedicated its systems to detailed sensor readouts, comprehensive battle mappings, environmental readings, radiation levels, atmospheric pressures, and a whole list of things that wouldn't matter prior to our battle because I had no one skilled enough to sit in the seat. If we got back home, I'd need to train a crew to help me fly this hunk of metal. But for now, I'd put Juan in charge of the tactical station and hope for the best.

Lost in the controls, enjoying the thrill of being back on the stick, I didn't hear Carla enter. She cleared her throat, startling me from my chair.

"You scared me," I said.

"Sorry." She took the copilot seat next to me and looked out at the galactic expanse. "Never thought I'd be an astronaut."

I chuckled. "Hadn't thought of it like that."

She sat there, silent. After a while, I couldn't take it.

"How's Juan?"

"His mom's dead. How do you think?"

"Yeah."

"I'm sorry," she said. "I shouldn't treat you like that. I don't like feeling this way."

"You have the right."

"I suppose there's a lot of history between us."

"Think they call that an understatement."

She laughed sadness. Sighed. Then asked, "What are we going to do about him?"

"Juan?" I swallowed hard, unsure. I hadn't really thought that far ahead. "If we survive all this, we'll have to try and find his dad, I guess."

"If what you've told me is true, I can't imagine the military will be all that accessible."

"Then we'll take care of him. Watch out for each other. All we can do."

She looked at me for a long while, picking me apart, planning her next move. I knew it all too well; the lawyer in her. She couldn't help it. Always looking at life as a chess match, trying to stay one move ahead of her opponent. A habit you could admire in a person when you were in love. But when things got rocky, it became the first thing to drive you up the wall.

The tranquil whir of the machines hummed all around us. The peace and quiet was unbearable. I shifted uncomfortably but bit my tongue, sensing I needed to let her speak.

"You've changed, Raines," she finally said. "Haven't you?"

I didn't answer.

"Juan looks up to you."

"I know."

"I've got half a mind to tell him it's a bad idea."

"Think he already knows."

Carla grumbled something to herself, not convinced.

"I'm going to earn back your trust, Carla. If it takes me the rest of my life, I will."

"We'll see." She brushed her hand across my shoulder as she stood, an intimacy there we'd lost long ago. Then she left me in the cockpit without another word.

Despite all the misery between us, I smiled.

* * *

The computer beeped incessantly, waking me from a nap I hadn't realized I'd fallen into. I didn't like that. Bad portent to sleep before a battle. At least for me. That grip on my chest tightened a little, smothering me with the weight of responsibility. My entire body tingled. I shook it off, roused my senses from that torpor, and tried to clear my head. The panic did no one any good.

I checked the controls for what that damned alarm was all about. Finally figured it out; the ship's proximity warning. We were approaching the Mars fleet.

No more worry. Only action.

Then the real horror took hold because I no longer flew alone. Next to me, the little Iraqi boy sat—his face a bloody mess as always. He smiled a broken-toothed smile, the hole in his head still smoking from the shot I'd fired decades ago. "You're going to get everyone killed," he said in Arabic that somehow I understood.

We were old friends, this kid and me. He'd been my companion through some dark times, and his arrival in this moment of trial and tribulation was nothing new. Really, I'd expected it. His presence felt oddly right, though unnerving. But what put me over the edge was the man standing behind him. My Shade.

How'd he find this place?

What do you mean? He's one of us.

An impostor. He'd penetrated my very being and discovered my dirty little secret. The whole truth of which I'd only shared with Carla. This was where everything about my world started to break down. Because my stability, the belief in my sanity, all hinged on a reality where my murder victim visited me on a regular basis to demand tribute for my transgressions. And that was crazy.

But if I knew it was crazy, then I couldn't possibly be unhinged, right?

Are we really going to debate this now?

Fair enough. I'd had this argument with myself a million times over. Even what I'd told Carla had been a half-truth. The truth of my deeds but not of the constant haunting. If my shrink hadn't killed himself, and I'd told him about the visions of the boy, he'd have had me committed for sure. And that truth probably answered any lingering doubts about whether my version of events could really be trusted.

Maybe I should've told my doctor. Gotten on some good drugs and saved us all the trouble of this little adventure. But I never had. Mistakes were made.

And there my Iraqi friend sat. Watching. Judging. My cohort. My consummate drinking buddy. My everlasting reminder of impending damnation.

You knew he'd be back. Blood demands blood. Fate always gets paid.

The boy embodied my hurt. My guilt. And if you want to know the truth, I loved him. Because deep down I knew he was all I had left. He might have been the proof of my madness, but he also kept me grounded and reaffirmed everything that made me sane. Strange contradictions. He represented my driving force. The taskmaster of Death that kept me moving towards a goal of redemption.

Our very own Eternal Watcher.

My Shade placed his hand on the boy's shoulder and smirked our father's grin at me. He didn't say anything. He didn't have to.

The dead boy was right. We were going to die today.

Took a deep breath. Didn't help. My hands shook. Clenched my fists. For the first time since I'd traveled across the brink and passed between the barriers that separated universes, I needed a drink. The old demons reared their ugly heads, showing me my true self. The ghosts chattered at me, reminding me of my failures.

But they were just that, weren't they? Ghosts. All in my mind. Whispers of my insecurities.

Swallowed the fear and tasted that bitter bile. Closed my eyes.

This wasn't real.

They clamored louder, crushing me. They sounded real enough. I tried to focus, run through my breathing techniques. But it didn't matter. They were me. Only I could shut them up.

"Enough," I shouted into the darkness.

Silence.

I opened my eyes. They were gone. I was alone again with that ceaseless beeping.

A button flashed on the control panel, demanding my attention. I pushed it, shutting that damned alarm off, and then activated the intercom system. My voice echoed through the cavernous ship, a slight quiver beneath it: "All crew, this is the captain. Battle stations."

A serene drone of an alarm sounded throughout the ship. The lights dimmed, illuminating everything in the red hue of battle. I hit another button, and the shields of the frigate armed. On a screen to my left, the defensive barrier ignited around a diagram of the vessel specifying that status of primary systems. The entire ship displayed in a crisp white, surrounded with solid dashes of the same color indicating the shields were at maximum.

White good. Red bad. Check.

Out of a console in the armrest of my chair, a retinal device rose up for my use. Designed to fit snugly over the ear, with a long protrusion that jutted forward to scan a single eye, the clunky machine reminded me of an outdated wireless headset for a cell phone back home. I put it on and tapped it once.

A microscopic yellow light danced into my eye from the gadget, and instantaneously a tactical readout of the battle lay before me in three dimensions. But this was far more than a holographic representation. The computer plugged directly into my mind. I could have immediate information from any-where on the battlefield. And here with the ship, my thoughts and the computer became one. Melded with its systems, my reflexes and responses enhanced. I thought about reviewing my secondary radar readouts, and suddenly they scrolled in front of my eye. This system wouldn't give the detailed reports the station behind me could, but it would give me up-to-date information on incoming weapons fire and enemy ships. It just might help keep us alive.

My real-time tactical display zoomed in on the space around the Gateway, showing me what we were up against. The fleet above Mars included five battle cruisers, similar in design to the ship my Shade had brought through the worm-hole. In addition, an array of defense mines surrounded the anomaly's event horizon. But the mines were meant to keep the bigger ships out. A small maneuverable ship, like the one I flew, had a shot at getting through the minefield quickly and with negligible damage. Nose to nose, my vessel could never stand up to all the firepower those dreadnoughts packed. But hopefully she wouldn't have to. We weren't here for a battle. We were here to make sure we never had to fight that war.

On my screens, I picked up an incredible amount of energy emanating from the ring of pylons constructed around the anomaly. The computer told me they were the charging nodes meant to stabilize the anomaly and allow one of the larger ships to pass between our two realities. And then I saw the reading that I didn't want to see. I stood quick to check it at the rear sensor console. Confirmed. The Gateway was fully energized, and they were already sending another battle cruiser to join my Shade's flagship. If that ship went through, it would close the wormhole until another charge could be generated—essentially stranding us on this side. With the element of surprise lost, our attempt at destabilizing the anomaly would be lost forever.

We were too late.

The shock of the loss hadn't even had time to settle when, as if from nowhere, three ships appeared on my readouts in orbit above Mars. The normal warnings that should have accompanied ships of that size had been nonexistent. In layman's terms, they shouldn't be there, their arrival impossible in both speed and stealth. I checked my Shade's memories for a clue as to how this had happened but found nothing. If I had to guess, the other Duster Raines would be just as surprised by their arrival as me.

The ships broadcasted call signs from Livia's fleet and had materialized right on top of the other armada. Their massive size was a striking contrast to their elegant splendor of braided metal that shown even at this distance, reflecting the light of our sun back out from the empty darkness of space. Miles in length, the ships bore a thin and elongated design that created an hourglass silhouette with bulbous sides that had reminded me of blown glass the first time I'd seen one. Those elliptic ends, narrowest at their center, came to deadly points at the fore and aft of the vessel, like a double-bladed knife.

Without ceremony, Livia's fleet opened fire on my Shade's task force. A full-fledged space battle had just erupted around the Gateway. Frankly, I couldn't believe our luck. This civil war might just buy us the time we needed to get through the worm-hole before those ships could use all its energy.

But where had her ships come from?

My mind raced. Badger had mentioned previous attempts at harnessing the stones' energy to create a fold in space-time—it had to be that experiment—not traveling between realities but rather two points in a single universe, just as the Stone Tails had teleported around the hangar bay like magic.

Carla, Burke, and Juan all entered the cockpit. Juan huddled beneath a blanket despite the fact the life-support systems maintained a comfortable seventy-two degrees throughout the ship. Carla had an arm around him, though I don't think he even noticed. He looked exhausted, his eyes swollen from crying. Kid deserved better than this, but it was the hand we'd all been dealt. I only hoped I could see the boy through to better days.

"Juan, I need you to run the secondary weapons." I indicated the computer terminal he'd operate. Without a word, he took a seat. I began explaining how it all worked but he cut me off.

"I think I got it." He pointed to a few different buttons. "Main firing trigger, proximity detector for mines, anti-missile defenses here, shield power indicator there. Piece of cake."

Carla, Burke, and I all laughed in disbelief.

Juan shrugged. "I play a lot of video games."

"All right," I said. "We were just given a gift. Livia's fleet crashed the party. My Shade's fleet has engaged her ships. It's mayhem out there."

"How is this good news?" Carla asked.

"Because," Burke said, "they won't be paying much attention to little old us."

"Precisely," I said.

"How'd they get here so quickly?" Juan asked. "I thought we had the faster ship."

"No clue. Faster-than-light travel doesn't exist here as far as I know. That technology is science fiction for them, too."

"Things keep getting better and better," Burke said. "But I for one say we blow the thing to hell so we don't have to worry about it anymore."

"Agreed," Carla said.

With a few quick commands, I took back control of the ship from the computer. Pointed the frigate's nose straight for the Gateway, into the battle, and gave the vessel everything it had. Even with the dampening fields at maximum, keeping the g-forces placed on our bodies at a minimum, I pushed the ship to its max, and the systems couldn't keep up. Both Carla and Burke nearly fell over. Dragging themselves into their seats, they harnessed themselves in. Juan and I did the same. I gritted my teeth and watched the sensors as we flew into the lion's den.

"We need a name," Juan blurted out, breaking my concentration.

"What?" I tried to focus on the battle that, according to my computer readouts, we'd enter in one hundred and eighty-seven seconds. Eighty-six. Eighty-five . . .

"For the ship. All good spaceships have a name. *Serenity. Millennium Falcon. Enterprise. Challenger. HAL.*"

"HAL was a computer," Carla corrected.

"Yeah, she's right," I said. "Think the ship in that movie was *Discovery One.* But I'm impressed you saw it." Juan seemed more relaxed, forgetting his mom for at least a second. Those moments would be few and far between in the months and years to come.

"Are you really encouraging this?" Burke demanded.

"Ease up," I said.

But Burke didn't look good. He white-knuckled his chair's armrests, and his color didn't seem right. Maybe flying wasn't his thing. I gave the ship a quick adjustment, and he reeled back, swallowing whatever had just come up. Definitely not his thing.

"Pick a point to focus on," I told Burke. "It'll make you feel better. And I'm all for a name, Juan. But you'd better make it quick. We've got"—I checked my instruments—"about two minutes before this all gets a bit hairy."

Juan thought for a minute. "How about *Pigeon's Fury?*"

"*Pigeon's Fury?*" Burke laughed. "What kind of a name is that?"

"Well, my mom always used to take me down to Griffith Park to feed the pigeons. It was sort of our thing. And fury because, you know, we're tough. Sorry, I can think of something better."

"No way," Carla said. "I think it's great."

"Yeah," I said. "I like it. *Pigeon's Fury.* Has a nice ring to it."

"Suppose it does." Burke turned back and gave Juan a curt nod, which I guessed was about as touchy-feely as Burke got if he wasn't trying to beat you to death with his bare hands.

"Thanks." An alarm began beeping on Juan's tactical station. He checked it. "Incoming missiles from that main cruiser."

Leaping back into combat mode, I checked my controls. According to my readouts, we still had thirty seconds before we'd be in their weapons' range. But the incoming missile had a different opinion about that. Somehow my computer had miscalculated our trajectory. Maybe this ship needed more maintenance than I'd realized. Hopefully it wouldn't be a problem.

I kicked the ship to port and put her into a sharp nosedive, pushing the inertial-dampening system past its limits and pinning us all against our chairs. The frigate handled great, whipping back up on a hairpin. This vessel was sleek and fast, its design like a bird of prey, reminiscent of our own stealth bombers, making our new name all the more fitting. The missile pursued, I could see that on my tactical display. I gave the ship's engine a reverse thrust and spun her around on our y-axis, firing the blasters as we went.

The missile exploded from a direct hit. Our ship rattled from the explosion as we whipped back through the burning debris of the projectile. A near miss but still a miss.

I swung us around and pointed the *Pigeon* straight at the maw of the wormhole. It glowed there, a pulsing green and blue eye above the red planet. The ships all around it were frozen from this distance, a light show of delayed explosions kicking up around them.

"Hang on back there." I boosted the ship to full throttle.

We were amid the explosions seconds later, the battle cruisers no longer frozen but moving at incredible speeds. They spun around themselves in a blur of motion, like garden spinners catching the wind, creating their own gravity but also never exposing one portion of their hull to their enemies for too long. Brilliant.

The dreadnoughts' weakness was their tail end, the engines being the most volatile point, so their tactics were meant to keep noses forward. But these vessels were juggernauts and maneuvering them was easier said than done. This was how I imagined nautical battles from the 1700s had looked. Wooden ships battling the sea and wind, slowly trying to outpace the other vessel to win position. In the end, the upper hand depended on one daring move, unseen by the opposition until it was too late.

But I didn't have time for such nonsense. I plunged straight at the nearest ship, strafing it with laser fire. The trail of explosions I left in my wake were satisfying but did little to harm the behemoth. And that elegant simplicity was what made the battleship's construction a stroke of genius. The braided coils of metal created a cocoon of protection around anything we'd want to damage, all vital systems hidden deep within its womb. Layers of smooth metal jigsawed around one another like a corkscrew, strengthening one another, while simultaneously creating something artful—a flowing sculpture of metal, pure beauty in its design—rather than a deadly tool of war. But in battle, that graceful magnificence vanished, the smooth metal opening to reveal her fangs. The entire hull pocked as weaponry emerged from within: thousands of gun turrets, radar detection systems, and missile launchers. The once-smooth ship now covered in structures, like a city had sprung up atop the twisted metal. And as those weapons fired, they lit up the darkness of space.

The dreadnought's sensors detected a threat in our approach and turned a section of that city of death towards us. The readings went red, and I sent the *Pigeon* into evasive maneuvers as the battle cruiser opened fire. The first salvo exploded around us in bursts of shrapnel, sending millions of tiny metal fragments in all directions. Our shields handled them easily. But those shots weren't meant to destroy us. Rather, they were meant to keep us from getting too close and slow down any assault we could muster. Eventually, those bursts would overwhelm our shields but their immediate purpose was to delay. My Shade's cruisers were on defense, tactically playing the long game and buying their ship time to escape through the portal.

Livia's fleet, on the other hand, threw everything into offense. Her ships fired torpedoes meant to overpower the dreadnought's defensive shields and penetrate its braided hull to more critical systems. A direct hit from one of those torpedoes would send our little ship to the next life. But they were slow and cumbersome weapons, meant for the battle between titans and not intended for a spry ship like ours. I easily avoided the incoming missiles as their trajectories and eventual points of impact were fed to me from the *Pigeon's* computer.

We handled ourselves well but little of this maelstrom was meant for us. We weren't an immediate threat to these larger vessels, and their tactics reflected that, the idea being to hold our attack at bay until fighters were launched for direct ship-to-ship dogfighting. I just needed to make sure I didn't accidently make these stalling tactics winners by getting us blown up. We needed to reach the wormhole fast before those fighters arrived.

"Mines away," Juan shouted. He didn't really need to yell but he was having fun. Belonged in the heat of battle. A kid after my own heart. I was having fun, too.

"Keep them coming, Juan," I shouted back.

"Anything I can do to help?" Carla asked, already knowing the answer as she held on to her chair for dear life.

"No time to teach you," I said. "Just hold on tight. We're almost there."

I put the ship into a steep descent as one of the torpedoes slammed into the battle cruiser we'd just strafed. A massive explosion of fire erupted from a tear in the larger ship's hull where the *Pigeon's Fury* had just been. I ignored the bodies of personnel now spilling into the coldness of space. War meant casualties; I needed to make sure we didn't join their ranks.

Checking my sensors, I expected to see a torrent of fighters on my tail. But neither fleet had launched their defensive squadrons. I couldn't understand why. We were a small threat but still a threat. Standard rules of engagement necessitated we be destroyed to minimize the damage we could cause if left unattended. But they weren't coming.

Burke saw it before my sensors did. "Is that big ship making a break for the Gateway?"

The alarms changed tone, warning me of the computer's calculations on the energy output of the Gateway. They weren't good numbers.

"What's that new alarm?" Juan asked.

"It's the computer telling us the wormhole's stability is questionable based on the trajectory of those ships."

"What the hell are you talking about, Raines?" Carla demanded. "And how do you understand any of this?"

"Long story," I said, ignoring the question. "Basically, too much mass in the anomaly means the entire thing could blow up. Good for our mission but bad for us ever seeing home."

"What are we going to do?" Juan asked.

"Hope for the best."

No time to waste, I took the ship straight at the wormhole, across the firing patterns of two of the battle cruisers and through the primary minefield meant to prevent exactly what we now attempted. *Pigeon's Fury* jostled in all directions as explosion after explosion tickled our shields. The old frigate responded to every command I gave her, avoiding most of the mines and weapons fire. But despite some incredible flying on my part, the computer screamed about our imminent demise—the dashed white outline of our shields now flashed red on my monitor—we couldn't take much more of this.

Pigeon's Fury blew through the last of the minefield and sped past Livia's command ship—I knew in my gut she was aboard that vessel, going to face my Shade directly—and headed straight for the Gateway. Livia's ship held its fire, most likely not wanting to destabilize the anomaly before she could pass through it, too. The other ship from my Shade's fleet entered the wormhole in front of us, its structure stretching out like taffy in a carnival display. It vanished. Any moment the anomaly's energy would dissipate, and the Gateway would close.

Hold on just a little longer.

"Fifteen seconds until we reach the event horizon." I checked my instruments. "Shields are depleted but holding." I turned back and looked at Juan. "Get ready to drop everything you've got. Set a five-second delay so we can pass through before detonation."

Juan punched in some commands.

"Ten seconds." I readied my torpedoes, watching the instruments. Five. Four. Three. "Fire in the hole."

The torpedoes streaked out in front of us. But we never saw them detonate as we entered the wormhole and were flung across the edge of reality. We'd entered a swirling vortex of pure energy. The wormhole glowed all around us in a cloud of every shade of green imaginable. That vortex of swirling greens blended together with hints of blue energy reminiscent of the shields and blasters of that other universe's human-made technology, likely created by the pylons' attempt to harness the power of the stones. A kaleidoscope of hues. Beautiful. I checked my sensors, but they were all static, making it impossible to know if our bombs had worked.

Unlike my trip through the mechanism that Dr. Andrews had built—where time and space had warped, nearly pulling my atoms apart—the space between all of us here on the bridge of the *Pigeon's Fury* held stable. Except that this time, I could see every possibility. As I moved my hand across the controls, I saw thousands of iterations of that hand reaching for thousands of options. Infinite possibilities. Endless choice. I saw Carla hugging me as we passed through the anomaly safely. I also saw her screaming as the ship broke apart around us. We lived and died a million times in a fraction of a second, the fragility of life unfolding before my very eyes. But this wasn't my imagination. I could see all of *what might be.* And all of it in

an instant. Thousands of Juans, Burkes, and Carlas ran around
the cockpit, doing different tasks. But I stayed seated, knowing
that nothing I did would change what would be, the outcome
of this trip had already been determined.

And then, everything returned to normal, snapping back
to the one possible reality of what had occurred. The sensors
came back online. Only the four of us were in the cock pit.
The tunnel of light we'd been flying through no longer existed.
We were back in the infinite void of space.

My sensor readings danced before my eyes, warning me
of the *Liberator*—my Shade's flagship—bearing down on our
position. It had worked. We were back in our galaxy.

I didn't have time to dwell on it long as the proximity
alarms screamed in my mind. I sent the *Pigeon's Fury* into a
hard nosedive as we narrowly missed slamming into the battle cruiser we'd chased through the wormhole. Fortunately, my
Shade's ship wasn't in firing range yet, so we only had to avoid
the onslaught of weapons fire being unleashed by the closer
dreadnought. I brought the *Pigeon's Fury* across the giant ship's
underside, firing as we went, and came up across its bow. We
passed beneath its moniker, painted in stark red across its hull:
Peacemaker.

Like a jump cut in a badly spliced-together B movie, Livia's
ship blinked into existence in front of the wormhole. Her
ship appeared in my tactical readout, its name clearly marked:
Imperial Might. This other universe didn't lack for its melodra-
matic ship names.

Having just come full about under the attacking
Peacemaker, I could now see the anomaly. It appeared to be
pulsing the same blue and green as it had on the other side.
Our bombs had failed. The extra mass of Livia's ship hadn't
done the trick, either. The Gateway would remain open, and

more ships would spill across the rift in space-time. That other universe's civil war would become our own.

We'd lost. I'd failed.

A blaze of blinding light enveloped everything. When it cleared, the anomaly had collapsed in upon itself. So sudden, I wasn't sure it had happened. But it had.

Juan jumped up from his chair. "We did it!"

Everyone cheered.

But as usual, it was a short-lived victory. Slowly, from a microscopic point where the anomaly had been, a wave of blue-green energy began to expand out. It reached Livia's ship first, enveloping that vessel in a bubble of jade-colored lightning as its ship's systems failed before they could compensate. My sensors indicated the cruiser's shields had collapsed, and all its systems were offline—the energy pulse acting like an EMP from a nuclear blast, crippling the vessel's electronics. But the shields had done their job, taking the brunt of the energy and allowing the *Imperial Might* to survive.

I didn't need to wait for the computer calculations to know our own *Pigeon's Fury* would not be so lucky. I took the ship hard to starboard and gave it everything it had to get away from the expanding shockwave.

Hitting a few commands on my panel, I brought up a rear projection of the expanding energy wave on the main viewport in the cockpit. We all watched as the explosion reached the *Peacemaker* and did to it the same thing it had just done to Livia's ship. As the energy wave passed over that dreadnought in a storm of electricity, its pace quickened. Alarms sounded on our ship, warning our current speed would be insufficient to outrun the tsunami of energy. It was gaining on us.

I rerouted minor systems into our ship's engines. The inertial dampeners began to fail, and the ship shuddered under the added stress. With our increased velocity, the computer now gave even odds on escaping.

Then, the storm of crackling green-blue energy reached Mars. Unlike the ships, the red rock didn't fare so well. Parts of the planet disappeared into the anomalous vortex, sent across space-time to who knew where, while larger parts of the planet broke apart. Unceremoniously, it ended in a few seconds. Mars obliterated. All that remained of the red planet was a chaotic collection of asteroids spanning in size from pebbles to small moons. The sensor readings began spitting out new warnings as the gravitational forces in the area completely shifted from the loss of the planet's mass.

"My God," whispered Carla.

"What about Earth?" Juan stammered.

Burke and I said nothing. Everyone knew the answer to that question.

The *Liberator* had also turned around, fleeing from the quickly expanding energy field. We sped past it, neither ship bothering to fire at the other. As we came close to my Shade aboard his vessel, I could feel his anger; his fear of the unknown shockwave palpable; the misery of losing his road back to his home world raw.

Then, I heard a thought directed at me as clear as if it had been said in the cockpit I now sat in: *What've you done, Raines?*

Our ship sped on, moving past my Shade's vessel and out of range of any direct connection I had to that other me. No time to worry about my double's feelings. I kept rerouting systems, trying to put distance between us and the expanding swell of crackling energy. We couldn't outrun it forever. I'd made a losing bet, but I had to keep playing because I was all in. No options left but to try.

Moments later, the energy field reached the *Liberator* and crippled the ship.

The wave of destruction sped up again, as if feeding on the energy of the dreadnought. The alarms roared throughout the *Pigeon's Fury*. A male voice with an Australian accent spoke through the intercom: "Analyses of the current surroundings indicate imminent danger to the ship. Please take drastic measures to alter current scenario. This is a recording. Analyses of the current sensor readings indicate that—"

I hit a button, turning off the voice. Who the hell had thought that recording was a good idea?

Quietly, Burke said, "We aren't going to make it."

"No," I replied, accepting our fate. I swiveled my chair back so I could look directly at Carla and Juan. "I'm sorry."

She met my gaze straight-on, a lingering love behind those eyes mashed up with hate and pity. She didn't say anything. Our final moment together. I'd failed her again. I tried to think of something profound to say, but it had all been said. What I needed now was time to mend our wounds. Time I wouldn't have.

"Look." Juan pointed excitedly at the viewport behind me.

I spun back around to see the energy field disappearing before our eyes. I checked the sensors. The readings confirmed it. The blast had dissipated, its power spent. The wave wouldn't reach Earth. It wouldn't catch us.

Leaning back in my chair, I let out the breath I hadn't realized I'd been holding. I heard Juan clamoring over to Carla, imagined him hugging her. We'd done it. I'd done it.

Juan's arms wrapped around my neck from behind. I grabbed his hand, squeezing tight. For the first time in my life, I was truly a hero, though I didn't feel like one. That's what surprised me most of all, the sadness of victory.

"Thanks, Raines," Juan said.

"No big deal."

Numb. An emptiness still loomed within me, despite all we'd been through. And maybe that should've been a warning of the tragedy still to come. But I couldn't see it. Instead, I clung to Juan's arms wrapped tight around my neck—desperate to feel that connection. I'd always been an outcast longing for a chance to belong, wishing for once that I could feel normal.

CHAPTER 30

IF ONLY THIS WERE THE END. BUT SADLY, IT'S JUST THE beginning.

Nothing would be the same. Even the sway of the trees, the splatter of the rain, the pulse in the stars felt different to me now. It'd been changing for a long while. Warning us. Shouting at us to wake up.

Those of us with Shades had known it was coming. Some deeper meaning existed in the link between those doubles, stitched into the fabric of the cosmos, a truth we haven't yet gleaned. But we could feel it in our guts, hear it in our souls, waking us from our slumber of sanity to the reality of the unbelievable.

But who are the crazy in a multiverse of the insane?

Maybe now we're all lost in this folly together, circling in an endless labyrinth of the mind around that place between reason and mania, the division of the two razor thin. Most ignore that unpleasant truth to survive the day-to-day. But some of us choose to step into the light. To know. And we teeter on that edge, dancing back and forth. Perhaps that was the silver lining in all this death and destruction. Because maybe now we all danced to the same tune. Finally, everyone would hear that endless beat of the metronome of the gods, driving our lives towards oblivion.

The tempo picked up a while back. Did you feel it?

Be honest with yourself. The truth will set you free.

Clenching my fists, I tried to shake off those thoughts. Banish that impending sense of disaster that anxiously clutched at my chest. I stared out the cockpit of the *Pigeon's Fury* at the perfect blue orb of Earth. It hung there, frozen in that pristine black, a beacon of hope. That was what Carla had been to me. What Juan had become. A light that sparkles in your soul through the despair and gives all this suffering meaning. Something worth fighting for.

Behind us, out among the stars, the loss of all hope readied itself. Wounded, yes. But coming. They would be the harbinger of our demise, rolling down through our lives in an avalanche of change and destruction. My Shade. Livia. Badger. Torian. Jacobs. A band of futuristic imperialist wannabes. They would rise from the ashes of Mars, turning their ambitious eyes towards our home. Their war would consume us all.

Do you hear it? Those footsteps?

Soldiers marching to the front lines. Their trumpets herald the coming of our doom.

No? Strange. We do.

I'd heard it all my life yet had been unable to act. But now, I had purpose.

My Shade would seize power, the Eternal Watcher reborn, of this I had no doubt. The silver tongue would be his mask. Tyranny would be his sword. I knew him better than he knew himself. We were connected—both my envy and my scourge—the shackles of our link unbreakable save in death. I heard his call even now. A promise of friendship. Fortune. Power. But it was a lie. A trick to betray the ones I loved. Still, the allure of that offer was intoxicating. A new kind of addiction. If I lost that battle, I may not be myself anymore.

Were you even now?

But he was right to fear me. I'd been reborn. Found strength and abilities beyond reason. Call it a religious awakening. You were witness. I would be the speaker of truth against his lies, a new kind of sage. Time would be my ally. I would rise to meet the moment. Powerful. The man destiny demanded, defending our world against the shadow of the Eternal Watcher.

What had Varnok called me? *A Dream Walker.*

Here, staring past our world into the infinite black unknown, I knew we would push back against the siren's call of death. We would scream into the void and reject the nothingness. We would resist. A storm approached. No avoiding it now. We'd bought ourselves time, but it couldn't last. The tide would roll in, bringing the inevitable. We may have won the battle, but the war for Earth—*for our Earth*—had only just begun.

THE END

GRAND PATRONS

A Tom Wood
A.S. Ganser
Aaron W. Covington
Albert C. D'Amico
Ana Egatz Gomez
Andrew J. Melaragno
Anne Mistler
Anthony Carlston
Barbara Van Poole
Barry F. Kramer
Belinda Des Jardins
Bradley D. Turk
Brian Fitzpatrick
Brianna R Stump
Cassie Marks
Catherine Smith
Charles J. Maes
Cheryl L. Kvasnicka
Claudia Castello
Clyde Huffman
D.R. Whitson
Dan Hrey
Dan J. Manucci
Daniel Diaz
Daniel K. Cozzetto
Danny Fedo
David E. Brown
David Houze

David M Krieg
Dee Dee Trosclair
Derrick Jue
Dianna Kokoszka
Dr. Tyler Barratt and Mr.
  Christian Riley
E. James Bodmer
Elena Bechtholdt
Emily B. Ferenbach
Eric Bucklin
Forrest Moore
Frank H. Turpin
Greg Alaestante
Heather T. Taylor
Helen Hwang
Holly L. Harris
Jacob Shapiro
James Balazs
James Bruske
James Carusone
James Connor
James Lawson
James Moore
Jamie Marincola
Jason Reuben
Jeanette Szafran
Jeffrey Breese
Jeffrey C. Mc Clain

Jesse Keller
Jim Dunning
John Michalic
John Prescott
John Walko
Jonathan Beard
Jonathan Castellanos
Jonathan Ma
Jonathan Sahnow
Joseph Cocklin
Joseph G Melaragno
Joseph Sacavitch
Joshua Symons
Josie and Evan Schrodek
Jude Mendoza
Jules Mugema
Katelynn Coleman
Katharine Brennan
Katherine Immerman
Keith Smith
Keith R. Alba
Kelli Royer
Ken Schneider
Kevin Kauffman
Kim Healy
Kim Valdivieso
Kirk Miles
Larry Estrada
Li Hong Wattel
Lou Ronayne
Margaret Bowerman
Marie Parsey
Mark Hewitt
Marsha Morris
Mary Mendoza
Marylee S. Hoffman
Matthew C. Brown
McKenna J. Mendoza
Michael J Mendoza

Michael Shawver
Michelle Lapaglia
Pablo Abad
Pamela Jacobson
Pamela Kum
Paul Davidovac
Paula M Colemere
Peter Hall
R. Bruce Hadden
Rebecca Beaird
Regan and Brian Bergmark
Richard Barker
Richard Neil Laser
Ricky Khamis
Rj Daniel Hanna
Robert L Smith
Roger D. Ziegler
Ron Capalbo
Sandy Mermelstein
Scott Agnew
Shannon Cook
Sherri Hummel
Spencer Crossland
Stephen Parsey
Steve Moore
Steven E. Michael
Susan Lieser Frederick
Theresa Jay
Todd R Goldman
Todd Traina
Tracy Worischeck
Tyea Doty
Victoria England Patton
Whittak Sun
Will Kotterman
William Witt
Xuan C Smith

INKSHARES

INKSHARES is a community, publisher, and producer for debut writers. Our books are selected not just by a group of editors, but also by readers worldwide. Our aim is to find and develop the most captivating and intelligent new voices in fiction. We have no genre—our genre is debut.

Previously unknown Inkshares authors have received starred reviews in every trade publication. They have been featured in every major review, including on the front page of the *New York Times*. Their books are on the front tables of booksellers worldwide, topping bestseller lists. They have been translated in major markets by the world's biggest publishers. And they are being adapted at the biggest studios and networks.

Interested in making your own story a reality? Visit Inkshares.com to start your own project, connect with other writers, and find other great books.